"5 stars**** ... created an enthralling story with all the characters of Destiny's Present. I was riveted to the pages from the first to the last …I want to know more. I enjoyed this book a great deal. I would highly recommend it."
Kathryn Bennett for Reader's Favorite

Read2Review on Destiny's Past: "The flow of the story was very well planned; I didn't want to stop reading! I loved the characters; each one had heart and their own voice. However, what really stuck out for me was that while I was reading I could actually picture the places the story was set in and I could clearly picture the characters. Patricia's use of description, for me, helped bring this brilliant story to life."

From the Paranormal Romance Guild: **Reviewer's Choice 2016 2nd place winner** "This is an amazing series and I can't recommend it enough…it has everything you could want if you love paranormal and fantasy." *Linda Tonis*

"Patricia C. Lee has a gift for plot and character, and readers won't need to read much into the work to realize this as they are immediately swept away by the engaging descriptions, the poetic allure of her language, and the powerful narrative voice right from the opening lines of this beautiful story. The story also touches on a good number of very interesting themes and they will speak to many readers because they are very close to their own experiences. Love, sacrifice, betrayal, and a sense of duty are among the most recurrent ones. I loved the way the characters evolved throughout the story. They are engaging and fully-fledged. Destiny's Future is one of the very few novels I have read that deals with time travel, and I found it greatly satisfying." *Christian Sia for Reader's Favorite*

Other works

Daughters of the Crescent Moon Series

Destiny's Past

Destiny's Present

Destiny's Future

Without a Paddle: short stories about life's struggles

To Rita,

FIRST GEAR

A Sadie Hawkins Mystery

by

Patricia C. Lee

Enjoy the read!

Phoenix Literary Publishing
phoenixlitpub@gmail.com

This book is a work of fiction. Any references to historical or current events, real people or real places and events are products of the author's imagination, and any resemblance to actual events or places or persons, living or dead, is entirely coincidental.

Copyright ©2020 by Patricia C. Lee

All rights reserved. Any scanning, uploading and electronic sharing of this book, or any parts thereof, without the permission of the publisher constitute unlawful piracy and theft of the author's intellectual property.

Cover design: Cathy Walker - Cover Artist
(cathyscovers.wixsite.com/books)

ISBN: 9781777156305   print

ACKNOWLEDGMENTS

My thanks go to these fantastic people who helped form this book: my editor, *She Who Shall not Be Named*, - your suggestions and guidance are appreciated beyond words. Sandra D. Polk from the Briar Shoppe in Houston for teaching me the finer points of cigars. Cover artist Cathy Walker who took my ideas and made such a brilliant cover. Ashley Boler - Creative Director, one of my beta readers and über friend. Meghan Sloane – converted romance reader and good friend – thanks for all your suggestions. And Dianne Burns – beta reader and awesome friend who has been with me from the very start of my writing career.

DEDICATION

To Diane Hill, my inspiration for Sadie and Brad MacBride because I couldn't have Sadie at some mundane job. Oh and thanks for the help on baseball.

And for *K* – always and forever my love.

CHAPTER ONE

I stared at my desk which should have been cluttered with invoices and payments received, but sadly none were there and I couldn't help the spear of apprehension which pierced my gut at the stack of bills that spilled over one corner. I could have sworn they were multiplying like rabbits in springtime.

"We may need to consider hiring you out as a stud muffin." I eyeballed my brother Blaine, five years older than me, who stood in the doorway of my broom-closet of an office. Tall, slim, a solid force in my life, he had a runners build although didn't partake in that sport.

A wry grin tipped up the corner of his mouth as he wiped his hands on an oil-stained rag. "The wife may have something to say about that."

"It'd be for a good cause."

He chuckled and shook his head. "Takes time, Sadie."

"Time is what I'm running out of."

When I first took over this business, I'd done a few small hauls, mostly for friends in exchange for beer or dinner. But if I didn't get more jobs lined up soon, I'd be using the company cube van for sleeping instead of hauling. I could picture it now, roll-away cot in the corner, a little end table and a propane lamp, spending my nights parked at the local mall with the rest of the RVs that popped up once in a while. A real mobile community. Slap on a pair of sweatpants and extra large tee shirt, sit out on my lawn chair and I'd be set.

Kill me now.

"All I need is for someone to call."

As if fate had listened, the phone on my desk rang. With a start I went to grab for it but hesitated.

After the third ring Blaine nodded his head in the direction of the unit. "Things not going to answer itself."

"What if it's one of my creditors?" I'd been dodging them for over a week.

"Never knew you to back down from anyone, sis. Despite your size."

At just over five feet and with more curves than the Daytona International Speedway track, I'd had my share of dealing with bullies growing up, both male and female, but they'd learned I could fight like a cornered dog if the need arose.

And it had.

Once.

"My inner Chihuahua wants to take the day off." My Alabama accent, which I'd tried unsuccessfully to tame once I went to college in Texas, came on even stronger when irritated or stressed. "If it's Mrs. Paisley from the credit and loan I'm offering her your services as a bribe."

"Just as long as it's strictly vehicle related."

I snatched the phone before the caller decided to give up. "Hawkins Freight."

A voice with more twang than a well-plucked banjo barked over the line. "Yeah. It says in this here ad that you haul stuff. Is that true?"

Hallelujah. "Sure do." I wanted to add the obvious 'why else would I advertise' but instead tacked on a question for the benefit of the caller. "Did you need something relocated?"

"Yeah. Hester's gotta be moved but my truck broke down and we have to get it done right away."

Pen and pad of paper in hand I flipped past the list of bills that needed to be paid, which was as large as the pile on my desk, and started a new sheet. "Okay. Do you have everything packed or would you like me to hire a crew?"

"One person can handle it and I'll be here ta help. Not much ta take."

"All right. From where to where?"

"Pickten Meadows to Lakeland County."

"Can you guess a total weight? We charge by distance and weight."

"Around seven hundred pounds."

Easy as pie. I did a quick calculation and gave him a rough quote. "I'll be able to give you an exact dollar amount when we weigh in before we leave. Payment is half up front, half at destination. Will there be someone at the drop off point?"

"Yawp. No problem."

"Okay."

"Can ya come now?"

Guy didn't waste any time. With a quick glance at my watch, I figured if all went well I'd get to Lakeland County around dinner and I didn't want the client going to a competitor. "Sure. What's the address?"

My brow scrunched at the directions he gave me.

"And your name?"

"Lester."

Lester and Hester. Sweet. "Great. See you in a bit Lester. And thanks for hiring Hawkins Freight."

I hung up the phone, a wide grin crossing my face.

Blaine leaned a hip against the desk, stuffed the rag into a pocket and gave a dimpled smile that had broken the hearts of a few females over the years. "Let me guess. The entire state football team wants to move across country and they called you."

"I wish. Nope, it's a small job but it's a start."

"Good for you."

"Now if only I could get a back haul we'd be laughing."

"When you headed out?"

"Right now."

"Need help?"

Getting up, I eyed my notes. "No. This one's pretty simple. Plus the guy said he'd give me a hand."

"Fair enough. I'll reroute the phone when I leave, so take your cell."

"Yes, big brother," I grinned, shoving his almost six foot frame out the door.

"I'm glad things are finally looking up for you. Talk to you tomorrow."

Before I could grab a clipboard and contract the phone rang again. I cradled the unit between my ear and shoulder while pulling open desk drawers. "Hawkins Freight."

"Hey, Sadie."

My hand stilled momentarily before continuing to leaf through papers. "Hi, Clayton." Hearing my ex-husband's voice always brought a quick stutter to my heart. We had a good relationship, still do, but no matter how amicable our divorce he will forever be tied to part of my past through no fault of his own.

"Calling to see how the new businesswoman is making out."

"She is doing fine. The business could be better but things are picking up. In fact I'm on my way out to do a job. Is there something you wanted to talk to me about?" I mentally crossed my fingers, kept pawing through drawers.

"No. Only wanted to say hi."

My shoulders relaxed and the edges of my mouth tipped up in a smile. "Thanks. How are things at the office?"

"Busy as usual."

I panned my tiny surroundings while mentally comparing his professionally decorated office to the four slate grey walls encompassing a desk, two chairs, a four drawer filing cabinet and a framed picture of my Uncle Stan and my father. It wasn't much but it sure as heck was a sight better than when I had taken over. The upkeep of the business had been attainable, positively and negatively, because of the man at the other end of the phone conversation. Silence hung across the line, something I knew neither of us would fill with idle chatter or words of melancholy regrets. Our relationship wasn't like that.

"Glad to hear." I resumed my search, found the contract folder and a clipboard. "You make partner yet?"

"No, but a position might be coming up soon."

"I'll keep my fingers crossed for you. Listen, I have to run."

"Of course. Take care, Sadie."

"You too. Thanks for calling."

I disconnected, paused, tapped the edge of the phone against my lips, considered calling him back but decided now was not the time to inquire about past events that still haunted me.

Clipping my cell to my waist, I slung my purse across my body, grabbed the items and headed out the door.

* * *

Later, with the sun angling through the windshield, I drove down a scrub-lined rutted lane, one eye on my pad of notes while the van bucked and jerked like a wild horse. This was the right address but I hadn't expected the client to live so far off the highway. As I got closer to my destination, a house in dire need of paint appeared, the well-worn porch missing a few spindles and the accompanying red barn was weathered to grayish ochre. A man in a short sleeved faded plaid shirt and overalls covering his significant paunch stood in the yard, motioning to the barn.

A sinking feeling started to form in my stomach when I switched off the engine.

Eyes peered from an aged face tanned from a lifetime in the sun. "Yer a little small for the job."

I disembarked. "Determination more than makes up for size." The comment was a standard answer to the multitude of height remarks from over the years. "Are you Lester?"

"Yeah."

"You said you wanted to move some things for Hester."

"Ain't some things. I need ta move Hester."

The sinking feeling grew.

"She's in the barn." He led the way and heaved open a rolling door, the metal screeching in protest.

Annnnnd the sinking feeling exploded into full dismay.

Dust motes danced in the sunlight that spread across the barn's floor to the center where a huge pig stood, rooting around the hay-strewn floor with a series of grunts. Lester grabbed a length of rope hanging from a hook on a nearby beam, secured the animal and led it outside.

"This here's Hester."

With a sigh I quelled the desire to close my eyes and pinch the bridge of my nose. "I see. You never mentioned I'd be hauling livestock."

"What difference does it make?"

For one thing, my insurance didn't cover moving live animals which meant if something should happen to the load, besides not being paid for the job, the client could sue. But if I turned him down there was always the possibility that farmer Lester might be inclined to spread a nasty word, possibly jeopardizing any future prospects.

I pasted on my best smile. "No difference at all. Best if you could throw some straw on the floor of the van. And we'll need extra rope to tie her off."

While he ventured back into the barn, I squatted down and looked the sow in the eye. "You're not going to give me any grief are you?"

Hester gave a short oink.

"All right then."

I opened the back door of the van and tugged out the ramp attached to the undercarriage. While the farmer tossed straw across the floor, I got the clipboard from the front and started to fill out the information.

"I'll put in the weight after I hit the first set of scales."

Lester jumped down from the back. "No need. Had Hester weighed last week. She's six hundred and seventy pounds."

"Okay. Not many people know the exact weight of their stuff. Makes it easier to calculate the cost."

"Had to know the weight," he nodded to the pig. "You'll be dropping her off at the slaughter. Need the cash."

Well, hell.

This time I did pinch the bridge of my nose. I wasn't a vegetarian, I liked a good steak or pork chop as much as the next person, but that didn't mean I particularly cared for hauling a pig to a death chamber.

The farm owner raised a pair of bottlebrush eyebrows. "Somethin wrong with your nose?"

"No, I'm fine." I inhaled and turned so I wouldn't have to see the pig's eyes. I did the calculations, considered Lester's threadbare coveralls, the sorry state of the buildings, the dilapidated broken-down truck and with a sigh gave the man a discount before showing him where to sign. The guy was struggling to make ends meet, I knew what that felt like.

Taking back the documents, I went to the front of the van and tossed over my shoulder, "You can get Hester loaded. There are a couple of rings on either side of the van to tie her off."

Hester, however, had other ideas.

As if sensing her impending doom, the sow refused to move an inch. Figuring if I didn't lend a hand I'd be there all night, I tugged on the rope while Lester pushed from behind but the pig still wouldn't budge.

"Maybe she needs to see you. I'll nudge her from the back."

He went into the barn and returned with an apple. With fruit in one hand, Lester hauled on the rope with the other while I shoved from the back. The animal held fast but as I dug down and leaned into the task with my shoulder, the pig moved forward.

And I went with her. Right onto the ground.

"Shit." Muttering, I struggled to stand.

"Naw, just dirt," Lester grinned, backing up the ramp. "Be glad we weren't in the pen, you'd be pulling crap outta your pretty red hair."

I dusted off my jeans and tee shirt, waited for the man to finish saying his goodbyes then secured the ramp and closed the door of the van before I changed my mind.

Lester fished out a folded envelope from the pocket of his coveralls. "Here's the down payment. Walter at the slaughter will give ya the rest. I've already called him and set it up."

I took the cash, mentally made a note to apply the man's savings at the receiving end and held out my hand. "Okay. Guess we're good to go."

His meaty, calloused hand shook mine. "Thanks…ya know I didn't even get yer name."

"It's Sadie Hawkins."

"Well now, ya certainly don't live up to that name. You're far prettier. Nice doing business with ya Sadie."

I smiled. "Thank you Lester. And thanks for using Hawkins Freight."

"Be tellin' my friends to call ya if they need things moved," he hollered as I hopped up into the cab and waved.

"As long as it isn't a fricken cow or bull," I mumbled, started the vehicle and drove away.

* * *

I turned onto the slaughterhouse property three hours later. Although the van was retrofitted so I could reach the pedals better, my numb butt made me realize I should have gotten extra padding for the seats. I sat, engine off, the relief upon arriving without incident evaporating at what I was about to do.

For a minute I considered calling Blaine for moral support but what could he do? He certainly wasn't going to suggest keeping the sow and I was long past the age of hand holding.

I slapped the steering wheel, snatched up the clipboard and thrust the door open. "Not your pig so yank up your big girl panties." Actually the undies were a lacy deep purple from Victoria Secret, my one vice. Well, make that a second vice, high octane cola being first and foremost.

Trying to ignore the unholy stench, I quickly strode across the dirt to the beige door marked office and marched in.

"Is Walter here?"

"That would be me." The middle aged man in a green shirt rose from behind a desk.

"Have a delivery from Lester. He said you'd be expecting me."

Walter eyed me up and down. "Yes, well, I certainly didn't expect someone so…"

"So, what?" I pressed, launching hands on hips.

"Capable."

Smart man.

"Let's get the animal unloaded."

I handed him papers to sign, he gave them back with payment from which I returned a portion because of Lester's discount, stating as such.

At the van I jumped up on the bumper, unlocked and opened the doors then yanked out the ramp.

"Definitely capable," Walter commented quietly as he strode into the back and untied Hester.

I understood how an operation like this worked and the reasoning behind it; meat did not magically appear on store shelves wrapped in plastic, but guilt still made me stand stiffly off to the side, unwilling to watch the animal being led to its demise. I hoped it would be quick for the poor thing. Once man and pig were clear, I secured the ramp and closed the doors with more vehemence than necessary.

Walter glanced down to the sow behind him then regarded me. "Piece of advice, little lady?"

I bristled at the endearment but said nothing.

"If you plan on doing this again, never look them in the eye."

He gave a short nod, turned and walked away, leaving me to wonder if I would be able to haul livestock to slaughter again, coverage or no.

If I did get another call for this type of job, what choice would I have? Most of what I received from my amicable divorce with Clayton was tied up in the company, a mechanism to assert freedom, independence and some sort of control over my life. He'd paid me out, kept the house. Since there were no kids involved, I was able to take the money and make a fresh start. And what I wanted was not to be tied down and especially hemmed in.

Been there, done that.

In more ways than one, and it hadn't been pretty.

However, with independence came responsibility which included paying Blaine to work on the vehicle. Well, hopefully vehicles if the company could make it past the first two years. Hells bells, all I wanted was to make it past the first six months. And I was bound and determined to do it even if it meant hauling livestock I admitted with a sigh.

Back in the cab, I put the clipboard with payment into the slot in the door and decided to head toward the nearest gas station to sweep and hose out the calling card Hester had left in the back.

Instead, my cell phone rang before I could start the van.

"Hawkins Freight." The message on the screen indicated the call was rerouted from the office.

"Yes. I am calling to inquire if you would be able to move some items as soon as possible," said a cultured male voice.

"Depends on where you're calling from and how quickly you need me to be there."

"Houston and preferably today."

What was it with people who waited till the last minute?

I stifled a groan. That meant going back the way I came. It was past six so I wouldn't reach the place until after nine, perhaps closer to ten pm.

"I've just finished dropping off a load and can't make it there until very late tonight."

"Hmm. I really need to have the items at their destination in Pampa tomorrow."

I could tell by his insistence and how his voice drifted off at the end, as if he was already contemplating phoning another company, that I was about to lose this job.

"How about early in the morning, say eight."

Silence.

"Or seven. I can be there for seven am." Sounded like I was bidding at an auction.

"Well, I...I suppose that will have to suffice," he conceded. "I doubt I could get anyone else at this time today anyway.

"Great." The reflection of the slaughter house in the side mirror got me thinking. "Is your cargo alive?"

"It was, but not anymore."

What the…

"You want to run that by me again?" Oh lord, please don't let it be cadavers.

"So sorry," he chuckled, "my attempt at humor. I am an antiques dealer and require the delivery of some pieces, one of which is a sarcophagus. Rest assured, the mummy has been dead for a very long time."

Bet he hasn't seen the *Mummy* movies.

"You are not superstitious are you?" he added.

My death grip on the phone loosened. "Not at all."

Black cats were fine and as long as said mummy was secured inside its fancy coffin and locked in the back, I was okay with that. I got his name, Lionel Stanton, the address of pick up, went through the particulars and gave him a rough quote.

"How soon do you need it at the destination?"

"By mid afternoon the latest."

Depending on loading time I'd be hard pressed to make it. "That's a fair ways to go in that short of time."

"I'll pay double."

My ears perked up with that but also on the hint of desperation in his voice. "This is strictly official isn't it? I mean, you have the proper documentation for these pieces don't you?"

"Yes of course," he assured. "This was a last minute transaction and the purchaser is quite eager to get these items. The crew I usually hire is on another delivery."

"And the person receiving the goods will have someone to help unload?"

"I'll be catching a flight tomorrow morning and will be on hand at the destination so there's no need to worry, everything is arranged."

"Okay then. Looks like we have a deal Mr. Stanton. I'll see you around seven tomorrow."

I hung up. With the amount the client was willing to pay I could get caught up on bills and even give Blaine a paycheck. I started up the vehicle and put the pedal to the floor. I still had to clean out the back of the van and drop off the paperwork at the office. Not to mention having not eaten yet. But with this job I'd at least be able to stock up on groceries.

* * *

Lionel Stanton took a dark blue linen handkerchief from his breast pocket and mopped his brow, wishing he could wipe away his troubles as easily. He strode around his office and double checked things were in order before leaving to get a good night's rest – something he hadn't been able to obtain recently. He noticed the door to the room next to his was now closed. As he passed the receptionist at the filing cabinet searching intently through the top drawer, she refused to meet his gaze or acknowledge his farewell, so he left quickly for the elevator.

At the lobby of the building, he almost knocked into the janitor in his haste to exit the elevator and returned the main floor's receptionist's brief nod with one of his own.

But as he left the building and walked to his car, he was oblivious to those watching, of the three separate individuals who eyed him with anger, hurt, suspicion and malice.

CHAPTER TWO

After downing a Live Wire – my own concoction of a double shot espresso, four teaspoons of sugar in a mug of cola with a healthy dose of chocolate syrup made from eighty-five percent dark chocolate I had found at a specialty supply store – I was raring to go. I created the drink in college to help me cram for exams. It was potent enough to wake someone from a drug-induced coma and I was going to need it to get through the morning.

Although I tolerated driving in the city, maneuvering a cube van into the downtown core of a metropolis with over two million people ranked right up there with going catfish hunting at night with my cousins as a kid – stinky, sweaty and constantly on the lookout for things coming at you from all sides. The only saving grace was that I beat rush hour and the furnace like heat that would hit in a few hours.

The office district in downtown Houston is a maze of one way streets. Restaurants, trendy clothing stores, hotels and cathedrals jostled for space with multiple high-storied buildings in the concrete jungle

There wasn't a man waiting for me at the address on Capitol Street when I arrived, a mere one minute late, thank you very much. Instead, a very slim Asian woman stood in front of a multi-glassed building, impeccably dressed in a dark pencil thin skirt and crisp white blouse. At spotting the van, she glanced at her watch and moved across the still shadowed concrete in purposeful strides, her black hair cut into a smooth wedge style and flawlessly in place. I pegged her for around mid twenties.

"Are you who Mr. Stanton hired to haul the items?" Her cool professional tone had no hint of a Southern accent.

"Yes. Sadie Hawkins from Hawkins Freight. Is Mr. Stanton here?"

"No. He caught an earlier flight and left last night. I am his secretary, Ms. Ing. He asked that I meet you this morning and get things underway."

I thought it odd he never called to let me know but then figured he was probably rushed and since he had someone meet me here anyway it didn't matter. Besides, I didn't care who I dealt with as long as I got paid.

"You and your crew can get loaded at the back of the building. At the corner, turn right and I'll meet you there."

I touched the secretary's arm as she turned to leave. "Wait a minute. Mr. Stanton told me he'd help me load so I don't have a crew with me."

"I see." Dark, almond shaped eyes took in my snug jeans – a cleaner pair than what I wore last night – and loose fitting blouse. "Perhaps I should make alternative arrangements."

My stomach lurched. I couldn't lose this client. "Wait. I can get a few people here within half an hour."

A thin brow arched upward. "At this time in the morning?"

"No problem. Just give me a few minutes."

I pulled out my cell from the pocket of my jeans. Contacting Blaine wasn't an option; having a two year old child and his wife, Karen, pregnant with another on the way, it was a sure bet he hadn't even cracked an eye open yet.

I chewed my lip, observing Ms. Ing's impatient frown. Who to call? Then, as if hearing a voice in my head, I smiled and punched in my best friend's number. The phone rang six times before a sleep-heavy groan answered.

"Unless you are J.Lo, don't even bother leaving a message."

"Tanya."

"You're not the one from my fantasy," she intoned. "Goodbye."

"No!" My yell garnered a dubious look from Ms. Ing. "It's me, Sadie. Pull that ridiculous eye mask off and haul your ass up. I really need your help."

There was a muffled curse, some rustling and then Tanya rasped over the line. "Girl, do you have *any* idea what time it is?"

"Seven in the morning."

"Jeez, I only got to bed three hours ago."

I could picture her reaching for the one thing that would make the woman able to cope from lack of sleep. "And don't go popping a smoke in your mouth while you're still in bed."

"You woke me up. You don't get a vote. What's wrong?"

"I need two or three of your people to help me load some stuff for a haul within the next half hour or I'll lose this client."

"Seriously? Like now?"

"Seriously."

"Okay." There was a pause and I heard the tell-tale deep inhale and exhale of smoking. "I'll see who I can extort into coming. What's the address?"

I relayed the info. "Thanks. I owe you."

"I'll add it to your tab," she deadpanned and disconnected.

I pocketed the phone and turned back to Mr. Stanton's secretary. "All set. I'll have people here by seven thirty. Any place open close by for a cup of coffee."

Ms. Ing cast her eyes to the diamond studded Cartier on her wrist and headed to the building. "Not until eight. I'll meet you out back in half an hour."

I shrugged and watched the woman enter the building. Good thing I made extra Live Wire.

* * *

A white paneled van screeched to a halt twenty-five minutes later and a tall black woman stepped out of the passenger seat. Dressed in light grey blazer over a loose fitting burgundy top and trim black pants, all of which complimented her almost six foot frame, Tanya Woods had the coloring of light chocolate, a model-perfect body shape and a stop-traffic gorgeous face that could have graced the cover of any fashion magazine. I said as much to her one day as we were waiting in line for a movie and I spied a well-known model-turned-actress in a poster.

"The last thing I want is someone to see only the surface and believe it is the only redeeming quality," she'd said indicating the poster I had been pointing at.

"But people do that now to almost everyone, especially gorgeous women. Surely you must have come across that from time to time?"

She gave me a wicked grin and set her hands into claws. "Yes. And once I pounce they realize their mistake."

I was ten years old when we'd met. She'd come peeling around the corner in my hometown of Oxford, Alabama and had crashed into me while running from a pack of girls who were ready to beat the living tar out of her. I could hear their shrieking voices coming closer, filled with anger and hate, taunting punishment. One glance at her tear-streaked face, skinned knees, the wild, panic-filled eyes, and I knew I couldn't let that mob get a hold of her. I pushed her into the building I'd just left, instructed her to stay quiet and had just turned around when the group came into view. I told them she'd taken off into the department store across the street and when they'd blasted through the glass doors, I yanked Tanya from the hiding place and high-tailed it in the opposite direction. Once we were about a block away, I'd found a phone and called Blaine to come get us. We got her cleaned up, took her home and from that day on, twenty years ago, we were best friends and I loved her like a sister.

She doesn't run from a fight anymore.

Pulling me out of my memory, Tanya came to stand beside me and said imitating Lurch from *The Addams Family*, said "You rang."

A sliding door on the van opened and two young adult males plus a female exited, joined by the driver. The group was part of StreetSmart, which Tanya was the director, and one of a half dozen facilities where offenders could make a fresh start by helping mentor those on the edge of stepping over the crime line. Tanya ran a tight ship and took no crap from her charges but she was also fair.

"You made good time," I grinned.

"Rico was driving."

"Thanks for coming. Talk about pulling my butt from the fire."

"You're racking up quite the tab, friend," she said but gave me a wink. "Let's get this show on the road. I have to be back in juvie court by ten."

"Anything to do with why you only got three hours sleep?"

She shrugged.

I knew better than to pry. Besides it being confidential, Tanya was fiercely loyal to her people and would defend them to the end.

"Fair enough. Follow me around the building. Can't have you late for court."

The two vehicles circled the block and went down the alley to where Ms. Ing impatiently tapped her foot. I reversed to the loading area, jumped out, and opened up the back.

"What needs to be taken?"

The secretary cast a wary, almost disdainful eye at the hired muscle then led the way. "These crates need to go but the sarcophagus, which is in its own container, should be loaded first. However it's much too heavy to carry. Does anyone in your…group know how to drive a forklift?"

"I can," piped Rico Espenza, his Hispanic voice full of bravado. Baggy beige pants rode low on slim hips and a matching colored muscle shirt draped his trim body.

Tanya shook her head. "I don't think so."

"Hey, I got us here, didn't I?" he objected.

"Barely. Jessie." Tanya singled out the girl of the crew, dressed in ripped blue jeans, fashionable military style laced boots, and bright orange shirt. "Follow the lady. And if you goof off, I'll call your P.O. and have you hauled back into custody so fast you'll get whiplash."

Her comrades sniggered.

"Knock it off or I'm not buying breakfast," the StreetSmart director barked. "Will, get some work gloves from the van and then everyone wait by those crates. Last thing I need is to have one of you run over. It'll be your body in that mummy case instead."

Will Ellington, the tall, GQ special, dressed in designer label garb, ventured to their vehicle for the gloves. He looked vaguely familiar but I couldn't place where I'd seen him before.

I looked up, fluttered my eyelashes and crooned to Tanya. "My hero."

She smirked. "They love me."

"She can drive a forklift?" I nodded my head in the direction of the retreating two women. Not that I was stereotyping but I hadn't come across many female forklift operators.

"You should see her work on cars."

Storing and securing the sarcophagus and crates went by without a hitch. Vic Russo, the last crew member sauntered up to me as Rico shut the back doors of the cube van and flipped the lever down.

"Want me to ride shotgun with you?" he asked.

I shook my head.

"Come on," he urged, leaning in. His toned body was clad in black clothes that encased him like a second skin. Blue eyes sparked as he lowered his voice to a suggestive purr. "Girl can't be too careful these days. You might need some protection."

Stifling a grin, I had to hand it to younger people today, they sure were confident.

"I think I can handle myself."

With a flick of his wrist and a wink, he handed me a business card with only a phone number on it. "Call me if you change your mind."

I was sure more than one female had been entranced by his bad-boy image but there were a few years difference in our ages. I put the card in my jeans pocket anyway.

"Once I get weighed at the scale I'll come back and you can sign off on the contract," I said to the secretary.

"Just give me the papers and I'll sign them now."

"But I can't give you a precise quote."

"I don't care about the cost, just fill in the amount once you have it figured out," the woman said testily. She glanced at her sparkly timepiece with impatience. "Mr. Stanton's last minute departure has left me with three appointments this morning, the first of which I will be late for if we don't finish this immediately."

"Oh, okay." I handed over her clipboard. "And I'll need the documentation for this cargo as well."

"Yes, yes." Ms. Ing shoved a manila envelope at me. "The address is on the front. Mr. Stanton left a check on his desk for the down payment. It's in there as well."

I took the envelope, held out my hand. "Thank you for using Hawkins Freight."

She turned and left without another word.

Okay then. "Y'all have a good day now," I called out.

My fingers went to open the flap on the envelope when Tanya appeared at my side.

"Sadie, we have to go or I'll be late for court."

The time on my own watch made my eyes gape open. Between loading everything and waiting for Tanya and her crew to come, it was later than I expected and I was way behind schedule. Slipping the envelope under my arm, I disregarded Tanya's protest and fumbled with my wallet to pay her and the group for helping me. After a quick hug, she strode to her vehicle while I secured the van's back doors with a lock. I hopped into the cab and broke into a huge grin. The heavy weight of uncertainty I'd been carrying since getting into business started to dissolve. Once I completed this job I would ask Stanton if I could use him as a reference. Who knows what doors that could open?

The clock on the dash screamed the lateness and I brought the engine to life with a roar. I'd have to drive like a bat outta hell to get to Pampa within a reasonable time. I flipped on the radio and zipped out of the alley in a squeal of tires.

CHAPTER THREE

"A possum in a three-legged race could move faster than you. Get the lead out!" My frustration level maxed at the rusted beater of a vehicle driving ahead of me. I'd been stuck behind the car for a while and with each progressive mile that I hadn't been able to pass, my patience dwindled.

"Screw it." I checked the side mirror, zipped into the oncoming lane, cutting off a pickup that had the same idea. With Brooks and Dunn booming across the airwaves, I floored the gas pedal and managed to cut back into traffic to the protesting blare of horns.

"Yeah, yeah, I know, but I'm on a tight schedule."

I cranked the music higher, floored the pedal and rocketed down the highway.

Until the strobe of red and blue lights accompanied by a siren appeared behind me.

Muttering a string of curses, I flicked on a signal and pulled over to the side of the road. I did not need this. At all.

From the side mirror, I watched the officer exit his car and walk my way. I took a second to fluff my short red hair, wet my lips, pasted on my most sincere smile and rolled down the window.

"Clocked you at thirty past the speed limit," the man dressed in a dark uniform, complete with reflective sunglasses said. "I'll need to see your license and vehicle registration."

"Of course," I replied, laying on the accent. I flipped down the visor, took out what he wanted and handed them to him.

Cars and trucks continued to whir by.

"Please step out of the vehicle ma'am."

I hedged. Oh, come on.

He waited.

Sometimes, a girl's gotta do what she has to. I couldn't believe I was about to stoop so low as to use feminine wiles.

I opened the door, turned to back down the step and purposefully missed the running board, losing my balance.

I hoped the guy was quick.

He jumped to my rescue, steadying my back as I fought to find my footing.

"My goodness, thank you," I gasped and stood on the pavement.

He said nothing but I caught the suppression of a smile. I barely came up to his mid chest.

The officer took a short step back, peered down. "Have you been drinking today, ma'am?"

"This early? No way. Besides, everyone knows you're not supposed to drink and drive."

The edge of his mouth twitched.

"You do realize you were speeding."

Trying to look properly chastised, I stared at my Dan Post turquoise triad water snake cowboy boots – a gift from Clayton when we were still married - before meeting the cop's mirrored eyes. "I know and I'm truly sorry but I need to get this delivery to Pampa as soon as possible or else I may lose the rest of the payment. If that happens I might as well fold up shop."

He eyed the lettering on the van. "What are you hauling?"

"Antiques."

"Do you have the proper papers?"

"Yes."

"I'd like to see them please."

When I turned to go into the van, he interrupted. "Uh, do you need a hand up?"

I flashed a brilliant smile. "No, thank you."

Grabbing the handlebar screwed into the doorframe, I actively stuck my jean-clad butt out, retrieved the documentation and hopped back down.

His gaze snapped up from where it was zeroed to my behind.

He scanned the papers, handed them back with my license and vehicle registration which I took with a pleading expression. "Are you going to give me a ticket?"

This time he let go the grin. "I'll let you off with a warning. This time."

"Thank you so much."

"Watch the lead foot. And don't forget to buckle up." As he tipped the brim of his hat he added. "Oh, and nice boots," then walked away.

I scooted up into the van and waited until the cruiser passed, then merged into traffic with a satisfied smile.

* * *

I reached Charles Street behind schedule and hoped Mr. Stanton wouldn't dock anything from my fee. The map navigation app on my phone left a lot to be desired but I finally pulled up in front of what could be classified was a stately mansion.

Two square brick columns, each topped with a black carriage style light, stood sentinel to the paved driveway that bisected a surprisingly green lawn when compared to the rest of the houses on the block. Round ornamental bushes, so perfect they looked like massive green billiard balls marched along both sides of the drive. The biggest Montezuma Baldcyprus I had ever seen towered over an expansive section of grass across from the house.

I backed the van up the part of the drive that branched to the front of the house on the left while the rest of the blacktop continued on to a structure at the back. Probably a garage.

A low whistle parted my lips as I climbed the bricked portico steps and rapped the huge front door three times using an ornate doorknocker. I inspected the well manicured grounds, which included a beautiful landscaped garden that circled the house. People with serious money lived here.

No answer. Maybe the servants had the day off.

I rapped again, waited. Perhaps, because of the size of the massive three story structure, no one heard my knocking. Not finding a doorbell I used the knocker again and added a few thumps of my fist.

Nothing but silence.

I meandered around the house and spied a window. Stepping through the pristine garden with reluctance, I slipped between the ornamental shrubs and peeked through the glass. The room, a parlor by the looks of it, was decorated in expensive furniture of some sort with thick area rugs and it appeared vacant. I crossed the lawn and headed to a three bay garage farther down the paved driveway but whatever windows I found were too far off the ground for me to see into.

Figures.

I headed back to the van, pulled out the contract and dialed the number for Mr. Stanton's office.

Maybe the personable Ms. Ing could shed some light on what was going on.

But after six rings the machine kicked in and I left a message to contact me as soon as possible.

On the off chance Blaine was at work, I called the office but there was no answer. However I did get him at home.

"Hey," he said in lieu of hello.

The temper tantrum scream of a child assaulted my ears. "Hi yourself. Sounds like world war three over there."

"Karen's at class tonight and I'm making dinner. Apparently my macaroni and cheese isn't as good as mom's."

"Oh yeah, I forgot tonight was course night. How much longer before she gets her CGA?"

"Not soon enough. Shanty, stop," he admonished his two year old daughter, Shantelle. "What's up?"

"Did you receive a call from Stanton's office today?"

"No. I got the message you'd left early this morning but haven't heard a word. Why?"

I glanced at the house, brow furrowed. "There's no one at pick up."

"Maybe he got waylaid."

"It's at a house. You'd think someone else would be here."

"What are you going to do?"

"Wait for a bit, I guess."

"Can you drop the load?"

"No way. First off I want payment and secondly I can't do this by myself."

"I'm sure Stanton will be along," he assured.

"Probably. Think I'll get a bite to eat and come back. Someone should be here by then."

"Keep me posted."

"Will do. And Blaine, try feeding my niece creamed corn. It was always your favorite." I smirked. The first and only time my brother ate creamed corn it came out just as fast as it went in.

"Very funny. Talk to you later." He disconnected.

I turned over the engine, ventured down the drive and out into the street. I spent the next half an hour hunting for a fast food outlet to take my meal to go and finally returned to my destination with a meal in a bag on the passenger seat.

But the situation remained the same.

"This is just strange."

From where the van was parked in the driveway between the house and garage, I kept checking around for any signs of activity while I ate my burrito but everything remained quiet.

As night began to settle in, I phoned my brother and reported what was happening. Or rather not happening.

"What are you going to do?"

"Stay the night, I guess."

"Is there a motel close by?"

"The seats recline a bit. I can sleep in the cab of the van."

"Taz…" he warned, using his childhood nickname for me.

"What? I can't afford a motel. I'll be fine."

"Okay, but call me in the morning."

"Goodnight."

I shut off the phone to save the battery and stared out into the Texas night. There was virtually no traffic on the street. A breeze, still warm from the mid-day heat, floated through the open windows, carrying an orchestra of cricket song. Before long, I got bored with nature's symphony, reached over and scanned channels on the radio until I landed on one that stopped me cold.

"Sweet Georgia brown." The breath left my lungs at hearing the DJ's voice. It was smooth, rich and deep, like a mixture of James Earl Jones and Sam Elliot. The resonance brought instant images of sultry languid nights tangled in satin sheets.

The man could talk down a treed raccoon with a voice like that. I turned up the volume.

"Now I know anyone tuning in has their own opinion of good, even great guitarists," crooned the mystery man. "But if you've studied them, as I have, and really listened to their technique, you'd have to agree no one can touch Clapton. Let's give a listen to the Slow Hand."

I gazed at the radio dial. If I had to stay up all night I was going to find out who he was.

As *Layla* belted out of the speakers, I sat back, closed my eyes and got swept away in audio bliss.

My head bopped to song after song of classic rock. I'd always thought myself more of a country gal but each tune this magical maestro commented on made me want to say goodbye to the steel guitar and venture over to the dark side of electric.

Just as long as Mr. Heavenly voice led the way.

"This is Jackson Steel on KRDL and I'll catch you on the other side of midnight after a short news break. And if any of you night hawks want to hear something, give me a call and I'll see what I can do." The velvet speaker proceeded to rattle off a toll free request line.

My bleary eyes sprang open and I launched for my phone, turning it on. I didn't care if I was acting like a teenage hormonal twit, I wanted to hear this man talk to me. Even if he only said hello. What I didn't expect was that he would answer on the second ring.

"KRDL. This is Jackson."

Holy Hannah, his voice was even better over the phone. Even my ears got goose bumps.

"Hi."

"Hello there. Thanks for calling in. How are you this fine evening?"

I was going to melt into a puddle right there in the cab of the van. "I'm fine, thank you." I almost choked. Nervousness made my Southern accent so thick, the 'u' sounded like I was a queen madam at a whorehouse.

"Is there something I can play for you?"

For me, to me, even on me, I didn't care.

"Umm, I'm not sure. I thought I would have to stay up longer but it looks like the person who was supposed to pick up some items isn't coming tonight." Good grief, I was babbling.

"Did a guy stand you up?" he said in good-natured disbelief.

"Well, ahhh…"

"Just a second."

While on hold, Jackson did a lead about the couple of songs he would play back to back and then he was on the line again.

"Sorry. Had to set up the next few titles. Don't tell me some guy left you high and dry?"

His voice didn't carry a Texas drawl, but it wasn't a Boston accent either. From what I could tell, Mr. Jackson Steel wasn't a native from these parts.

"It's not like that. I have a delivery but the client didn't show. I run a freight business."

"No kidding. You're a mover and a shaker."

"Well I don't know about shaking." Unless it's on the dance floor I wanted to add but didn't.

"Not many women in the moving industry. Lifelong dream?"

I stifled a laugh. "No. It's a family business."

I wasn't about to elaborate to a total stranger on how I'd become owner of Hawkins Freight. I'd won the business in a poker game because my Uncle Stan, my father's brother, had drunk and gambled himself into an early grave. All because of guilt over an accident he couldn't have prevented.

My father, Jerry, and his only brother were extremely close growing up but Stan left Alabama in his early twenties and moved to Houston. The man had been a wheeler-dealer but he had a heart of gold and loved all of us. On one of his visits, dad ended up giving Stan a hand with a move and there was an accident. My father died and Stan spent some time in the hospital. There was no evidence of wrong doing; it was just an unfortunate accident. Uncle Stan never forgave himself, changing from the warm, caring individual who had taught me to play cards at an early age, to a shell of a man. He slid into the bottle and despite my attempts at trying to reassure him no one in my family blamed him, he blamed himself. Once I moved to Houston I'd visit him as often as I could but the evidence of his guilt was plain; the business was sinking and Stan, the casual poker-night-with-his-buddies player, started to gamble heavily. He'd win some, lose some and then he lost it all. The next time I saw him, he was so drunk I almost couldn't make out the name he mumbled of the new owner of Hawkins Freight.

A week later Stan shot himself.

It took me a while before I finally connected with the owner of my uncle's former moving company. I didn't have enough money to buy the business and the proprietor wouldn't take installments to pay for the purchase. He did, however, love to gamble and agreed to a poker game. It was poetic justice that Stan's passion for playing cards, which he taught me, was the catalyst that gave me back the family business the same way in which he had lost it. I'd had to wait to reopen the business though, because at the time I was married to Clayton and again didn't have the money to keep it operational. A tiny voice whispered to me that I could win at poker to get the cash I needed but seeing what it had done to Uncle Stan, what he had become, scared me into not crossing that line – that lure of possibly winning a bigger pot. Some of the funds from my divorce had gone into getting the business open again. Hawkins Freight was the only connection I had left of my dad's family.

Jackson's voice brought me back to the present. "So, what now darlin'? You going to stay up for the next few hours with me?"

I literally bit my tongue so as not to blurt out what I'd love to do for a few hours with this man. Instead I tempered my answer with a hint of flirtatiousness. "As appealing as that sounds, I should hang up and try and get some sleep."

"Well, I'm sure my listeners won't mind if I play something different, especially if it's for a good cause." I could hear his smile across the line. "Maybe something soft and low."

Don't tempt me.

"That would be mighty nice of you."

"If I'm going to send it out, I need your name."

His voice level deepened. This guy took flirting to a whole new level.

For a second, I could have sworn I caught movement in my side mirror. I strained, peering into the darkness by the bushes but saw nothing. My tired eyes were playing tricks on me.

"Hello? You still there?"

"Oh, sorry. Thought I saw something in the shadows but nothing is there. My name is Sadie."

"Okay, Sadie, I'll see what—"

An awful screeching yowl of a cat nearby made me yelp, making me drop the phone and it clattered under my seat. Heart clamoring against my ribs I mentally cursed the feline. That was probably the shadow I had seen and scrambled down to search for my cell, desperately hoping Jackson was still on the line so I could at least thank him for the dedication. His voice lured me to my device and just as I reached for it, the driver's door sprang open. On instinct my fingers brushed past the phone, kept moving until they reached the baseball bat I always had beneath my seat and then I was yanked out the door, pulling the bat with me.

"Hey!"

I landed on my ass and came up in full swing with the twenty-five ounces of sanded and polished wood, aiming it at whatever or whoever was within range. The thirty inches of solid ash I held felt like an extension of my arm. I had played ball for most of my life, making it to one of Texas' Single A fastball leagues before I got married, becoming the top female batting champ in the state and second best overall in the league. Although my small stature gave me the advantage of being a fast runner, it was swinging line drives for double hits where I really shone.

And right now whoever had yanked me out of my van was going to get a taste of my 40/400 average.

The sound of bone exploding on impact with a sickening crunch came before a roar of pain ripped through the air. I dodged to the side, ready for another swing but before I could make it more than half way around, something that felt like a Mac truck slammed into the back of my head and the world turned to darkness.

CHAPTER FOUR

"Ma'am, ma'am, are you okay?"

"I will be as soon as the herd of buffalo stops square dancing in my head."

With a muffled groan, I gingerly peeled back my eyelids. A blurry figure swam in and out of focus in the night and for a second my not-quite-working brain considered the person was the attacker who gave me this Grand Canyon size headache. But reality resumed when I figured my assailant wouldn't be so considerate of my well-being.

"Can you stand?"

My gaze zeroed in on a dark uniform and a badge. The police officer gave me a hand, helped me to my feet where I staggered slightly. My shaking hand touched the goose egg bump on the back of my skull and I winced. What did I get hit with, a wrecking ball?

He aided me to the van's back bumper. "Do you know what happened?"

"Someone cold-cocked me."

"Why?"

"I have no idea, jollies maybe."

My Good Samaritan stood back, inspected the surroundings including the vehicle, noting the name on the side. "This your van?"

"Yes."

"You have a load?"

I nodded. Big mistake. Things wavered in and out of focus.

"Could be an attempted robbery," he suggested.

"Yeah, well I wasn't the only one who got whacked. Someone's going to need a new kneecap." I gestured to the handle of the baseball bat sticking out from beneath the van. I'd named it Louis, for the Louisville Slugger, and had always kept it with me no matter what vehicle I was in or where I went.

Eyebrows shot to his hairline. "You averted a robbery?" The officer stooped, picked it up, tested the heft, ran a hand along the shaft. "Nice. Good weight." He brought the bat closer. "No blood."

"Trust me, I nailed him. I heard bone shatter."

"Him. So it was a man you hit?"

"From the howl of pain, yes."

"Did you get a good look at him?"

"Sorry, no."

He tilted his head, inspecting me. "There's more to you than meets the eye. You're lucky you got away with a bump on the head. You could have been killed. Did you want me to call an ambulance?"

I touched the tender spot again, thought about the cost of going to emergency and concluded unless I was bleeding or unconscious I could handle it and told him so. But I wished I had an Aspirin. No, better an extra strength Aleve. Throbbing echoed in my ears. On second thought, nothing short of Morphine was going to get rid of this killer headache. Or perhaps a fifth of Wild Turkey.

He scanned the area. "There was no one else at the scene when I got here."

"Cowards."

"Would you rather they had stayed and finished you off?"

"Good point."

Adrenalin must still be in my system because I sure wasn't thinking clearly. I was more mad than scared. I pointed to the bat. "You're not going to keep it are you?"

"Considering it was self defense, no." He handed me the piece of wood. "Can I ask what you're doing here?"

"This is the drop off point for what I'm hauling."

"And that would be?"

"Antiques. I have documentation in the door of the van."

He walked to the front of the van, reached into the still open door, pulled out the envelope from the slot and retrieved some papers. After a quick perusal he replaced the contents and returned the envelope to the slot.

"But why are you here, at a house, in the middle of the night," he said walking back to me.

"The person I was supposed to meet wasn't here. In fact no one was, so I thought I'd wait until morning in case Mr. Stanton, my contact, would show up. I was about to get some sleep when this all happened."

"Still doesn't explain why you decided to stay here instead of finding a motel."

I averted his speculative gaze. "I've slept in the van before." I didn't have a problem admitting to myself I didn't have enough money to afford a motel room, it was entirely different saying it out loud.

The officer noted the doors above my head. "Lock's still intact. Looks like you thwarted their plans."

"Thwarted?"

"Cop jargon, ma'am," he smiled.

Really? Thwarted? I'd have to remember that one.

"You may want to rethink the motel. What if those men come back?"

"Well, considering one can't walk, I doubt it and I can't believe they'd be dumb enough to try again. Besides, I plan on backing the van up to the garage so they won't get in."

"They could try and take the van from you," the man pointed out.

I shook my head. Pain lanced through my skull. Gees, I didn't learn. "There was nothing stopping them in the first place when I was knocked out. It was probably a couple of young guys who saw an opportunity to do something stupid."

He paused, eyed me. "I don't know if I feel comfortable leaving you here alone for the rest of the night."

"As you can see, I can take care of myself. Please, Officer, it's too late for me to head back to Houston and I still have to drop this load somewhere. I'm sure everything will straighten itself out in the morning."

"Well," he turned around, surveyed the house and grounds. "I can't make you leave as you have a legitimate reason for being here, in a sense. You're not planning on robbing the place, are you?" he added with a quirk of an eyebrow.

I laughed. Another error. Oh, my aching head. "First, I'm not a thief and second if I had planned to rob the house, why would I still be here?"

His demeanor changed, softened. "How's the head?"

"I'll live."

"Did you want to file a complaint?"

"No. As you said the lock is still on the van. Looks like nothing was stolen. Besides, I can't give you a description."

I stood. "Wait a minute. How did you know to come here? I didn't dial 9-1-1?"

"Station got a call from some guy on the radio, said you'd been talking to him when things started to happen."

Jackson Steel. A warm sense of appreciation tickled across my skin.

"Good thing you didn't disconnect. We were able to trace the signal because he kept the line open."

For the first time in my life I was glad I dropped my phone. I stuck out my hand. "Well, I guess I should thank you Officer…?"

"Timmins, Wayne Timmins." He shook my hand. "But it's not me you should thank. If the guy hadn't contacted us, the perps could have come back. In case you think of anything or change your mind, give me a call." He handed me a business card. "And I'll see if I can have a unit drive by occasionally, just to be safe."

He took down my name, place of residence and contact information for his notes in response to the 9-1-1 call. As he stuck the small spiral notebook into his breast pocket, he hesitated, gazed into my face, as if he wanted to say something, but gave a light tug on his hat instead. "You take care now." He turned and left, his footsteps echoing sharply in the quiet night.

I tucked the business card into my pocket and sat on the bumper, trying to decide what I should do. Going back home right now was out of the question. Besides getting home around dawn, I didn't trust myself on the road with the way my head was feeling. And I still needed to find out where Stanton was and what to do with the cargo. Guess that meant staying in the van but the first order of business was chugging down a couple of Aspirin.

My normally agile entry into the van was hampered by incessant shaggy quadrupeds thundering around in my skull. I pawed through the glove compartment and practically wept for joy at detecting a bottle of pain relievers. Dry swallowing three, because downing the medication with a Live Wire was just asking for trouble, I started up the van and backed the whole way up the drive until my back bumper almost kissed the garage. Let's see if the buggers could get in now.

Learning from my mistakes, I locked the van doors, rolled up the windows so there was enough space to let air in and not some nutcases' hand and reclined my seat. As much as I wanted to listen some more to Jackson's voice still coming over the wire, I had to get some sleep. But that didn't stop me from thinking of various ways to personally thank him for looking out for me.

* * *

Rule number one when approaching someone whose head felt like it was used in a game of Whack-a-Mole while their body was contorted into a human pretzel from sleeping in the front seat of a vehicle; do not thump on the windows to wake them up.

The idiot scaring the living bejesus out of me didn't get that memo.

Rule number two, don't yell at them.

The idiot didn't get the addendum either.

After picking myself up from the floor, where I'd landed from jumping two feet into the air, I scrambled to find Louis under the seat, ready to do battle again. This time, it wasn't a shady character wanting to punch my lights out standing on the other side of my door, but an elegantly dressed woman in about her mid-forties who peered quizzically at me.

She took a step back when she spied the bat in my hands and hollered through the glass. "Are you okay?"

I forced air into my lungs and lowered the bat a bit. "Yes."

We stared at each other for a moment, not saying anything.

She broke the silence first. "What are you doing here?"

Figuring I had the upper hand in the situation, I reached over and rolled down my window, checking her out for hidden weapons. Unless she had a switchblade in her slim fitting Capri pants I was pretty sure I was safe. She appeared a bit disheveled like she'd been up all night.

"I'm here to make a delivery. Do you know where the occupants of the house are?"

"*I* live at this house, but I don't recall ordering anything recently."

"Oh. I arrived last night but no one answered the door."

"We've been away and I returned this morning." She did the full body scan, narrowed her eyes on my hair which probably looked like a Medusa special. "Just who are you?"

"Sadie Hawkins from Hawkins freight. Actually the delivery I have is for Lionel Stanton. Do you know where he is?"

"Who?"

I repeated my client's name.

"I'm sorry but I don't know anyone by that name."

"Perhaps someone else does. You said we've been away. Would that be you and your husband? Maybe you can ask him."

"He is still on holiday. I returned early. Look, this is not a convenient time. I've had a very long flight and am tired."

"But…but…"

The woman's tone hardened, her eyes pinched in frustration. "Please, Ms. Hawkins, the past few days have been quite stressful and I'm going to have to ask you to leave. I assure you, when my husband returns I will inquire if he is expecting a shipment. Do you have a card?"

The synapses in my brain were as tangled as a May Pole dance gone wrong and I struggled to make a coherent sentence as I fumbled with the visor, withdrew a business card, handed it to her. "But…what…why would Mr. Stanton tell me to bring the delivery here if it isn't for you?"

"That is not my problem. If the items have been ordered by my husband, I will contact you and pay your travel time. Now, if you don't mind I would like to go into my house and get some rest. Good day." She turned and marched off.

Well, didn't that beat all.

As it seemed I wasn't going to get any answers, I drove down the asphalt, onto the street but I knew one thing for sure. Someone was lying to me and if there was one thing I hated, it was a liar.

CHAPTER FIVE

Before I left Pampa, I wanted to meet my guardian angel. According to a web search, the office of KRDL was listed as a single story building on Banks Street. When I got there, the tell-tale electronics and the large bronze call letters on the front told me I was in the right place. I parked the van close to the door where I could keep an eye on it, took a few minutes to run a finger over my teeth, wished for a toothbrush, and tried to get my hair into some semblance of order. A quick peek into the visor mirror made me shudder, so I scooped out a ball cap stuck into the pocket of the passenger seat and slapped it on my head and headed into the building.

Music streamed through invisible ceiling speakers, ostensibly what was currently playing on the airwaves. The lobby was painted in various hues of blue. A light grey couch and chairs sat along one wall that had pictures of various DJs. I headed straight there, delicious anticipation tickling through my veins at being able to see what Jackson Steel looked like, only there wasn't a shot of him. Merely a frame with a blurred silhouette and his name underneath. Dang.

I crossed the tiled floor to the receptionist, a perky blonde who looked like she should be in high school instead of manning a multi-lined telephone console. She gave me a show of perfect white teeth that probably put her orthodontist's kids through private school.

"Hi. Welcome to KRDL! How can I help you?"

I tried to be as polite as possible without the benefit of my usual morning beverage; two cans of high octane cola. "Hello. I was hoping to speak with one of your on-air personalities, Jackson Steel."

"I'm sorry," Ms. Perky replied without a hint of remorse. She could be the poster child for Barbie. "Mr. Steel works strictly nights and isn't in the building."

That didn't come as a surprise considering the time of day it was when I'd almost dissolved into a blubbering mass of hormones at the sound of his voice. "Do you know where I can get a hold of him?"

"I'm sorry," she repeated with the same enthusiasm. "We can't give out that information."

Although that shouldn't surprise me either, I was a tad disappointed. Anyone could see with my lack of height I wouldn't make a very good axe murderer.

"Okay. Can I leave a message?"

"Absolutely!"

If she grinned any wider, I'd swear her face would split apart. I waited for her to give me a pen and paper. She just stared at me.

"What's the message?"

"It's kind of personal. Do you have anything I can write it on?"

"Absolutely!"

I closed my eyes briefly, made a mental note to never step foot out the door and meet these types of challenges without having the prerequisite amount of cola pumping through my system, and waited for her to give me what I needed to leave Jackson a note.

I stepped to the side, pressed my lips together as I tried to formulate what I wanted to say. Guaranteed, as soon as I left the building, Ms. Perky would read what I had written, so I had to put my point across without sounding like a love-struck groupie.

Or a stalker.

Or both.

I hemmed and hawed and finally settled on 'thanks for sending in the cavalry' and finished off with my phone number. The last bit was added on as wishful thinking. I didn't expect him to call, why would he? But if he did it would be because he wanted to and not because it was part of his job. I handed the folded paper to the girl, nodded my thanks and strode across the lobby.

"You didn't sign your name," she called out.

Wow, not even out the door. The gal worked fast.

"That's okay, he'll know." I kept on going. At least I hoped he'd know who the message was from.

Back in the van, I mapped my route out of the city, keeping an eagle eye for the closest convenience store. No way was I going to tackle the freeway without downing two cans of cola. Better make that three.

* * *

In Houston, I made a beeline for Stanton's office. I'd had enough of being jerked around and didn't appreciate wasting gas on some type of wild goose chase. I maneuvered through early afternoon traffic, shaking my head at how rude people could be and parked at the loading dock of the office building beside another larger truck. There wasn't anyone to open the locked door so I made my way to the front and entered the building. After the stifling heat from outside, the air conditioned lobby was like an oasis. Cream and tan marble flooring spanned the large room, meeting walls painted in soft beige. A janitor was dusting two sets of dark brown chairs that bracketed the glass entry doors. A solid mahogany desk presided close to the center, manned by a mid-forties woman dressed in business attire and currently on the phone. At her back was a makeshift waterfall of Plexiglas rising to the second story. Elevators were on the right and a hallway probably leading to other offices exited to the left.

I spied a building directory beside one elevator and saw a listing for Back in Time Antiques, which I thought was catchy. I entered the elevator and hit the third floor button. The doors swished open a moment later to a carpeted hallway that branched in both directions and a brass plaque that indexed office numbers either left or right. I ventured right, found the door for my client, gave a short knock and entered.

Expecting something like out of the Victorian era, I was surprised to see an ultra modern glass and metal reception desk. Dove grey walls held an assortment of paintings, some reminiscent of the ancient masters, while others would take me a year to figure out what they were supposed to represent. Dark grey carpet spanned the room. On a white square pedestal an object d'art held homage within a solid glass display case.

I went to the reception where a woman in her forties with light brown hair curled tightly to her head sat typing on a computer. I wondered if her hair was naturally that curly or it was a perm gone wrong.

She glanced up. Tired hazel eyes and a worried expression met mine briefly before calm, professionalism slipped into place. "May I help you?"

No perky blonde. I was making progress.

"Yes, I would like to speak with Ms. Ing please."

"I'm sorry, she is not in today. Is there something I can help you with?'

"Do you have a way of contacting Mr. Stanton?"

She stared at me. "Who?"

"Stanton. Mr. Lionel Stanton. He owns the business."

"There is no one here by that name and Back in Time Antiques is owned by Jeffrey Rogers."

Okay, what the Sam hell was going on?

I gaped at her long enough that she edged back in her chair and reached for the phone. "Perhaps there is someone I can call for you?"

She didn't wait for me to reply, hit a button on the phone and softly spoke into the receiver. "Could you come to the lobby please?"

My stomach started to form into a knot. The situation was more confusing than a Father's Day picnic in my home town.

I sat down and waited. And waited. Apparently whomever the receptionist phoned was taking the stagecoach from the other end of the country. I smiled at the staff member, hoping my pleasantness would persuade her to inquire what was taking so long. The phone rang, but instead of announcing the arrival of the party I was supposed to meet, it was a personal call.

The receptionist turned slightly, lowered her voice. "Thank goodness you called but I can't talk right now, Francie. Are you still out of town?"

Pause.

"Yes, I know I sound upset."

The woman began tapping her finger on the desk.

Although she was trying to keep her voice low, she didn't realize how much it carried in an otherwise silent room.

"I've done something awful and I'm scared I might get caught. I don't know what came over me. I really need to speak with you. When are you back?"

A door down a short hall closed.

"No, I can't talk about it now. Meet me on Monday at The Maple Diner. I get lunch at one. I have to go," hissed the receptionist and hung up the phone. I still kept my gaze averted to a piece of art on the wall.

A tall, slim, distinguished gentleman came striding toward me. Light touches of grey were dispersed in his dark wavy hair. A set of smart-looking black glasses rested on a straight nose, framing his green eyes. The tailored deep blue suit covered his six foot frame, complete with a light grey shirt and black silk tie.

He extended a hand in greeting. "I am Jeffrey Rogers. What seems to be the problem?"

"Sadie Hawkins." I finished the introductions with a shake. "Mr. Stanton hired me to deliver some crates carrying antiques and a mummy to Pampa yesterday morning. He said he would be there when I arrived. He wasn't at the destination and the woman who actually owns the house where I was supposed to deliver the items doesn't know anything about the delivery nor has ever heard of Lionel Stanton."

"As I'm sure my secretary has already said, there is no one by the name of Lionel Stanton in my employ."

"But I was *here*, yesterday morning. I got loaded from your loading bay out back."

"I see." His brows pinched together and he crossed over to the desk. "Perhaps we can check for any outgoing deliveries. Mrs. Yates, please pull up the manifest of the last three days. I'm sure there is some valid explanation for all this."

The older woman didn't look at him as she tapped on her computer while I watched Rogers but he didn't meet my gaze.

Within seconds she ran a finger down her monitor. "A couple of deliveries went out three days ago and one the day after. Nothing for yesterday."

"Stanton said his crew was out on another delivery. That's why he called me. He said it was a last minute transaction. Now I have cargo but no place to deliver it to."

"Do you have any documentation?" Rogers asked.

"Yes. In my van which is parked out back."

"Why don't I accompany you and I'll have a look at it." He glanced to the secretary. "Mrs. Yates, I'll be back in a minute."

"Don't forget you have an early dinner meeting with Ms. Ing to go over details before your departure tomorrow," Mrs. Yates said a bit frostily. "And you asked me to remind you about the theatre tickets."

Rogers did not reply but his lips compressed for a moment and I caught a quick narrowing of his eyes in irritation before it was gone. A ripple of icy tension followed us out the door. Someone was miffed.

As we walked to the elevator he said, "Is it possible you have the wrong name?"

I don't have Alzheimer's I felt like saying. Then I had an idea. "I have proof. Ms. Ing said Stanton wrote out a check for half the cost so you can see for yourself."

He nodded but said nothing and we rode down the elevator in silence. At the lobby, instead of going out the front, Rogers escorted me through a door behind the reception desk and down a long florescent-lighted hallway. Perhaps because of what had happened in Pampa, my gut tightened in panic. I realized no one knew exactly where I was. I hadn't called Blaine or Tanya and this guy could shove me into a room and no one would know. I lagged a bit, trying to decide if this was such a good idea when he opened a heavy metal door at the end of the hall and I spied the familiar loading bay. A rush of relief made me quicken my steps.

He let me through and I noticed the forklift we had used to load the crate containing the sarcophagus was in use, this time moving a pallet of large boxes with some type of writing on them into a truck beside mine. Another two pallets of boxes lay in wait.

We went to the outer door and down the stairs to the van. The lack of breeze and stifling heat slammed into me. I unlocked the door and pulled the envelope that contained the documents from the door's pocket. I withdrew the papers and handed them to Rogers.

As he scanned the first sheet his gaze narrowed. He quickly flipped through the remainder of the pages and jerked his eyes to mine.

"This isn't right. Where is the check?"

There was no paperclip on the documentation so it must still be in the envelope. I dug to the bottom and tugged it out but when it cleared the envelope, Rogers yanked it out of my fingers.

"Hey!"

His lips formed a thin line. "Did you examine this before you set out?"

"Ahhh…no." I was going to when Ms. Ing gave me the packet but then Tanya needed to rush off and I had been running so late I never got the chance. As I drove to Pampa, I remember thinking I should check but what with the attempted theft and me mooning over Mr. Velvet voice, aka Jackson Steel, I totally forgot.

"Why? What's wrong?"

He flipped the paper for me to see. The check was from Back in Time but it was completely blank. No signature.

"I think you'd better open up the back. Now."

I didn't care for his tone or the menacing glare on his face. Something was really wrong and I pulled the keys out of my pocket with trembling fingers. We went to the back and I jabbed the key into the lock. It wouldn't turn. I gave it another twist. Nothing.

My heart went into overdrive.

"I don't get it. I put this lock on myself. Why won't the key work?"

"Let me try."

He took the keys but had the same result.

The line between his brows deepened. Instead of handing me back my keys, he clamped onto my arm and started hauling me back up the stairs into the loading bay.

"Now just a cotton-picking minute!"

"You, Ms. Hawkins," he stated emphatically, "are coming back up to my office and we are calling the police."

I dug in my heels but was no match for the death like grip he had on me.

"Tell me what's going on!"

He mutely marched me to the elevator and back into his office where he instructed Mrs. Yates to call the authorities. He sat me down in a chair at the reception and stood guard, as if challenging me to escape. I knew there had to be a logical explanation but I still felt like a kid being hauled into the principal's office and shifted between panic and outrage.

Rogers must have had some pull because the police arrived within what seemed like minutes. Funny, they never did that when I'd needed them.

Two uniformed-clad police officers, one of which was a female, listened with interest as both Rogers and I stated our sides of the story. When we finished, the male, Officer Daniels, faced Rogers.

"And why did you call us in?"

Rogers arrowed a finger at me. "Because, according to the documentation she provided, Ms. Hawkins is in possession of stolen property."

I whirled at the company owner, thinking I hadn't heard right. "What!? Are you nuts? How can I have stolen property when I have the proper papers?"

"These items were in my care, yes, but they were not sold by me." He jabbed his finger to the papers. "This is not my signature."

Daniels' partner, Officer Thomas, interceded. "Let's go down to the van and check."

I turned to face her. "Can't. For some reason the key doesn't work in the lock."

"I'm sure I can find a pair of bolt cutters somewhere," Rogers smugly suggested.

After locating a tool, the four of us went back down to my van and I stood with hands on hips. Daniels tried the key but the lock wouldn't open. He hefted the cutters and snapped the bolt in two. With a flip of the handle, he tugged open both doors and we all peered inside.

To an almost empty space.

I sucked in great gulps of blistering air. The only thing left in the van was the huge container that had the sarcophagus. Everything else, all the other wooden cartons that had been loaded, were gone.

I'd been robbed.

"What is that smell?" Rogers covered his mouth with a handkerchief.

Daniels and Thomas instantly went on alert, their bodies tense. Thomas immediately put a hand on her holster and kept it there. Daniels searched the loading bay and came back with a pry bar. My heart was pounding like a cornered rabbit as he approached the huge crate. He went to slam the end of the bar under the lid of the crate but found no need.

The lid was no longer nailed shut.

The pry bar clanged as it hit the floor of the van and Daniels heaved up the wooden lid, covering his nose with his elbow. He felt around for a minute then grasped and yanked open the elaborate cover of the mummy case. The most noxious stench filled the van and I almost gagged. I had a feeling, without being told, that the body in the sarcophagus wasn't hundreds of years old.

Daniels slammed both lids back down and strode directly to me.

"Sadie Hawkins, you are under arrest for theft and suspicion of murder."

Officer Thomas spun me around and I experienced the uncomfortable yet familiar sensation of being in very deep trouble.

Well, hell.

CHAPTER SIX

"We've got to stop meeting like this."

I locked gazes with Clayton Bellows across the metal table that was bolted to the floor at the Houston Police Department. Florescent lights washed out dark beige walls to a dirty off-white in the eight by ten interview room. There was no window.

The corner of my mouth lifted at my ex-husband's attempted levity. His dark brown hair cut conservatively short was neatly in place. Moss green eyes held mine and although his handsome triangular face remained impassive, I caught a glimmer of concern before he sat back and folded his arms across his chest.

"Just like old times." My smirk was half-hearted. Although I was innocent, I was in a crap load of trouble and because of my past, I wondered if I'd be spending the night in jail.

Or more than one. The thought left me cold.

He leaned forward and opened the file folder in front of him. "Grand theft and suspicion of murder.

You sure don't do things half way. Take me through it."

I explained everything, starting with Stanton's phone call until the events that lead to my arrest. His mouth quirked at the part about hitting the guy in the knees with my bat and I could tell he was trying hard not to laugh.

"I'll get someone to check emergency room visits in Pampa over the past twenty-four hours, see if I can get some corroboration."

A thought hit me. "Talk to Officer Timmins." I pulled out the card still resting in my pocket. "He was the one who answered the 9-1-1 call. He'd have to file some type of report, right?"

His hand brushed mine when he took the card and his fingers twitched ever so slightly. Those long, slim hands that used to caress and knead, stroke and lay claim. But not anymore and for a brief moment I wondered who was sorrier.

"Yes, plus there will be a record of that call but it still looks like an attempted robbery."

"I don't get it. How could the stuff be gone?" The notion had been bugging me ever since the back doors were open and I saw the almost empty van.

"Any other way into the back?"

"No."

"Was there any time you were away from the vehicle?"

"No."

Except when I went to the radio station to try and see Jackson Steel I'd been in the van the whole time. "Well, other than when I arrived back at the antiques dealer."

He frowned, pursed his lips and there was the lawyer I had come to depend on. I could almost hear the gears turning in his head, his mind looking at angles, outcomes.

"How long were you away from the van?"

I shrugged. "I don't know, maybe fifteen minutes, twenty at the most the first time I went in. And I have no idea how long it was from when Rogers pulled me upstairs to when the police arrived and we went back down."

"Hmm, might be possible to take what they wanted, if they had enough people. Even if they had to go in twice, both times you were up in the office."

"Sorry to burst your bubble, hon, but the door was locked. In fact the police had to break in."

"Why? Did you lose the keys? Wouldn't be the first time."

"Very funny. The keys didn't work. Even Rogers couldn't get the lock open."

Clayton sighed. "Why didn't you say so in the first place?"

"Guess I had other things on my mind, like the dead body in the sarcophagus. The *fresh* dead body." I shuddered. Wonder if I'd ever get that smell out of my nose.

"One thing at a time. The lock. You're sure you secured it when you first left yesterday morning?"

"Yes."

"What type was it?"

I gave him a description of a well known brand.

"Your basic lock found at any hardware store."

"Meaning?" I leaned forward, spread my arms wide. I couldn't see where he was going with this.

"Meaning, someone switched the locks, putting the blame on you. It could have been when you were knocked out in Pampa or even here in Houston. Three or four guys could easily clean out the crates in twenty minutes. You said yourself it was only the sarcophagus that required a forklift. And that also tells me it was planned."

I sat back, stunned. "Son of a bitch."

"Did you get a chance to look around the loading bay at the antiques place?"

"I was a little busy at the time." I was pissed. Royally pissed and the comment came out with more sarcasm than I intended.

"Sorry."

Clayton tugged back the sleeve of his navy blue suit jacket and glanced at his watch. "You can bet if whoever took the stuff while you were away from your vehicle and temporarily hid it in the loading bay, it's gone by now."

Did the thieves put the crates I'd been hauling into larger boxes like the ones on the pallet which were being moved onto a truck when I'd first come down with Rogers? If so, it was a ballsy move, like hiding in plain sight.

I placed my elbows on the table, put my hands over my face and sighed heavily. I couldn't believe this was happening. I wasn't one for hysterics but a bubble of panic started to form, threatened to creep up and overthrow the hold I had on my nerves.

"Hey," Clayton said softly, reaching over and pulling my hands away from my face. "We'll get to the bottom of this, including the murder charge."

"I didn't do it, any of it." The implication of what was happening hit me full force and my voice cracked in an anxious whisper.

"Of course you didn't."

There was a short knock before the door opened and a uniformed officer poked his head in.

"Times up, Counselor."

Clayton squeezed my hand. "Hang in there. I'll see if I can get you out tonight."

The uniform came in, holding a set of handcuffs. I rose and put my hands behind my back.

"Can you call Blaine, tell him what's going on and not to worry." I imagined my brother would have a fit once he heard.

Nothing like history repeating itself.

Clayton nodded, grabbed his briefcase from beside the chair, stuffed the file from the table into it and rose. He may have been an overworked and under paid public defender when I'd first met him but since then one of Houston's top legal firms enticed him over and he'd been making a name for himself ever since.

His smile of assurance gave me hope. It was one of the things I liked about Clayton, his unfailing belief in me. We may not have made the perfect husband and wife, but he had stood by me before when I really needed him and I knew he'd do it again.

CHAPTER SEVEN

Clayton did manage to get me out of jail but it was late afternoon the next day when I finally stepped out of the Houston Police Department's multi-storied concrete detachment on Reisner Street.

Although heat waves shimmered from the sidewalk beneath my feet and the air lay still and heavy, it was a heck of a lot better than the stale, almost dank atmosphere I'd experienced over the last twenty-four hours.

I spent most of last night awake in my six by eight cell, complete with metal toilet that chilled my butt when I finally broke down and used it, trying to make sense out of the debacle from the last two days. All I received for my efforts was a raging headache due to high octane cola withdrawal and list of questions longer than a preacher's sermon on Sunday.

"I made some headway." He turned his BMW out of the police station's parking lot followed the street and then right onto Houston Avenue.

"Can this wait until after I have a shower, change of clothes and get something to eat?"

He eyed me briefly, probably sensing from my closed off expression and the fact that I was staring out the side window that I wasn't in the mood to talk. My short incarceration brought back a lot of memories, ones I had tried very hard to suppress.

"We'll swing by your way. You can get washed up and then I'll take you to my place and make dinner."

I turned to him, lifted my eyebrows but didn't respond.

"We need to discuss some things which I'd rather do in private and I certainly don't expect you to cook."

I nodded my agreement and went back to watching cars zip by, the people inside on their way home or to some appointment, oblivious how life could change for them, for anyone, at any moment. I was withdrawing, a self defense mechanism I did when things got out of control in my life, and was grateful Clayton sat beside me and not Blaine. There were some things even an ex would understand more than a sibling and although my brother would believe me when I said I had nothing to do with the theft and murder, I wouldn't be able to handle seeing pity in his eyes that I was in trouble yet again.

At my home I showered and changed my clothes and then we headed to his condo.

Once inside, he dropped his keys and briefcase on the lacquered table in the entranceway and headed straight for the kitchen. I felt kind of awkward being in such intimate quarters so I left him there, busily chopping and cooking while I wandered the two thousand square foot space and marveled at the view.

A black leather couch and two matching chairs, their hides rich and soft like butter, sat perpendicular to a white marble gas fireplace that was currently unlit in the Texas summer. Recessed lighting threw a muted glow over a few pieces of modern art hanging on walls of cool blue-grey then pooled into soft halos on the bleached grey wooden flooring. A rectangular glass dinner table with four metal chairs took residence on a step-up riser, giving an unobstructed view through the floor to ceiling windows that looked out over the Houston skyline.

In a little while, Clayton emerged from the kitchen wearing an apron over his black pants and pale blue shirt, minus the suit jacket, quickly set the table for two and then carried in a couple of steaming plates with a chilled bottle of white wine tucked under an arm. He waved me over to the table and I sat down. Memories of shared dinners like this when we were married came back in a rush and I struggled to push then away.

Fried okra and catfish were piled on trendy contemporary plates and an unexpected wave of gratefulness swept through me, but instead of saying so for fear my voice would crack, I fell back on my failsafe wit.

"Domesticity suits you, apron and all."

He tossed the noted garment onto another chair and poured wine into glasses. "If a man wants to eat, he should learn to cook. Besides, I had a feeling you could use some comfort food."

The jolt of gratification returned, so I took a sip of wine. The crisp, fresh vintage tingled on my tongue. "Nice wine. Nice place, too."

"Thanks. I like it."

"Different. Didn't realize you cared for monochrome and leather."

"Styles change. People too."

Sometimes.

Despite his growing up in an affluent family with deep roots in Texas and my heritage from a small Alabama town, our differences, even uniqueness were what had initially drawn us together.

After we married, I tried to bring some southern atmosphere into the big house his parents bought both of us as a wedding gift. In the beginning Clayton had accepted my style, both in furnishings and clothing. But as time wore on and he moved from public defender to one of Houston's most prestigious law firms, his outlook and mine started to travel down different paths. He never criticized outright, but his discomfort and alternative suggestions increased and it felt like the Sadie Hawkins from Oxford, Alabama became more and more smothered. Eventually, we both realized that coming from different worlds was what pulled us apart.

I gazed out at the Houston skyline punctuated with yellow and neon. "I'm surprised you didn't stay in the house."

When we split up, Clayton had paid me out. I'd taken that money, got a small apartment, not nearly as grand as his, and used some of the remainder for my business. I was lucky, most divorces weren't as amicable as ours and he and I were still comfortable in each other's company.

He wiped his mouth on a napkin. "The condo is more my thing and also closer to work."

"No female touches."

Clayton's brow quirked. "Fishing?"

I pressed my lips together, cringing at how my foot likes to take up space in my mouth all too often. Why I had said that was beyond me and I certainly didn't want to analyze the reasoning now.

"Just making an observation." I hurriedly changed the subject. "Thank you for getting me out so quickly. I'm sure it wasn't easy."

"I pulled a few strings and told them I'd be responsible for you."

"Some things haven't changed."

The corner of his mouth lifted and he pointed to my plate. "Eat."

I took a bite of fish. "You mentioned making a bit of headway."

"Some. One of the staff at the office contacted the officer in Pampa and your attempted burglary story checks out. And according to your timeline of that day, a person would be hard pressed to get rid of the crates in the van. Doable, but it'd be tight."

"In other words, we haven't found out anything new."

He put down his fork. "It's only been a day, Sadie. Give me time. I'm waiting on the coroner's report on cause of death."

I picked at my food, all appetite gone. I'd hoped Clayton's people or the police would have found the missing antiques so at least one of the charges could have been dropped.

"What about the body in the sarcophagus?"

"Right now he's a John Doe. No ID on his person, and I think Houston PD is running his prints but if the guy had no priors he won't be in the system, so they won't get any hits."

A sick feeling welled up. It was a bit of a stretch but what if the body was Stanton? I said as much.

"Possible," Clayton conceded.

"If it is, I had no reason to kill him. Hell, I hadn't even met the man yet."

"You and I both know that." He sipped his wine. "Playing devil's advocate, the way the prosecution will look at it, they'll say you killed him to fence the stolen artifacts. And, still under the supposition the body was Stanton, whoever did kill him set it up quite well. It could have been days before his body would have been found, if at all, had the sarcophagus not stayed in the van and begun to decompose so quickly because of the heat."

My throat seized at his words and I took a few gulps of wine before I could breathe. Set it up. Had someone actually targeted me specifically to take the fall for Stanton's murder, or was it just circumstance? But then how would they know I was going to move the load? I'd gotten the call from him only the night before. Was he being watched? Then another thought hit me with the force of a southern hurricane. How did I know if it really was *Stanton* I talked to? Since I'd never met the antiques dealer maybe the voice belonged to one of the killers and they needed a fall guy, or in my case, gal.

"You're over-analyzing it."

I started. The fork hovering half-way to my mouth threatened to clatter against the plate and I rescued it just in time.

"What?"

"It's what you do whenever you come across a problem."

"No, I wasn't." I stabbed a few chunks of vegetable, the tines of my utensil making loud chinking noises as it met the plate.

"We were married Sadie, I know all your tells."

"Can't play poker with you." The joke failed badly, probably due to the tremor of defeat in my voice. I stared at my almost untouched food, not wanting him to see the panic that was trying to slither up my throat.

"Sadie…"

Whatever Clayton was about to say got cut off with the ringing of my cell phone. I went to rise but my ex laid his hand on mine.

"Let it go to voice mail."

Green eyes held mine, concern drawing tiny lines across his forehead. I eased my hand away. "The call could be a potential job redirected from the office and I can't afford to ignore it." I stood with a sad smile. "God knows it certainly isn't someone asking me out on a date."

I pulled the phone from my purse on the fourth ring and noted the call display and turned slightly away. "I have to take this." The conversation was brief and to the point after which I hung up and went to gather my things.

"I have to go."

Clayton crossed the distance between us. "But we still have lots of things to discuss."

"Tomorrow. If you can't take me back to my place I can get a cab."

"Of course I'll drive you home, but Sadie…"

"I have to leave, Clayton. Now."

He must have noticed the rock hard set of my jaw and how rigidly I stood at the door. "The facility?"

"Yes."

"I can take you."

"I don't know how long I'll be. Just get me back home and I'll drive myself." My hand was on the doorknob. My voice lost a bit of its tension. "Thank you for dinner, it was very thoughtful."

He nodded, grabbed his keys and followed me outside.

CHAPTER EIGHT

I had travelled the route to the facility so many times it was as familiar as going to work and when I received the type of phone call that had summoned me, my mind always ventured down the dark pathway that had created the situation. When I arrived at the four-story building on Richmond Avenue almost an hour later, I pulled my pick-up truck into a parking space, sat for a moment to gather my inner strength then hopped out and strode quickly to the front glass doors of Windhaven and punched in a code. The automatic lock clicked and I went in. The woman at the reception desk nodded at my passing and I bypassed the elevator for the stairs.

On the second floor, I went directly to the last room at the end of the hall and paused just outside the door. I could hear murmured voices, one soothing, one in a state of distress saying she wouldn't go. I knocked briefly before going in.

The nurse standing over the bed came to me, the light purple cat patterned uniform sat snugly around her overweight frame.

I peered over the woman's shoulder. "How bad is she?"

"A bit stressed. Wouldn't eat or take her medication but I think she'll calm down now that you're here." She moved to the doorway. "Come get me when you leave and I'll give her something to help her sleep."

I waited until the nurse left before stepping to the bedside.

I took her hand, the skin smooth but thin. "Hi momma."

The person sitting up in the bed stared blankly at me. "Who are you?"

"It's me momma, it's Sadie."

A frown wrinkled my mother's brow. "Sadie?" Her eyes traversed my face, searching, searching, until her features eased and she said in a sing-song voice. "Sadie, Sadie, my pretty little lady."

"That's right momma. I'm here."

She smiled mischievously. "Will you tell me a story?"

I pulled up a chair. "Sure. What would you like to hear?"

"Oh, you pick something. You always have good stories."

I may have good stories to relate to my mother but the one of how she got here was like something from a horror crime novel.

Ricky Best had been my mother's on again/off again boyfriend for a number of years. I was going to Houston Community College, or HCC as it was a heck of a lot easier to say, at the time and my mom, Jolene, had come to visit from Amarillo. We'd moved there from Alabama shortly after my father died because that's where my mother's brother, lived and he got mom a job.

It was during her visit while I attended HCC that I started to notice the change in her. The once vivacious woman had become subdued and jittery and even though I tried to assess what was going on, she said nothing was bothering her. The plucky southern belle who had raised Blaine and me since our father's death was gone. When I spied the bruises on her body as I passed by the bedroom in my apartment while she was changing, I suspected the cause of her personality alteration.

Ricky was using mom as a punching bag.

He never left signs of the abuse in any overtly obvious location and she denied he was the cause of the marks on her body but I knew better.

On the last night of her visit I took mom out to a Tex-Mex BBQ Block Party being put on as part of Houston's fall celebration. We were having a great time dancing to a local band outside on a huge portable dance floor. My mother was kicking up her heels and I caught a glimmer of the person I knew before dad died. As we were leaving and heading to my car parked on a side street a number of blocks away on that warm night, Ricky showed up.

A few years younger than Jolene, Ricky was very different than my mother. Smooth, charming, even overconfident in a quiet, mysterious sort of way, he owned the department store where my mother had worked. After a couple of polite refusals for a date, he'd eventually worn down her resolve and they became a couple.

"Ricky." Mom's eyes widened. "What are you doing here?"

"I had business in Houston, thought I'd catch some of the local flavor."

I eyed him with speculation. The odds of him just happening to be here and finding us on the street were something I wouldn't even take to Vegas. It wasn't a secret that I was attending HCC and since they'd been an item for a while she would have mentioned either him or her friends and coworkers where she was heading.

Although not in a three piece suit, his slicked back hair, dark dress pants, tailored silk shirt and Italian shoes would hardly fit in with the jean clad, boot stomping, Stetson toting crowd we had left behind.

"Really?" I did little to gloss over my disbelief.

He didn't rise to my bait. "Hello Sadie." The tone was the same he probably used when meeting any new buyer for the first time instead of the daughter of the woman he'd been seeing for the past few years.

It wasn't as if we had started on the wrong foot when we'd first met. But from the very beginning, Ricky and I had kept each other at arm's length. Perhaps unconsciously we were both vying for my mother's attention and considered the other as competition. Whatever the reason, I had never warmed up to the man but kept things as cordial as possible for mom's sake.

"Well," he flashed his perfect white teeth in a smile that although was friendly, certainly wasn't filled with love. "As luck would have it and you're here, perhaps we could get a drink together and talk."

Out of the corner of my eye, I saw mom stiffen. What was that all about?

"I'd prefer to go home with Sadie, but thank you." Her words were said more like a statement than the warmth of apology I'd expected. Apparently they were on the off again stage in their relationship.

His lips thinned briefly before they smoothed in a hopeful gesture. "Surely one drink won't hurt."

Mom turned to me. "I'm tired, let's go." She glanced back to Ricky. "Enjoy the evening."

We went to the car but he continued to follow us. "Jolene, please. I only want to talk to you."

My temper reared its ugly head. "Look Rick," I started but felt a restraining touch on my arm so dialed it back a bit. "She said no."

He eyeballed me. "I don't believe this conversation involves you."

Condescending jerk. "Perhaps, but the conversation is now over."

He stepped closer. "I will talk to my wife however and whenever I wish."

"First off, she isn't your wife."

Jolene tried to pull me aside. "Sadie."

"Mom, he's got no right to speak to you that way. To anyone for that matter."

"Freedom of speech," he pointed out with an air of authority as if sensing my mom might relent.

"Okay, then get lost."

He leaned down, his face inches from mine. "You mind your mouth little lady."

"Freedom of speech," I repeated sarcastically and turned to unlock the car door.

He grabbed my arm, shoved me hard against the vehicle. My mother shrieked and as luck would have it, two couples rounded the corner, perhaps going to the same festivities we had just left and strolled our way. A smug smile turned up the corners of my mouth because I knew Ricky wouldn't cause a scene in front of others.

I walked around to the passenger side. "Come on, mom. We're leaving."

She hesitated, perhaps thinking by conceding she'd diffuse the situation but she matched my gaze and slid into the seat. I rounded the car, gave Ricky a mock salute, climbed in and pulled away from the curb.

"You shouldn't have antagonized him," Jolene said as we drove through the crowded streets back to my place.

I gripped the steering wheel hard. "And you would never have let a man speak to you like that before."

"Honey."

"No, mom. He's an ass and he's hit you."

"You wouldn't understand," she sighed.

I made a left turn, flicked my eyes in her direction. "You're right, I don't, so please, explain it to me."

She stared out the window. "I don't want to argue. Let's just go home."

When we got back to my place, I made tea but the pleasantness of the evening was ruined. We talked about superficial things then got ready for bed.

It must have been over an hour after I fell asleep that I woke up. Something had awakened me and I sat tense, alert, straining to hear the sound. The muted sounds of a party down the hall filtered in through the walls but the noise was different.

"Mom?" Thinking she might not be feeling well, I rose and made my way to the bathroom.

"Mom, you okay?"

A whimper pulled me to the room where she was sleeping. I eased open the door and crossed the threshold. "Momma?"

The room was dark and I didn't expect to see anyone else but someone behind the door yanked me inside before throwing me against the wall. My head snapped back against a picture frame, making it tilt crazily to the side. I didn't even have a chance to yell before a fist collided with my face, sending an explosion of pain across my cheek. I gasped out in agony as another blow landed and I fell to the floor. A shoe met my midsection in a vicious kick. Nausea rose, thick, heavy and I heaved, gagged and heaved again, emptying the evening's dinner and drinks from the contents of my stomach. A further assault to my body brought darkness to briefly take me away.

When I awoke, I peeled back my eyelids, pain simmering everywhere. From the glow of the streetlight streaming across her pillow, I saw my mother lying limp on the bed, almost in a catatonic state while a beast of a man violated her in every way possible. She was a mess, bruised, bloodied but it was her total lack of defense that scared me into action. Ricky, his face in a demonic grin of power, was so intent on crushing the will of the woman beneath him that he didn't notice me crawling across the floor to the closet. Every second it took to get to my destination echoed with sounds of abuse, helped me push past the pain that seemed to permeate everywhere inside my body. I reached into the closet, closed my hand around one of the four baseball bats I kept there for when I played, and eased myself up, shoving the agony from my ribs to the furthest recesses of my mind.

Ricky leaned forward, braced one hand on the bed, violating my mother while he drove punches to her side. His threats of retaliation for her denying him were filled with fury. With the shadows around the room and his attention on the terror he was inflicting, he didn't see me creep up to the edge of the bed until I had the bat in mid swing. The movement must have caught his attention because he shifted which made the weapon connect with his shoulder instead of the head I was aiming for. He grunted, swayed to the side and I took that second to leap onto the bed and deliver as many hits as I could. I don't remember screaming, perhaps I didn't, but a blood red haze enveloped me and it wasn't until my mom touched my leg and I finally glimpsed her lying there, that I snapped out of my rage and let the bat go.

I fumbled off the bed, went to her. "Mom! Mom!"

Her vacant stare horrified me but I saw her breathing. She slowly raised a hand and I slid an arm beneath her, pulled her up and out of bed, sheets tangling around her legs. I dragged her from the room, hell bent on getting out of the apartment, away from the monster still in its premises. I couldn't take a full breath for the agony on my left side. Once in the living room, I shouldered her up and half walked, half dragged her out the door and across the hall. The party was going full swing two doors down, music blaring, some of the participants leaning against one wall, sipping various liquids. I hollered at them but they must have been too inebriated to determine that I needed help and merely laughed drunkenly.

I pounded on the neighbor's door, yelling to open up. A few other doors opened, people stuck their heads out; one of them yanked his back in and shut the door. Finally, the portal I was thumping on opened and Mr. Reynolds, a fifty-something guy I had met only briefly, let us inside. I staggered in, shrieked about calling the police and slipped to the floor with my mother in tow.

In hindsight, it could have been my body coming to grips with the assault or my mind realizing we were somewhat safe, but I ended up losing consciousness again and I don't remember anything else but waking up in the hospital the next day.

They wouldn't let me see my mother for two days after, saying she was heavily sedated and needed rest. But no amount of rest would bring back the woman who had brought me life. Ricky had torn apart her psyche, broken the essence of her spirit, just as certainly as he'd tried to break her body. What remained was a damaged person who lived within the sheltered confines of her mind where she was finally free and safe from those who would do her harm.

"Sadie, tell me the story of Cinderella."

Mom's hushed words broke me from my internal nightmare and I smiled. "Once upon a time…"

CHAPTER NINE

The morning after my visit to my mother, I stumbled from bed, staggered to the bathroom, hit the shower with my eyes closed, and belatedly noticed I still had my sleep shirt on.

It was going to be one of those days.

The garment hit the shower floor with a wet splat and I finished washing. Once I towel dried my hair and checked the mirror, the dark circles under my eyes made me look like an albino raccoon.

"Nice."

I'm not one of those women who take an hour to get ready; some mousse in the hair, a quick finger comb, a light coat of foundation and I'm out the door. But my face needed some serious help and I hauled out the few cosmetics I had to cover up the tell-tale signs of a sleepless night or people would think I was trying out for the lead in the female version of the movie *Rocky*.

Forgoing the tee shirt and I usually wear when I'm doing a moving job, I slipped on a short sleeved light colored blouse and boot cut jeans, opened the fridge and lovingly embraced a bottle of high octane cola, twisted the cap and downed half the liquid in one long drink.

Thank the gods.

Since I'd turned off my phone once I'd gone in to see mom, I thought it best to check my cell for any messages from the Windhaven nursing staff but there were none. When I'd left last night, my mother had drifted off to sleep peacefully, which was usually the case when she became agitated and only needed to see me or hear my voice to calm down.

There was, however, a message from Clayton.

'Hey, it's me. Just checking to see if everything is all right. We'll talk more later.'

My heart softened a bit at his conscientiousness. I'd call him back sometime today, not yet feeling up to dealing with anything involving my mixed up life at the moment. Cowardly, yes but my southern chutzpah took a brief holiday while I was behind bars.

No message from my mystery DJ.

Dang.

Why did I expect one? He didn't owe me anything. I, on the other hand, owed him my life – you never knew – and would love to bear his children...on second thought, I'd love to practice what it took to bear his children. I sighed. Looked like I was relegated to be one of his many admiring fans where communication came from wanting to hear a special song. Maybe there was a reason he never called, like he was scooped up by an agent in Hollywood because of his voice.

There was still hope he'd call.

I struck my head on the kitchen counter a few times. I needed to get a life.

Since said life meant necessities like food, roof and clothing, I grabbed my purse and headed to the office.

Ordinarily getting to work took twenty minutes to half an hour if the traffic behaved. And on any other day that would be the case. But for some reason, fate, the sacrificial gods or the bad luck fairy decided today it would smack me down faster than a herd of girls going after the unattached male at the May Day picnic.

Once the bang and flub-flub-flub of the flat tire registered in my consciousness, I pulled over, jumped out and stood by the side of the truck, hoping some Good Samaritan would drive by in a tricked-out Dodge. A Ferrari? Hell, a Volkswagen?

Nope.

Maybe all the men thought I was standing out there for another reason; like using this stretch of road instead of a street corner despite not showing excessive amounts of skin. I wondered if swinging the lug wrench around may have had something to do with the lack of response as well.

After ten minutes with vehicles slowing down then flooring it past me, I yanked out my cell phone and called Blaine.

"Hawkins Freight."

"Hi, it's me. Listen, I hate to ask but could you come by and help me change my tire. I picked up a flat on the way and no one is stopping."

"Have you been swinging the wrench around again?"

The instrument dropped with a thud. "No."

"You know how to change a tire."

I sighed. "On a car, yes, but I wouldn't be able to get the tire into the back of the truck once I got it off, and then hauling the spare…"

He chuckled. "I'm on my way. You need to grow a few feet, Taz."

Eventually, his bright red minivan came into view, parked and he came up to me. "Got a last minute call before I left or I'd have been here sooner. It was Clayton."

Again. Maybe he had something on the case. I could use some good news.

"Did he say what it was about?"

Blaine fit the jack under the frame, started hoisting the truck up. "No. You're supposed to call him when you get in. He did ask about mom, though. Did you go see her last night?"

"Yes. The facility called. She'd had a bad night."

"When was the last time you talked to her?"

"A while."

I mentally backtracked and concluded it had been almost a week since we'd spoken. That was probably the reason why she'd been upset. Since the night of Ricky's attack and her subsequent admittance into an extended care facility, I'd either phoned or stopped in every other day. But with all that had happened, it had slipped my mind. Anger rose at whoever was behind my current predicament and I added another item on the list they'd have to answer for if I ever found out who they were.

"There's also another call on the machine, guess I didn't hear the phone ring at the time. It's a potential job." He grabbed the lug wrench and had the flat off in no time.

My day suddenly became a lot brighter. "Really! That's great."

Blaine lowered the tailgate, undid the spare anchored to the side and switched tires. "Yes and no. How are you going to haul anything? The police still have the van."

Hell.

Tears of frustration threatened to spill over. I hated this…this limbo land I was currently living in. I clenched my fists, spun around and wanted to scream. I couldn't catch a break today.

"Hey." My brother's hand gently settled on my shoulder. "We'll work it out. Depending on the load we can use your truck, my van and I can call a few of the guys from soccer and we'll rally the troops."

His immediate offering of help without hesitation threatened my pent up waterworks to let go. I sucked in a shuddering breath, swallowed the lump in my throat and faced him.

"Rally the troops?" A half smile formed on my lips.

"It was the first thing that came to mind. Come on, you're all set. Meet you at the shop."

I stayed his departure with a touch. "Thank you, Blaine."

My gratitude went beyond what he proposed and he knew it. Blaine had always been there, had been my strongest supporter when things had gotten bad right after mom's attack. He was the consummate big brother.

"Race you back." He ruffled my hair and jogged to his vehicle.

* * *

At the office I debated about calling Clayton first but business took precedence. The saved message was short and to the point. A woman wanted something moved and a phone number.

I punched in the digits and the call was answered on the second ring.

"Hellooo."

"Hi. This is Sadie Hawkins calling from Hawkins Freight. You left a message on our machine. I'm returning your call."

"Right on," the woman gushed. "Thank you so much for calling."

Wait, did she just say right on? Her voice was in a low octave and she spoke as if she had all the time in the world. A picture of a long haired woman clad in a tie-dyed hippie skirt sprang into my head.

"You wanted something moved, correct?"

"Yeah. I'm leaving the area and since the movers can't take my kiddies and I don't dare put them in the cargo hold of the plane, that's just inhumane, I need someone to take them to Amarillo."

I was taken aback at the mention of kids in the cargo of the plane but what I focused on was the location.

Amarillo.

Where mom and I used to live.

And Ricky Best.

I'd been back periodically when I was in college and before the incident with my mother but the idea of returning to the same city where he lived set me on edge. Immediately after what had happened, Best had stashed his money and taken off before the police could question him regarding mom's attack. Although the statute of limitations for violent sexual assault had no time limit, would he consider returning, even under an alias? Any sane person wouldn't take the chance, but then considering what he had done to my mother, I had to wonder if the guy was insane.

Regardless of how I felt, a job was a job and Amarillo was a decent size city. I'd be in and out.

"You said kiddies but what exactly would I be hauling?"

"Poodles."

Dogs, no problem. I think I could handle that.

"Are you calling from the Houston area?"

"Yes."

That would be a five to six hour drive without stops to let Fifi or Fido out for a walk, and could turn out to be a long day.

"You mentioned poodles, as in plural. How many are there?"

"Six, they're all brothers and sisters,"

I winced, thinking of my poor eardrums. Well, there were always earplugs or I could crank up the tunes.

"And would they be in their own cages?"

"No way, man!" the woman stated emphatically.

"Okay, that won't be an issue." They'd better damn well be litter trained.

I could use Blaine's minivan, take out the back seats to make room. Most importantly, I'd have to check with Clayton about going out of town. Since he'd told the court he'd take responsibility for me and I wasn't leaving the state, I'd doubt there would be any problem. It wasn't like I was going to take off – I had nowhere to go.

I got the client's name, said I needed to check on the schedule – a little white lie – and would call her back very soon with a quote.

"I've been told you are quite reliable so I'll wait for your call."

Far be it for me to brush off a compliment. "How did you happen to hear about us?" I had done a few small jobs so I was curious.

"Well," she said as if parting some secret gossip. "Lucy's cousin Frank who plays poker every Tuesday with a group of guys, I think they do more drinking than anything, was talking to his neighbor who is friends with Henry whose uncle happens to be Lester whose pig you hauled."

My eyes had glazed over once she got to the poker pals but they refocused at Lester's name. Good old Lester. I'd have to send him a thank you note or a peach pie.

"That's great. Like I said, I need to check on something and I'll phone you back."

I disconnected and rang up Clayton who luckily was still at his office.

"Hi. You called. Twice," I said when I was put through.

"First time was to see how things are with your mom."

"She's fine, thanks. What was the reason for the second call?"

"I've got some news."

"Really?" Even I could hear the hope in that one word.

"Now, don't get excited. We haven't found the killer yet but remember the guy whose knee you played t-ball with? Well, we tracked him down at a hospital in Abilene. It took some time because initially we contacted the hospitals in and around Pampa and along Interstate 27. Never figured he'd go so far away."

I pictured the man lying in agony in the back of a vehicle. Served him right, don't mess with me. "I'm sure that wasn't the most pleasant trip for whoever drove him there because he sure didn't make it on his own."

"He was admitted alone. Someone dropped him off and didn't return. The hospital picked up our wire about the suspect."

"Has he said anything?"

"Not a word and police can't really hold him because his prints weren't found anywhere on the van. He's left the hospital but local boys there have him under surveillance."

I didn't comment. I was hoping for something a bit more.

"But I do have other news that might be of interest to you. One of the antique pieces that was on your list from Back in Time turned up in Amarillo in a local pawn shop. Law enforcement in the city was on the lookout, put pressure on one of their known fences."

"Is he in custody?"

"Boys nabbed him last night, are holding him for questioning with regards to the antiques theft. He's not talking, though and the shops' video camera was *conveniently* broken at the time."

"Of course."

"If whoever dropped off the item was one of the two men who worked the theft together, maybe the shop owner will eventually roll on the other two. The really good news is that based on this info and the time line, odds are the prosecution will drop the grand theft charges against you."

"That is good news. But there's still the murder charge."

"One thing at a time, Sadie."

"Okay. Oh, listen, I have a potential haul out of town and I wanted to double check before committing to the job. There isn't a problem with me leaving town is there?"

"No. I know you're not a flight risk, just as long as you don't leave the state. Is it a long haul?"

"To Amarillo."

Silence greeted me across the line. I could almost hear his thoughts, something along the lines that it wasn't a good idea.

"You sure that's a good idea?" he queried as if plucking the words directly out of my head. If the topic wasn't so serious I would have chuckled.

"It's money. I don't have much of a choice."

A good portion of what I'd gotten from our divorce went into paying for mom's care.

"I can lend you some money if things are tight."

"You know how I feel about that, Clayton."

He'd offered to help before with my mother's care but we were no longer married and as generous as it was, I didn't want to be beholding to him.

"You're representing me for free. That's more than generous."

"Oh, didn't I mention the office needs a new computer system," he joked, then his voice became serious. "You're not going to try and find him are you?"

As much as I wanted to see that bastard Ricky in a cell for the rest of his life, it would be suicide for me to dig into the past.

My ex-husband was the only person on the planet who knew the truth, how I'd practically beaten Ricky

Best to death. Not even Blaine was aware of what really happened that night.

While my mother was recuperating from her assault those years ago, I was being detained down the hall in my hospital room for questioning.

According to statements from my neighbor, Mr. Reynolds, on the night of the attack, he had gone back into my place, took one look at Ricky lying there after I'd tried to break my bat over his body, and assumed Ricky was dead. He never checked for a pulse, claiming to have seen enough dead bodies on television to make a professional assessment. He'd called the police but it took Houston's finest a while to get there because the fall festival crowds had blocked a lot of the streets. When they did arrive, they mistakenly went to the party place instead of my apartment and by the time Mr. Reynolds set them straight, Ricky had vanished.

Enter Clayton Bellows, fresh out of law school and working for the public defender's office when he was handed my case. I had mistakenly surmised the tight-lipped, no-nonsense attitude he displayed was due to disinterest and a total lack of empathy. I couldn't have been more wrong.

Based on what Reynolds had said, Clayton informed me the local boys briefly speculated that I had someone get rid of the body, despite it being an obvious case of self-defense. However, when they contacted the Amarillo police to track down any info or next of kin for Ricky, they came back empty. Ricky Best's house was deserted, his department store locked up tight, all bank accounts and assets moved to an off-shore account. And the cherry on top – any and all documentation on the man ended up being falsified.

Ricky Best did not exist.

Even if I had killed Ricky and been charged with involuntary manslaughter, Clayton would have proved that on the night of the attack safe retreat had not been possible and I had used the force necessary to prevent further harm to my mother and I. Had a case against me been brought to trial he would have been able to convince the jury Ricky had found out where Jolene had gone, and since he knew I had a place in Houston, followed us to the barbecue fest in the hopes he could convince Jolene to come back to him. Perhaps some drinks, a little dancing, and she would change her mind. Considering mom had broken off the relationship just prior to the time of the attack and her doctor's prognosis that she would never fully recover, any jury would have acquitted me of the charges.

I had expected Ricky to come forward to hang me out to dry. Perhaps he'd kept quiet because he would be implicated and stand to lose it all if everything came out. Even the baseball bat disappeared, probably taken by the same person or persons unknown who had assisted in getting him out of the place. With the party going on, it would have been quite easy to pass off a slumping figure as an unconscious drunk being helped out by a friend.

The ease of his disappearance, the false life that was erased so easily, unnerved me.

Once it was all over I received some closure in a way – I was a free woman – but seeing my mother, thinking of what she had endured, how she changed, still kept it fresh, like a unhealed scar that reminded me of what I did. Those actions have remained a part of me and I still lived with the ramifications. Although I don't have any true regrets, regardless that the action was in protecting someone I loved, I have wondered whether that darkness would rise again.

And it scared me.

I had no desire to rake up the past and I said so.

I paused a moment. A comment over our dinner the other night refused to leave my mind and talking about Ricky now brought it to the forefront where it dug in harder, unrelenting, like a tenacious woodpecker drilling for bugs.

"Clayton. Do you…is there any possible way Best might be behind this murder and the missing artifacts?"

"What makes you think that?"

"You mentioned the other night the prosecution would say I'd killed Stanton, if it was him, to get to the stolen antiques but whoever *did* kill him had set it up. What if that person didn't want the items but was out get me? What if it was Best? What if this was his way of revenge?"

"That's a bit of a stretch, Sadie."

"But it is possible."

"I won't know anything until I get the coroner's report, which I'm hoping will be in the next twenty-four to forty-eight hours and a positive identification of the body is made. If it turns out there is no such person as Stanton, and theoretically someone is trying to put the blame on you for everything…"

He paused and I could hear the slight inhale of a breath.

"What, Clayton. Just say it."

He waited a beat or two longer before finishing his sentence. "Considering the skill involved in how quickly he got away and how efficiently he erased his tracks, then yes, it is feasible it could be Best."

Well, hell.

CHAPTER TEN

Never let it be said that friends can't be bought.

At nine the next morning, after a twenty minute walk to make sure there would be no accidents, Greg, Marcia, Peter, Jan, Bobby and Cindy were riding in the back of the van while Tanya alternately glared between me and the six individually identified poodles behind us.

"You didn't specify the Brady Bunch would be four legged." She moved to face forward in the passenger seat, a slight scowl on her beautiful features.

When I'd called my best friend the night before, practically begging for some company on the trip, I'd played to her nostalgic side. Growing up, Tanya and I used to watch reruns of the seventies television show and invariably argue as to why Marcia got all the guys while Jan was obviously the better person. When I'd found out the dogs I would be transporting were named after the characters of the same show, I knew I'd found my ace in the whole, the one thing Tanya couldn't say no to.

The chance to be up close and personal with the Brady crew.

I didn't lie; the dog's owner's last name was Brady.

I had been correct in my mental image of the woman I'd spoken to over the phone the day before. Sylvia Brady had waist length black hair liberally streaked with grey and a free flowing white peasant blouse over a denim skirt.

With down payment in hand, assurances that we would take lots of breaks for the 'kids' to do their business and wouldn't let them out of our sight, my bud and I drove off. Since Sylvia didn't drive, she'd be meeting us in Amarillo with her sister, who lived there, which was fine with me just as long as I didn't get stuck waiting with this load like my previous job.

Before hitting the Interstate, I drove to The Briar Shoppe on Times Boulevard, a specialty tobacco place to pick Tanya's vice of choice, a couple of Davidoff panetallas. A premium slim cigar with tobacco from the Dominican Republic, Indonesia and Brazil, it imparts a smooth, aromatic flavor and my friend looked like a sophisticated forties movie queen when she brought the thin cheroot to her lips. Although I didn't like supporting a habit that was detrimental to her health, it had been Tanya's price to ride shotgun with me this trip.

And an autograph from the Brady bunch kids. But that was before she found out they barked instead of talked.

I wondered how the dogs would like having their paws inked.

"I'm surprised you didn't have plans for a Saturday." I sipped my espresso spiked high octane cola. No chocolate syrup this time.

With mock indignation she glanced back when Jan began to whine at Marcia. "If I'd known about the minor *details* you'd conveniently managed to leave out I'd have thought twice about it. However, I think I'll have to charge you double." She took a deep drag from her cigar, smiled with bliss and blew the smoke out her open window.

"It would be worth it. We haven't had a chance to spend much time together, just the two of us."

"I was beginning to wonder if you slept at the shop."

A twinge of guilt had me inwardly wincing. I'd been spending so much time trying to keep the business afloat that I'd neglected my friends, not to mention dropping out of the baseball league I'd joined up months back.

Gone were the days when my worries consisted of keeping house and accompanying Clayton to required social gatherings.

Thinking of him brought up our dinner from the other night and I'd been trying to come to grips with the varied emotions I'd experienced since. Nostalgia, uncertainty. Desire even?

"Is this going to be a one-way conversation the whole trip, or are you planning to chime in every once in a while?"

"Sorry." I gave Tanya a sheepish grin. "I've got so much stuff buzzing around in my brain it's like flies swarming over dead catfish."

She wrinkled her nose at my analogy. "Lovely. Time to share, girlfriend."

I hesitated, darted a quick glance her way then pushed out in a rush. "Clayton invited me over for dinner the night before last."

She arched a perfectly shaped brow and drew out her one word response. "Really."

"Yes, really."

"And?"

"And what? We talked shop, as in my case. It was dinner, nothing more."

"Then why did you bring it up?"

Good point. Maybe because the whole sharing-food-he-cooked thing sat lodged in the back of my mind and I wanted to talk to someone about it but couldn't afford a psychiatrist?

"I…" I stopped, drew in a breath, tilted my head, screwed up my face and shrugged. "I don't know."

"Yes, you do. Just spill it. What's bothering you?"

"I guess how I felt being with him, at his place. I mean, I went so far as to comment there wasn't anything remotely female in his apartment. Why would I do that?"

"Did you go into the bedroom?"

My mouth gaped open. "No." Damn, missed that opportunity.

"Then how do you know there wasn't anything feminine in there?"

"I don't. But why the hell should I even care?" I was getting exasperated. Not with her but with me.

"That's what we're trying to figure out. Is there something else that brought on this way of thinking?"

Nothing came to mind so I merely shrugged.

She was silent for a minute, staring out the window. The dogs were blessedly quiet.

"My opinion," she started. "I think you look at Clayton as your knight in shining armor."

I snorted, opened my mouth to speak but she continued. "Hear me out. He was the one who 'saved' you from prison when your mom got attacked. He married you a little while later, essentially taking care of you. It was his money that gave you the opportunity to open your business."

"From the sale of *our* house."

"But the house came from his parents. Not saying you didn't deserve getting it but if you hadn't been married, you wouldn't have received the cash. "

Okay, point to her side.

"And now your ex-husband is representing you again on another charge."

"He is my lawyer, Tanya."

"He is *a* lawyer. You could have called someone else."

"What exactly are you saying?"

"Being at his place was the perfect opportunity to try and find out if Clayton has a girlfriend. You didn't have to invite yourself over or stalk him to get the answer. Did he say he was seeing anyone?"

"I didn't ask."

"Ahh, there you go. Subconsciously you made the comment about the lack of femininity in his surroundings because you were hoping the answer would be no. That way he'd still be exclusive to you. If another woman was in the picture he wouldn't be able to rescue you at the drop of a hat."

"Who are you, Sigmund Freud?"

I wasn't sure about her offbeat logic but I'd have to investigate things a bit further. Hell, all the confusing emotions about my ex could be attributed to loneliness.

"Maybe you just need to get laid." She flashed me a wicked grin.

That too.

"So, what is going on with your case? Can you talk about it?"

I brought her up to speed but there wasn't much to tell. We were waiting to hear from the coroner. Other than the one item, no other hits on the antiques showed up. Basically a standstill.

"Sounds like an inside job to me," she replied when I'd finished.

"Now you're Sherlock Holmes as well as Sigmund Freud? You should hang up a shingle."

"Smartass. Seriously, hasn't the idea of someone on the inside crossed your mind?"

"I guess, but I'm sure the cops would have checked into it already."

I was about to say something else when Greg started to howl. A full-fledged, from the belly, baying at the moon, howl. The sound was so sudden it ricocheted around the van with such force I almost careened off the road.

My girlfriend clasped hands over her ears and yelled over the noise. "Jeez, it sounds like he's being castrated."

"Maybe he has to go pee." I bellowed to be heard and checked for a place to pull over.

The rest of the Brady bunch got carried up in the charge and I had to take the next exit before my head exploded from the racket. I pulled into the parking lot of a gas station and Tanya and I leapt out of the van.

"Lord love a duck, that's loud." My poor ears throbbed. "Since we're stopped we might as well see if they need to go."

Tanya mumbled something about tiny bladders and before I could warn her, she pulled open the sliding side door.

"Wait! They're not…"

And a stream of white rocketed from the van.

"Whoa!" She back peddled as six dogs danced around her feet then took off.

"Grab the closest one and put them back in the van!" I ran to catch Greg as he lifted a leg to the tire of another car. When he finished and was secure in my arms, he gave a slobbery lick to my face. Cheeky little bugger.

Surprisingly agile in boots with two inch heels, Tanya streaked after Cindy and managed to scoop both her and Bobby at once. Double whammy. Into the van they went.

That left Peter, Jan and Marcia. My head whipped around and I spied one heading into the gas station as a customer opened the door to leave.

"One's in the store. See if you can find the other two."

I yanked open the door and was met by a fierce glare from the attendant behind a counter packed full of candy and chocolate. "Is that your dog? No pets allowed."

Tell me something I didn't know.

"Working on it."

I jogged down an aisle. A blur of white zipped around the end.

"Oh, no you don't."

I rounded the corner and barreled up. Jan yapped and tried to dodge around me.

"Jan. Sit."

The dog stopped dead and placed her white haunches on the floor. I stared, reached down and picked her up. "Good girl. You were always my favorite." I rubbed her ears for good measure and carried her out the door.

Tanya jerked her thumb to the vehicle when I arrived. "I got Peter."

Which left one more. She and I said in unison, "Marcia, Marcia, Marcia!"

But it wasn't funny since we couldn't see her and she was my responsibility.

Tanya and I walked around, calling, shading our eyes against the sun's glare. I felt the edges of panic start to squeeze against my chest when a teenager caught our attention from across the lot.

"You looking for a person or a dog?"

"Dog. A poodle."

"Small, white?"

"Yes." Thank goodness. I started forward.

She met me halfway. "Did the dog have a pink collar?"

Yup. Definitely Marcia. I nodded.

"I just saw it jump into a green pick up with an old camper on back and they drove off. Turned right out of the lot."

Great. Just great.

I sprinted back to the vehicle.

"Tanya, in the van! Marcia's been dognapped!"

My girlfriend looked at me like I was nuts but scrambled in when I cranked the motor over and was about to leave without her.

"How do you know?"

"The girl I just spoke to saw the whole thing." I zoomed off in a squeal of tires. "Be on the lookout for a green pickup with a camper."

She snapped her seatbelt in place and grabbed the door handle as I careened around a corner in the same direction of the truck. "A BOLO? On a dog."

"Yup."

Dang it. I couldn't believe this was happening. Just once it would have been nice to have a job without any type of complication.

"There! About five or six cars ahead. I think that truck is green."

I floored the gas pedal and gripped the wheel. No one was going to get away with taking Marcia. I dodged around two other cars and screamed down the road.

"Jeesus, watch the jeep!"

I maneuvered quickly into our lane away from the oncoming Wrangler.

I spied the bandit's truck plugging along, as if they didn't have a care in the world. A gap in oncoming traffic had me also checking my side mirror and I went back into the opposite lane and stomped on the gas, riding up quickly beside the vehicle. Tanya lowered her window.

I caught the driver's eye. "Pull over!"

His eyes grew wide and he gawked at us as if we were from another planet.

I inched closer to his truck. "Pull over!" I began to carefully force both our vehicles over to the side of the road. The last thing I wanted to do was to cause an accident.

With no other choice than to comply, he slowed down, turned on his signal, wow really, and came to a slow stop. I halted directly behind them.

"Stay in the van," I ordered Tanya as I opened my door. "If he tries to escape cut him off."

I was out of earshot before she could even take a breath. I jogged up to the passenger side because I didn't want to get clipped by passing motorists, and yanked open the door. A little old lady sat in the seat, hugging Marcia to her bosom.

"My word. What do you think you're doing?" Her veined hands shook while she petted Marcia's fur.

"That," I pointed to the poodle, "is my dog. Please hand her over."

Eyes behind thick round glasses peered back, startled. "But, but…this is our dog, Tinkerbell. I don't have your dog."

The woman who looked at least ninety shrank back when I tried to reach in and I stopped, showed my palms and then pointed to a pink collar around the dog's neck. "Look at the tag on the collar. It says Marcia."

"Now just a minute, dear." She squinted at the small round disc dangling from pink nylon.

The driver, her husband I presumed, rolled his eyes heavenward and shook his head. He remained silent but didn't advance on me like I expected.

After a minute, the woman's red face met mine. "I don't understand. This isn't our dog."

'That's what I've been trying to tell you. It's mine." Well, technically Marcia wasn't my dog but I didn't want to confuse this poor woman any more than she already was.

The passenger turned to her husband. "Harold. This isn't our dog."

Harold checked the rear view mirror into the back seat, shook his head again. "That's because Tinkerbell is in her cage."

"But you let her out for a pee at the gas station. I thought she'd gotten away from you so I grabbed the dog as it came running to the truck."

"No. While you went to the ladies room, I put Tinkerbell back in her cage and then I took a turn at the washroom. When I got back you were already in the truck and I figured Tink had wanted out of the cage to ride up here with us."

There was a moment of stunned silence as the three of us glanced at one another.

"Oh, I'm very sorry, dear." The woman handed back Marcia. "She's such a sweet doggie."

"Simple misunderstanding." I held onto the poodle. "Hope I didn't scare you too much."

"This was more fun than we had in a long time, isn't that right Harold. Wait till I tell the ladies at pinochle we were almost held up over a dog."

I took a step away. "Well, I wouldn't go so far as to say that." I really, really didn't need another visit from the police. "Y'all have a nice day now."

The truck and camper pulled onto the road and ambled off.

I held fast to Marcia's collar, jumped back into the van and set the runaway on the floor. "You're grounded."

The dog gave a little whine, circled three times, curled onto a blanket and lay down. Doggy version of giving me the finger.

I cranked over the motor, pulled into traffic, backtracked to where we'd pulled off initially and hit the Interstate toward Amarillo.

* * *

We got all the dogs dropped off safely and after many handshakes, doggie smooches – to Mama Brady, not me – and a forget-me-not from Peter against the back tire, Tanya and I headed for home. I thought about taking a cruise around Amarillo and check out my old stomping grounds but my passenger needed to get home.

During the return trip Tanya tried more than once to make me confront my feelings about Clayton but I wasn't ready to lay my heart open for investigation, by her or me, despite points she made that needed some serious consideration. Did I view my ex as a knight, saving me from others or even myself? The idea sounded hokey but it's kind of hard to separate oneself from the equation and look at it from a third party perspective. Unless you happened to be eyeing the bottom of a fifth of Wild Turkey. Then *everything* was clear, in a purely emotional, gut-wrenching 'I-love-you-Stella' kind of way.

After I left Tanya at her place with a promise to consider what she'd said, I swung by Blaine's to switch vehicles, declined his invitation for dinner and went home.

The truck's headlights splashed against the off white stucco building where my apartment sat on the second floor and a soft sigh escaped my lips. With all that had happened the past week, I was exhausted and needed a night of peace and quiet.

Inside, I hung up the keys by the door, toed off my Post's and eyed my place. It wasn't much, in fact, compared to Clayton's, it was downright dismal, but it was clean and I liked it. A one bedroom with corner kitchen, decent sized bathroom and a larger than average living room, I had decorated it with items and colors that reminded me of my childhood in Alabama. Dark laminate flooring held furniture in shades of the state's gemstone, Star Blue Quartz, with pillows and throws in Alabama peach to soften the tone, all of which were surrounded by walls of soft cream.

Flopped on my couch, a glance at my watch made me realize that if I wanted to speak with mom I'd better do it now, but when I reached the facility the nurse said she was already asleep.

"Any problems?"

"No. She had a good evening, even played a game of Snakes and Ladders. She won."

I chuckled, thanked the woman for the update and disconnected.

Stillness laid comforting arms around me and although I had planned to mull over what Tanya had said sleep stole me away.

CHAPTER ELEVEN

On Monday morning I woke up feeling groggy, perplexed and in need of more high- octane cola than the good old US could possibly manufacture. I'd spent most of Sunday trying to come up with ideas on how to drum up business and other than cold calling, which I hated, had composed a flyer I planned on plastering the college and university campuses for a cut rate on moving. That evening I tried watching television but nothing held my interest for long and I ended up going to bed early. However, my subconscious wouldn't relax because my dreams filled with bizarre glimpses of shady characters – not that they were nefarious but their faces were in shadow – freely going into people's houses while dressed as mummies and stealing items. That would teach me to fall asleep with only a couple of double shot espresso colas and not much else in my stomach.

My stomach loudly protested at being ignored and I stumbled to the kitchen. Despite the hunger pangs, caffeine addiction took precedent and I opened the fridge to grab a couple of cans of dark cola. Only there were none. In panic mode, I fled to my back up stock. Yes, it would be warm but I was desperate. But when I opened the small store room in my apartment I didn't see any bright, cheery welcoming cases of liquid refreshment. I was fresh out.

Just shoot me.

I slammed the door, hung my head and plodded to the shower, all the while promising my stomach and nervous system I would take care of them.

I was out the door in less than half an hour and headed for the closest convenience store where I grabbed a couple of icy cold, fully loaded caffeine drinks, slapped down my change and had half of one down before I got back into my truck. I finished the first while on my way to a java joint where I picked up a coffee and some toasted bagels. Next stop, Tanya's office.

At the first light, I dialed her number and put the phone on speaker.

The call was picked up on the second ring. "StreetSmart. Tanya Woods speaking."

"Hey, it's me. You in the office and will be for a while?"

"Good morning. Yes, I'm here for most of the morning."

"Great. I'm on my way over right now. I wanted to talk to you about your theory that the robbery was an inside job."

"I haven't decided if I'm still mad at you for the Brady bungle."

She may have said the words but I could hear her suppression of mirth. "I promise to get the picture of you and the doggie doppelgangers printed and framed soon."

"Very funny. See you in a few."

She ended the call. Obviously I was forgiven. Gotta love best friends.

At her office, Tanya opened her door to my knock and I raised my laden hands. "I come bearing sacrifices."

"You may proceed." She relieved me of the bag, closed the door and inhaled deeply of the fresh baked aroma. "Maple cinnamon French toast bagels, you really must be feeling guilty. So, what's up?"

I grabbed a bagel, sat down in a chair and opened my second high octane drink. I took a hefty gulp and sighed in ecstasy. One was never enough.

"Why do you think the theft of the antiques was an inside job?"

Tanya settled in behind her desk. "I don't know. I mean what are the odds someone knew where you would be and what you would have in the van? The heist was too easy."

"Don't you think the police have thought of that?"

"Probably." She took a sip of coffee and smiled. Girl loved her java. "But I'm sure they're more interested in the murder than the theft of some antiques."

Oh, yeah. The dead body in my van.

"If you ask me, I think the two are related."

I had wondered about that as well, ever since Clayton came up with the idea this whole affair was a possible set-up.

"Okay. Let's say you are correct with the inside job notion, how can I prove it?"

"It's not up to you. Leave it to the police."

Frustration and anger welled up, leaving a bitter taste in my mouth. "I haven't got the luxury of waiting, Tanya. This is my name, my business we're talking about. If I can't get cleared of these charges and figure out who took the cargo, let alone who killed the man in the sarcophagus, I won't have a business left."

She left her food and beverage and came around to kneel in front of my chair. "I get it. I know you didn't do it but there is nothing you can do."

"Yes, there is."

She stood, leaned back against the face of the desk and waited.

"If it was an inside job, which person would have the most to gain? The other partner, Jeff Reynolds, obviously, yet he said he didn't know Stanton. Even his secretary agreed." The brief conversation I'd overheard from Margaret Yates also put the receptionist under suspicion. She claimed to have done something terrible and was going to maybe confess to her friend, Francie, at lunch today. I planned on somehow listening in on that chit-chat.

"You think they're both in on it?"

"Possibly. And what about Ms. Ing? If no one was working at Back in Time Antiques by the name of Lionel Stanton, wouldn't she have said so? Maybe *she's* in on it too?"

"That's a lot of ifs. Do you have a plan?"

"I want to do a little snooping on my own."

"What exactly are you hoping to find?"

"Some connection between Stanton, whoever he is, and the business. I think the first thing to do is talk to Ms. Ing."

"Kind of hard considering they know you."

That thought had crossed my mind. For all I knew they probably had an Eastwood wannabe stationed at the office door just dying for me to make their day. But that didn't mean I couldn't go into the building to check things out. It was a public place with other offices, places I could feasibly visit.

Or, if not me, maybe someone else.

I paused, met her gaze. "But they don't know you."

After a second, her eyes widened. "You want me to start asking questions? What if they call the cops? I can't risk that with my situation here. I'd be fired in a heartbeat."

Tanya was right but that still didn't stop me from hoping she'd go to bat for me. However, considering what she had to lose, in reality, what kind of friend would I be if I pushed her into it? Shame lanced through me as I witnessed disbelief in her gaze.

The possibility of losing everything; my apartment, the business that had taken me so long to get back up and running, affording my mother's care, hell even my freedom, had me so wound up I was acting selfish and irrational.

Before I could say as much and apologize, we were interrupted with a knock on the door.

"Come in," Tanya said.

One of the young men who had helped load the van walked in. "Oh, sorry. I didn't realize you had someone in your office. I can come back later."

"Don't leave on account of me." I welcomed the interruption because it broke the subtle tension between Tanya and me. "You're Will right?"

He came forward, shook my outstretched hand and again I sifted through my mental filing cabinet to try and place where I'd seen him before. His slender fingers were smooth, nails trimmed, clothes of superior quality. With his looks it was an almost certainty he could have had a career as a cover model but I still hadn't figured out what his role was with StreetSmart.

"Hi Sadie." He turned to Tanya. "You wanted me to take a look at your computer this morning, remember?"

"Right. I guess I forgot."

"You don't look much like a computer nerd." I motioned to his shirt. "No pocket protector."

He gave me a mischievous smile. "I prefer the term techie."

Pride sparkled in Tanya's eyes. "Will here, is our technical guru. Made some great suggestions on streamlining my report filings. Even created our own website."

He cast his eyes downward, a hint of warmth rising in his face. The guy was a softie.

"Wish I had that kind of knowhow."

"It's quite simple. I'll show you. What's your website, perhaps I can give you a few tips?"

"I don't have one."

"With a business, if you don't have a website how are people going to find you? I could set up one very easily."

Now I was the one who felt self-conscious. "I don't have any money to pay you."

"He can use the time toward credit." Behind her desk, Tanya leaned over, quickly tapped a few keys.

"I've logged off and you can use this computer. I have to get going anyway."

Will sat down, started typing, and I met Tanya's eyes over his head with a don't-go-yet message. I didn't want her to leave, not with how our conversation ended.

She must have sensed my unspoken apology and her eyes softened slightly. "We'll talk later." She gathered her purse and briefcase. "And don't let him convince you to get something you don't need. He's a very smooth talker."

I touched her arm as she walked behind Will and past me. His fingers flew over the keys, like that of a master piano player.

"Looks like you've done this before."

"Once or twice."

He brought up a page, showed me different design layouts and I selected one that I liked.

"This is a free site and has limited selection but will do for the first while until you get better established or want to change. You'll need to create an account and password."

He continued, asking questions when needed, inputting data, all the while working faster than I could ever have imagined.

"Ever thought of doing this for a living?" Part of me wasn't joking.

Will didn't reply at first but cast a rueful glance to me before focusing on the screen. A few moments of silence followed and I wondered if I had said something wrong.

"I have made a living doing this, just not in the manner you think."

By the tone of his voice it sounded like a bit of a story there but I didn't press. Not everyone liked to be an open book.

I grabbed a chair, nudged in beside him and pointed out a typo. He corrected the error and clicked around the screen before sliding a sideways glance at me.

"I did a short stint for tech crime."

How should I respond to something like that? Sorry you got caught? Did you learn your lesson? I certainly wasn't lily-white either. I wondered how others reacted when he told them, if they looked at him with derision like someone who was dirty or foul. I thought it took guts to admit you were in jail to a stranger.

I met his blue-eyed gaze. "If you could go back to when it probably seemed like a good idea at the time and change something, would you?"

He studied me, lifted a shoulder in reply while the corner of his mouth tilted up. He probably asked himself that same thing as many times as me. I shrugged as well.

"You're all right, Sadie Hawkins." He grinned.

"Smooth talker."

A companionable atmosphere settled around us, punctuated by the odd inquiry and answer. Before long he sat back with a flourish.

"Ta-da. Say hello to your new website."

My eyes traveled around the screen, marveled at how professional and clean the site looked. "I must say, you do know what you're doing."

"You have no idea."

We both laughed.

He patted a pocket. "Hey. I didn't bring my cell phone. May I borrow yours to make sure the site can be viewed properly on a mobile device?"

"Oh. Sure."

While I clicked around the site, I could hear him tap-tapping on my phone. I was grinning like an idiot. I had a website! Before long he handed it back.

"Looks good. If you don't want to make any more changes, I'll log off on Tanya's computer."

"No, the site is fine. Thanks so much. Don't you still have to do some work on the unit?"

He logged off and stood. "Not enough time. I can look at it tomorrow. I have to meet up with some of the group, so had better get going."

As he walked toward the door, I burst out. "Will. What's next for you?"

Why I had asked that, I had no idea, but I felt a sort of kinship with him. Perhaps because of having been on the other side of the law line, same as he.

"Make amends. Find my way." He paused. "What about you? I read the papers, you know, about what's going on."

I came up to him because I was leaving as well. "Find my way out of the situation too, I guess." The words came out with less determination than I'd hoped.

He opened the door for me. His parents had taught him well. "I'd like to help if I can."

I studied him with a long, hard look. "Why?"

It appeared he was about to say something but paused for a second. "People are not always what they seem, Sadie. I get a sense you realize that."

Even though I was older, Will seemed so much more mature for his age.

I tried to make light of his comment. "I wouldn't ask anyone to put themselves in a situation for me. It could be very detrimental."

"Only if you get caught." He winked and headed down the hall.

I gaped after him for a fraction of a second, a wave of gratitude rising at his offer. However, what had transpired between Tanya and myself and also Will's bid to help didn't sit well with me. There was no denying I was frustrated, doubtful and scared but putting my friends – old and newly acquired – in a predicament that could be potentially harmful to them made me uneasy.

I passed through the building doors into the Texas heat, my mind jumping from one idea to the next. Clayton said he should have the results of the body's autopsy by end of day but I wasn't going to sit around waiting and hope something came up to deflect the suspicion from me.

In my truck while the air conditioner did a so-so job at keeping the sweat at bay, I began to formulate a plan. Speaking to the main players in this case wasn't a road I could travel at the moment but that didn't mean I couldn't probe into the second string. I sat in the truck, changed my voice, practiced what I was going to say to sound semi-legit and dialed the phone.

"Back in Time Antiques," a woman's voice answered, probably Mrs. Yates.

"Yes. I would like to speak with Ms. Ing please."

"May I ask who is calling?"

I came up with the first name I could think of, my first grade teacher. "Olivia Fieldstone. I am calling for my employer."

"One moment please."

I was put on hold. So far so good.

"Jiao Ing. How may I help you?"

The voice had a slightly different lilt. It was probably her professional telephone voice compared to the down-the-nose-at-the-hired-help tone I received the morning of pick-up.

"Yes. My employer is interested in selling a piece of art and has asked me to inquire if Back in Time would like to auction it off."

"Who are you representing?"

I didn't expect that question. Crap, why hadn't I thought this out more thoroughly? My eyes darted around. On one of the neighboring buildings, there was a pub called Popeye's, yeah like that was going to work. I zeroed in on a flyer on the floor of the passenger side, a take-out menu from a place near where I lived. I grabbed it like a lifeline, turned it over, and stifled a groan. Nothing popped out that could feasibly be used as a name.

"Hello?"

I was going to flub this. My hands shook as I flipped open the menu, scanning for anything I could use. There! I could make that work.

"So sorry, an assistant came into my office. My apologies. My boss is Herbert Berg." I held my breath. The moniker came from a dish on the menu called the Herbert Humphries Burger.

"I am not familiar with him."

"To be expected. He is not from here."

A beat of silence. Was she going to take the bait? Despite Ms. Ing not being able to actually see me anxiety made my heart thump wildly.

"No problem." Ms. Ing's voice warmed. "How can I be of service?"

Phew. That was close. "Mr. Berg would like me to meet with you and discuss the possibility of selling his piece."

"Certainly. What is the object?"

Jeeez. I wasn't cut out for this cloak and dagger stuff. I blurted out the first thing that came to mind.

"A Ming vase."

"Really?" My caller inhaled with interest. "What year?"

Oh-oh.

"Early." I crossed my fingers.

"Well, we would certainly be interested."

"Mr. Berg thought you might."

"When can you come by the office?"

By the note in her voice, the venerable Ms. Ing could hardly contain her excitement.

"I am in meetings with other potential auction houses for most of the day." I couldn't have her thinking she was the only fish in the sea. "Perhaps we could meet over an early dinner?"

This was crucial to my plan. I couldn't be seen entering the building housing Back in Time. If Ms. Ing really was interested, and I'd bet her diamond studded Cartier watch she'd flashed when we'd first met that she was, she wouldn't let an opportunity like this slip by.

"That can be arranged. There is a nice restaurant down the block from the office called Whitestone. Say around five?"

"That is acceptable."

"Will you have the vase with you?"

"No, it is safely tucked away under lock and key. But I do have some very good pictures. If we can come to an agreement, then I can supply the vase."

"Of course, how silly of me. Please excuse my rashness."

"How will I recognize you?" I knew what she looked like but I couldn't let her know that.

"Just ask at the host desk when you come in. They know me there."

"Good. I will see you at five. Thank you for taking my call."

"It was my pleasure." The woman hung up.

The object of the ruse was to meet Stanton's secretary face-to-face and see if she would at least talk to me. The authorities probably already interviewed her but if so, any information hadn't been passed onto me. I wanted to know if there was a specific reason why Stanton took and earlier flight and why he never made any arrangements to help load the antiques. Those things may be inconsequential to the investigation but the questions had been bugging me.

Scenario after scenario as to how I would approach her rolled around in my brain like one of those little white balls you needed to negotiate through a maze. Self-doubt churned acid in my stomach. Besides finding out what I wanted, what else did I hope to accomplish? Maybe I should have put more effort into the plan instead of grasping the first idea that popped into my head. But things were in motion so I was committed.

I was worried Ms. Ing might make a scene and refuse to see me if she recognized who approached her table. A disguise might give me enough of a chance to at least defend myself and hopefully get some answers before she demand I leave.

I left a message for Blaine on the answering machine at work saying I wouldn't be in. If people wanted to speak to me specifically, I knew he would redirect calls to my cell.

Since I had a few hours before one, I stopped by to have a quick visit with my mother before heading back to my apartment.

Planning my first undercover scheme, I figured the best course of action was getting to the restaurant before Margaret Yates would be meeting her friend Francie but since I didn't know the layout of the establishment nor where the women would be sitting, I would need to get as close as possible to hear any type of conversation. That would entail some type of disguise and since I was going to get made up to see Ms. Ing and didn't want to have to head back home to change, it was practical to use the same camouflage.

I worked on transforming my appearance. My head itched under the modified Cleopatra wig and stylish hat which I found stuffed in the bottom of my closet from an old Halloween costume. After applying enough foundation to my face it felt like it would crack, and going nuts with the eye liner, I inspected my reflection in the mirror. Still too recognizable. I'd made a quick stop on the way home and took the two products I had purchased from the theatre props store, added some rose colored makeup and topped it with a line of clear liquid. Once it dried, the liquid puckered and voila, a significant, bonafide, real-looking jagged scar jutted from the side of my right eye and went halfway to my ear. I slapped on a pair of dark sunglasses and checked out my reflection. Not bad, as long as I didn't have to take off the glasses. I purposefully put the scar coming directly from my eye so people would understand why I preferred to keep them protected and hidden.

The whole thing was a little convoluted but I had a pretty good feeling the police probably told the staff of Back in Time not to speak with me. God, I hoped this worked. I wasn't too worried about the lunch date with Margaret and Francie because I wouldn't be sitting at the same table as them but did have concerns the disguise wouldn't even get me seated with Stanton's secretary.

In my best skirt and blouse I hopped into my truck, not an easy task when compared to jeans, and after looking it up, drove to The Maple Diner. The location was close to the building where Back in Time had their office. It was quarter to the hour and once there, I stopped in front of some stores on either side of the diner and pretended to peruse the wares through the windows, all the while watching out of the corner of my eye for Back in Time's receptionist and at five minutes past one Margaret Yates came down the block in a purposeful stride. Dressed in a dark purple short-sleeved dress, her face pinched tight, she hunched her shoulders and clung to her purse as if it were her last possession. She did not come across as a woman about to enjoy a casual lunch.

I let her pass and waited a few minutes until some people arrived then ventured with them into the diner. I used the clutch of patrons as a shield thinking if I went in alone and Yates was sitting watching the door for her friend, there was a possibility she might recognize me despite the guise. I nonchalantly scanned the room and spotted Yates' purple dress at a table with another woman and as luck would have it her back was to the door. As the group in front of me broke away and went to claim seats, I tagged along and snagged a table. It wasn't as close as I wanted and as I was about to sit, the table just before Yates and her friend became vacant. Making a show of spotting something on the seat where I was, I walked to the table that was leaving and slipped into the chair closest to Margaret.

I inspected the menu although I wasn't hungry and avidly listened to the conversation already in motion behind me.

"Margaret, you must see that he isn't in this for the long haul."

That must be the friend, Francie.

"I know you're right but I can't help it. He's so smart and we have such wonderful talks like Eugene and I used to." This from Margaret directly behind me.

"But you work together," Francie pressed. "Have you ever considered what would happen when this ends, whether your husband finds out or not?"

When what ends? And who are they talking about? Stanton or Rogers? Or does the receptionist have another job besides Back in Time?

A waitress approached my table with a pad and pen.

"Just coffee, please."

She gestured to the almost full room. "It *is* the lunch hour."

"Okay. Your soup of the day, I don't care what it is." I needed the young woman to leave so I could hear what was spoken behind me. I had already missed something Margaret said.

The server left stating she would return shortly with coffee.

"Did you tell Eugene that?" queried Francie.

"No, not yet. But I will."

"When?"

No answer. Dang, what was Margaret supposed to spill to her husband?

"I gather you told *him*," Francie said with concern.

"Yes…"admitted Margaret.

A pause.

"And?" the friend prodded.

"Oh Francie, we had the most awful fight. He's going away and I offered to meet him, said I could tell my husband it was a business trip but he laughed and said no and he didn't want to see me. He actually laughed! I felt so ashamed, so used. And…and."

"And what, Margaret?"

I leaned back in my chair, mentally urging the woman to spill.

"And I did something awful. Something horrible! I was just so angry. Oh god, Francie, if I get caught, I'll go to jail!" Margaret sobbed.

My heartbeat rose in tandem with my interest. What had Margaret done that was so bad? I didn't know if the man she was talking about was Stanton, Rogers or someone else she worked with. Could she have killed Stanton? Or was I so desperate to pin the murder on anyone that I was hoping it was the woman behind me?

Francie's voiced filled with concern and compassion. "Would it make you feel better if you told me what happened? Maybe together we can figure something out."

Yes. Tell her, tell her!

The waitress returned with my coffee and an apologetic smile. "I'm sorry but we've already run out of the soup today, the chef miscalculated and it was very popular. You'll have to order something else. We make a really good French onion, if its soup you want. Or if you care for a sandwich, we have the best egg salad in Houston."

I wanted to strangle the polite but conscientious staff member. Her prattling drowned out Margaret's soft reply and since I didn't want to cause a scene, I agreed to the egg salad and the waitress left with a smile.

"I think you should talk to Father Williams. He'd be bound by the sanctity of the confessional and perhaps give you some advice. I'm just sorry I wasn't here for you last week," Francie commented.

Did Margaret say what happened? Perhaps not since the friend seemed calm. At least I presumed she wouldn't be so complacent if her friend committed murder.

"I think I should talk to a lawyer first," Margaret said quietly.

There was a pause in the conversation and then the topic turned to the reason of Francie being away the week prior.

My meal arrived and I was deflated. Not because of the food but I had learned nothing other than Margaret had some secret that she felt she needed legal counsel before revealing and it had to do with some guy. In other words a big, fat zero. But her reaction to whatever she did raised suspicion and kept her on my suspect list.

I ate quickly and thought it best to be gone from the table before the other two women left.

I still had time before meeting with Stanton's secretary but couldn't go into work because then I would have to explain the get-up to Blaine. I ended up going home for a few hours and tweaked the flyer I planned on posting around campuses.

I left my apartment for my meeting with Ms. Ing with lots of time to spare to make sure I would get there before her. Traffic wasn't that bad in the downtown core as most of the people were leaving work. Once I noticed that the Whitestone was only a half block away from where Ms. Ing worked, it made sense to me why the secretary suggested the restaurant. She had mentioned the staff knew her there, so she probably walked from work. After I parked the truck about half a block away, I steeled my nerves and walked down the street, wobbling slightly, partly because of the two inch heels and partly due to nerves.

Inside the restaurant, I let my eyes adjust to the dim interior before heading to the host desk.

A thirtyish guy, dressed in a smart suit greeted me with a professional smile. His gaze flicked to my face, widened imperceptivity probably because of the scar and darted away.

"Table for one?"

"Yes, thank you."

"If you'll follow me I can seat you near the back."

"I'd prefer something near the front." I stalled, scanned the tables nearby. "How about that one?" I indicated a small table with two chairs partly obscured by a piece of artwork on a pedestal. My reasoning was that I wanted to wait and approach Ms. Ing instead of her approaching me. If my disguise didn't work, there'd be no stopping Stanton's secretary from turning around and leaving the restaurant whereas if she was already seated I could get to the table before she might recognize me. Flimsy, yes but it was all I had.

"Of course."

He brought me to the table, laid down a menu and left with a nod. I chose the chair that would give the best vantage point to the door and skirted the seat even closer to the obstructing pedestal.

The restaurant carried subdued lighting hung over tables of two or four covered with linen white cloths. Subtle classical music drifted from hidden speakers. There were at least half a dozen occupied tables within my line of sight and I presumed the place would fill very soon. Well dressed men and women murmured in low voices over the tinkle of ice in glasses. More than meals were conducted here.

A waiter came by and asked if I cared to order anything but I told him I was still deciding. Time dragged. I checked my watch, ten to five. The waiter came back. I pretended to text on my phone and asked for a bit more time. Anxiety wormed up my spine. Would my disguise work or would Jiao Ing recognize me? I glanced at my phone, five minutes left.

Any time now.

As if she'd heard my thoughts, the door opened and a single person walked in. I raised the menu slightly, lowered my head to hide my face and peered over the rims of my sunglasses.

The host beamed. "Hello, Ms. Ing. Always nice to see you. Table for one?"

"Thank you, Richard. No, I am waiting on a potential client. Would you kindly show her to where I'll be sitting when she inquires?"

"Certainly. A potential client?" He turned and I inched my menu up farther. "Someplace quiet then. Perhaps near the back?"

"That would be perfect."

He strolled past and I lowered the menu, catching sight of Ms. Ing as she followed him. Although I knew I had my face mostly covered and there was no reason for her to be looking in my direction, my hands started to shake as I stared at her retreating back. Heart pinging against my ribs, I rose quickly, gathered my purse and high-tailed it out the door.

CHAPTER TWELVE

I stumbled out the door of the Whitestone restaurant and raced down the street to my truck, the two inch heels impeding my progress. It took me three attempts to unlock the door before I vaulted into the driver's seat and I sat with my heart pounding so hard it felt like a bass drum against my sternum.

What the bloody hell was going on?

The woman who walked into the restaurant moments earlier, whom the host recognized and called Ms. Ing, was definitely not the woman I had met claiming to be Stanton's secretary. Today's version of that person was well into her fifties, had a good forty pounds of extra weight and her wavy hair was cut short to her head. And she wore glasses.

Either Ms. Ing aged thirty years in the past few days, or the person I met on the street, who handed me paperwork, and watched while the crates and sarcophagus got loaded into my van, was an imposter.

Now what was I going to do? Go to the police? With what, the possibility that someone had impersonated Ms. Ing? Surely they had already questioned Stanton's secretary and surmised she was not the woman who met me last Tuesday morning because she would have no reason to lie. The woman who was being stood up in Whitestone had to be the *real* Ms. Ing because how else would she know to come here to meet me. And since I didn't give my real name, there couldn't be a major conspiracy plot between all the staff at Back in Time to implicate me.

The confines of my vehicle started to close in. My head felt like it was about to explode so I let it fall back against the head rest and stared upward. "Face it girl, you're as screwed as a cornered rabbit against a pack of hounds."

The jangle of my cell phone made me jump. Caller ID showed it was Tanya but I didn't pick up. The call went to voicemail and a few minutes later the phone rang again but I ignored it. I didn't want to speak with anyone. A layer of suffocating gloom descended as I sat and watched people drive or walk obliviously by, caught up in their own world. A woman across the street in a cream colored dress that looked like it cost more than my truck slid into a silver Lexus. I imagined she was on her way home to a six bedroom mansion where she'd join her executive CEO husband for martinis and they would swap anecdotes about their day but little did he know she was actually having an affair with his accountant. Or the man who was yelling into a cell phone plastered to his ear, eyes searching frantically up and down the street for a taxi. His fierce, grim expression spoke of a deal gone wrong and he was up to his yin-yang in hock.

This game, dubbed this-is-your-lie, was what Tanya and I used to play when we were kids at the mall, watching shoppers tote bags of purchases as they ignored two young girls who sat and whispered to each other and giggled.

Unfortunately, my current situation wasn't funny or a game.

Someone thumped on the passenger window.

My head snapped around so fast I nearly got whiplash and stared into a set of blue eyes peering at me from a drop-dead gorgeous face.

Will.

What the hell?

I scooted across the seat and rolled down the window looking at him like he appeared from Mars.

"What are you doing here?"

"I could ask you the same question. And what happened to your face?"

"Long story."

His features softened. "I've got time. Let's get a drink."

I blinked, startled he would make such a bold request. "Why?"

"Because I wanted to talk to you and also am curious about the whole Mata Hari thing you have going on."

"I don't know.."

"Come on, Sadie. One drink."

Why not? I had nothing else better to do. "Okay." I exited my vehicle and joined him on the sidewalk.

He smiled, steered me in the opposite direction of where my rendezvous with Ms. Ing was supposed to have happened, stopped at a place called Andro's and ushered me inside. "They make great dirty martinis here."

Since I didn't have to worry about anyone recognizing me, I took off my dark glasses and hat. My curiosity was killing me. What was Will doing here and how did he find me?

The host came forward. "Mr. Ellington. Good to see you again." He didn't so much as twitch at the make-believe scar on my face.

"Hi Richard. Nice to see you too."

"Your usual table?"

"No. We'll just sit in the lounge area."

Richard smiled and turned. "Certainly. This way."

I gaped at my companion.

"My father comes here often, has conducted a lot of business at this place so they know me through him. He always sits at a specific table regardless of time of day."

Wow. Obviously, Will's father had some prestige if he could claim his own table. Maybe he was the Rockefeller of Houston?

He lightly grasped my elbow and we followed the retreating host to a section separated from the main room by a low standing wall with a three foot privacy screen made of various interconnected squares. A long stand-up bar slid down the left side of the room, its sleek black surface supporting a variety of drinks to the patrons who sat on high stools. A mirrored wall ran behind with glass shelves housing what looked like every kind of alcohol known to man. Three bartenders zipped back and forth, creating concoctions for wait staff and customers.

Richard bid us adieu with a nod and Will led me to a table near the back. He pulled out my chair, the guy really did have manners, and sat down opposite me.

"Are you going to tell me—"

He held up one finger as a waitress came to take our order.

"Two dirty martinis, please."

She left and I stared at him.

"What?" The corners of his mouth quirked in an impish grin.

A mix of indignation that he'd ordered a drink for me without asking what I wanted and stupefaction at sitting in a bar with someone I'd just recently met, someone younger than me, welled to the surface.

"Are you going to tell me what is going on?"

"Sure. What do you want to know?"

"First off, what are you doing here?"

"Having a drink with you."

I grit my teeth. "Will!"

His grin widened.

I was about to open my mouth when he motioned with his eyes that the waitress was coming with our drinks. I held my tongue. She deposited them and when she left I opened my mouth again, only Will interrupted.

"Just take a sip first. Then we'll talk."

I practically growled at his evasiveness but figured a shot of something cold and wet would quell my rising anger and raised the glass to my lips and drank.

"Ohh, nummy." My lips smacked in appreciation.

"See, I'm not such a bad guy after all."

"It's not a question of bad," I interjected. "But of why you are here."

He lowered his glass, all playfulness gone. "I actually called you a little while ago but you didn't pick up. I wanted to talk to you."

The other call after Tanya. "How did you know where to find me?"

"I tracked your phone." The corner of his mouth twitched.

"You what?"

"I tracked your phone."

"I heard you the first time. What I want to know is how and why?"

He leaned forward, crossed his arms on the table. "Remember when I finished setting up your website and asked to borrow your phone?" At my nod he continued. "Well, I didn't need it to see how the layout was on a mobile device. I wanted to be able to find you so I set up a reverse ping to my own phone."

Okay, that was just scary.

He must have seen my eyes widen because he rushed on. "I'm not stalking you."

"In your definition, maybe."

He went to take my hand resting beside my drink. "Sadie."

I pulled away, startled. I was beginning to think coming in here wasn't such a good idea.

"How's the business going?"

"Ahhh, okay I guess." His question came out of the blue and I wondered if he was trying to throw me off track. "We're getting away from the subject. Why are you following me, why did you track my phone and so help me if you dodge the question I will go straight to Tanya and tell her what you did?"

"It's a long story."

"I've got no plans for the next couple of hours."

He took another sip of his martini, put his drink down and stared at me. His expression became serious, sad even.

"I want to help you."

"Help me in what way?"

"I want to help prove your innocence."

I stared at him in shock. "You don't even know me!"

He winced at my rising voice. "I may not have known you for long, but I know the kind of person you are."

"How? We only met a few days ago when I coerced Tanya for help with the moving job."

"That wasn't the first time I'd seen you."

"For someone who claims not to be stalking me, you're not doing a bang up job." I threw back most of my drink. Maybe I should go.

"I saw you the first time at the Women's Centre. You were moving someone in."

That was possible as I had volunteered my services on occasion. Since I didn't comment, Will took that as an indication he should continue.

"One of the women you moved was my sister Melissa."

That got my attention. "I wouldn't know who she was because one of the conditions of volunteering was a person did not know the client's name. For privacy and safety concerns."

Will described his sister and I vaguely recalled her.

"But I would have remembered if you helped me with her move, and you didn't."

"True. I was at the Centre that day doing some computer work for them. I volunteer there as well. Community service."

"Okay. So I helped your sister. That doesn't mean you need to repay the favor."

He steepled his fingers. "You didn't just help my sister, Sadie. You help a lot of women and you don't take any money for it."

I narrowed my gaze. "How do you know that?"

"I checked the Centre's financials." When I gaped at him he continued. "What? It's not like I stole from them."

"But…but it's still not right."

He finished his drink, saw mine was almost done too and ordered another round.

"I have no desire to use any of that information. Besides, I had a question I needed answered."

"What question was that?"

"Out of all the places to volunteer, why that one? And why you refuse to take any payment."

Our drinks came so I waited until after the waitress left.

"And?"

A hint of what could have been pity followed by pain passed through his eyes as he dropped their focus to the table momentarily before returning to look at me. "When I commit to aiding someone I try and get as much information as I can." He paused again. "I know what happened to your mother, Sadie. I understand the reasoning for your connection to the Centre because my sister went through the same thing."

I don't know what emotion hit me the strongest at first; anger for the invasion of privacy, disbelief at his audacity, shock that he was right or compassion for the pain he had gone through as well.

"How did you find out about her? Have you been following me or did you track my phone?"

His silence told me enough. I hissed at him through gritted teeth as I rose. "You had no right!"

He grabbed my wrist. "Sadie. I'm sorry. I know I crossed the line with my method but you have to believe me when I say I truly only want to help you."

The sincerity in his words and expression made me hesitate. I sat back down, not willing to concede to his assistance before getting more information. "Your sister, she was in an abusive relationship?"

"Yes, but she got out."

"Fine. I helped her. It still doesn't explain—"

He cut me off. "That wasn't the first time your family has come to her rescue so to speak."

Okaayyyy.

Will took a long gulp of his drink, set it down. His voice took on a rueful, almost sad tone. "Quite a number of years ago, my big sister decided she'd had enough of living under my parents' rules and moved out of the house to be with the guy she had been dating. Our father didn't approve of Melissa's boyfriend and cut her off financially. Of course she rebelled and waited until mom and dad went away for a weekend, then she called a mover. Between her and her boyfriend, they didn't have a lot of possessions and also not a lot of money. Lissa ended up phoning a small moving company by the name of Hawkins Freight."

I leaned forward, my voice softening. "How old were you?"

"Twelve."

"And you remember that?" I sure as heck wouldn't remember anything that happened when I was twelve, unless it was significant.

"Sometimes things bring back memories," he said quietly.

I searched his face, saw pain he was trying hard to mask. "What things?"

"I'll get to that. Anyway, your dad ended up moving Lissa."

Now it was my turn to mask the hurt but it still stung to talk about it. "Not my dad. My uncle owned the company."

"He was nice. Didn't treat me like some stupid kid. Said if I helped haul boxes I could ride in the front of the truck with him. Even let me drive in an abandoned parking lot after we were finished. It was a pretty good day. He paid for the four of us to have pizza after." A hint of a smile touched one corner of his mouth. "Is he still around? Do you work for him?"

"No. He died. The business belongs to me now." I could totally see my uncle doing that, taking a young kid for a ride, letting him have a go at the wheel, copping for the food. Despite the years that had passed, my heart still constricted when I thought of him.

"Oh, I'm sorry."

I gave a brief nod, took a hefty sip of my drink. A long beat of silence fell between us. Then another. I waited.

"Lissa and I are very close. She was – is – the consummate big sister, was there for me when my parents were not. In the beginning I was too young to realize the relationship between her and the boyfriend/husband wasn't the best. She was young - and in her words stupid - and kept the situation to herself, wanting to protect me and she refused to give my parents the satisfaction of 'I-told-you-so.' A little while back she called looking for the name of your moving company. It was a long shot, she knew that but couldn't remember the name and figured on the off chance maybe I did since your uncle had been so nice to me and wouldn't take any money for the move. At the time he'd said it was a gift and wished them good luck with their new life."

"He must have made quite an impression if your sister thought you'd remember his name."

"I talked about it nonstop whenever we got together. Every kid wants to be able to brag he got to drive at the age of twelve. The memory was a good one."

There was a lull between us and by the way he lightly rubbed the thumb of his left hand over the palm of his right, I had a feeling the topic of conversation was something he struggled with.

"You said sometimes things bring back memories. What did you mean?"

He downed the remainder of his drink, motioned to my now empty glass, raised his eyebrows. I nodded, definitely needing another one. He signaled the waitress for another round.

"Will?"

His gaze met mine and I saw a curtain of agony fall across his features so raw it made me take a breath.

"The asshole Melissa threw her life away for, gave her heart to, lost her innocence to, he tried to kill her. That's why she had to leave. He broke her confidence to the point where she relied solely on him."

"Oh, Will. I'm so sorry." Tears pricked my eyes. "Why didn't she call your parents to help get her out?"

"They weren't on speaking terms," he said quietly. "Dad called it tough love. I get the tough, but the love part of that equation he quoted to defend his action escapes me."

Another round of drinks came and Will took a sip of his and sighed. "Lissa had no money of her own then, still doesn't have a lot, and although I try to help her out as much as I can, my hands are *tied* financially."

He must have seen me eye the fine cut of his clothes because he gave a sardonic smirk. "I don't actually pay for my wardrobe. Ever since I got arrested for the tech crime, which was my form of rebellion, I am on a tight leash."

I said my sympathies again. I couldn't imagine having a family member, especially a father, have that much control. The men in my family, my dad, uncle and brother gave me nothing but love and support and although two of them were gone, I felt blessed to have had that. My heart went out to the young man across from me.

We sat in silence, the cocoon of surrounding genial conversation giving us a moment's distraction from our emotions. Which was fine because what he'd said was a lot to take in.

"But…but what has this all got to do with me?"

"I couldn't help my sister then but your family did. And now you. I am here for her these days as much as I can. I'm also here for you."

"What can you do?"

"Try and prove your innocence."

"That's what the police are for." Tanya had said the same thing.

He leaned close with a secretive smile and lowered his voice. "I have ways of finding out stuff the police can't."

CHAPTER THIRTEEN

My eyes narrowed on Will across the table from me in Andro's. A nervous twitch flittered in the pit of my stomach and I wondered, as a rehabilitated offender of the Streetsmart group, just what he implied by his comment.

"What exactly do you mean you have ways of gathering information the cops can't?"

My companion gave a cheeky grin. "If I told you exactly, well, I'd have to kill you."

"Very funny. Explain."

"Let's just say I use my…gift with technology and leave it at that."

I gaped at him. "You're a computer hacker?"

"Not so loud." His eyes darted around.

"Are you insane?! I can't ask you to hack into someone's computer. You could go to jail."

"You didn't ask." He firmed his lips. "I offered. And a person only goes to jail if he gets caught."

Talk about a cavalier attitude. "From what I remember of a previous conversation, you *did* get caught."

He shrugged, as if the notion of having a record didn't faze him. "I got sloppy. Won't happen again."

"Dang right it won't happen again." I jabbed my finger at him. "Because you're not going to have anything to do with this."

He gave a short bark of laughter. "Did you just say dang?"

I sat there glaring at him while he eased back. He seemed so relaxed, like I had already agreed to the idea and that what he proposed was the simplest solution to the problem.

"I'm not going to let you do it." There, that would show him.

"I'm not asking your permission, Sadie. I will do this with or without your help. It'd be easier if you were on board."

I wanted to wring his bloody neck. "Why? Why are you putting your life, your future in jeopardy for me? Because my uncle and I helped your sister?"

He paused, his eyes watching me. "My grandfather once told me that a man is defined by his actions not his words. May be sentimental but it's true. I've lost sight of that. What your uncle did before and what I've seen you do now makes me think of what I've done in the past. Some of those things were wrong but I plan on changing that."

I hung my head. Who would have thought my savior would have such staunch morals. I couldn't even begin to theorize what complications could arise if we were caught but from Will's hard, determined gaze, I had a feeling he wasn't bluffing.

"Okay. Let's just say I'll go along with this hare-brained idea of yours. I want your promise you'll only get info. No sneaky cyber attacks, no wigglies, no viruses."

He couldn't stifle his grin. "Wigglies? Don't you mean worms?"

"Whatever. Your promise. Now."

"I promise. I have no desire to crash Back in Time's systems. Strictly intel gathering."

"Jeez, you make it sound like some covert operation."

"Besides, it's an auction house not Fort Knox or the CIA. What kind of trade secrets would they have?"

Who knows? If the theft and murder was an inside job, then someone at Back in Time had something they didn't want to share, something they killed to protect.

"What happens now?"

"You give me everything you know about this auction house."

We finished the remainder of our drinks while I told Will the little I knew. All I had was the owner's name and two employees. Speaking of Stanton's secretary, I decided since it looked like he wasn't going to give up I might as well tell him about Ms. Ing magically aging almost overnight.

"Definitely sounds suspicious," he eventually said.

"There's no sound about it. It is suspicious."

"Okay. Leave this with me and I'll get back to you in a few days."

"What do I do in the mean time?"

He shrugged. "Carry on as usual I guess."

"Can I come with you to see how you do this?"

"The answers are not going to be found on a Google search, Sadie. It will take time. Besides, the place where I do my research is...secret. I'm sure you understand."

"Don't tell me you're going all 'Lone Gunman' on me?" I'd glued myself to the television for ten seasons watching *XFiles* as the skeptic and the believer confronted one conspiracy theory after another - with the help of their three apprehensive amigos from the underground.

"Who?"

"Never mind."

Will excused himself to go the washroom. I sat at the table, drumming my fingers, digesting what I'd learned the past few hours. First off Margaret Yates had done something she felt could get her arrested but didn't confide to her friend Francie and it may or may not be related to Stanton's murder. Second, the woman who introduced herself as Ms. Ing when I arrived to haul the antiques is an imposter. And third, I have a Lone Ranger wannabe who despite the ethics, wants to break the law because he feels it is morally correct in order to help me.

My life was so screwed up.

My partner in crime, I couldn't believe I was even considering the whole scheme, came back to the table. He signaled it was time for us to leave and paid for our drinks, against my protest, and we left Andros'. The intense Texas heat had abated but the air was still warm. Although not deserted, street traffic had diminished considerably. Our footsteps echoed as he walked me to my truck. I couldn't help but feel a tangled knot of fear despite his assertions that he knew what he was doing.

"No chance I could talk you out of this?" I tried one last time.

"None."

I unlocked my door, turned to him. "Please be careful, Will."

He smiled, a warm light entering his eyes. "I will. Trust me. I'll contact you when I have something. Good night, Sadie."

He waited until I got into my vehicle, then turned and walked away. I watched him go, torn between immense gratitude and guilt for his help even though what he was about to do was so wrong.

I drove home, my mind in a whirlwind of hypothetical situations where Will got caught and I'd be either implicated with him, on the run, or visiting him in jail. When I reached my apartment, I hopped into the shower and as I watched the remnants of my disguise swirl down the drain I couldn't help but feel the correlation to how my life was turning out. I finished washing, stepped out, toweled off, dressed in comfy light cotton pants, similar to surgical scrubs, and a oversized shirt then flopped on the couch.

I dialed Blaine to touch base and see what if anything happened today.

"Hey."

"Hi sis."

"So, which creditor came calling today?"

"The leasing company for the van."

Damn. And here I thought I was being facetious. "Did you tell him I'd sleep with him if he gave me another month?"

My brother played along. "Yes. But his partner wanted to watch and I didn't think you'd be into that sort of thing."

I sighed, all laughter going out of my voice. "I gather we didn't get any new jobs either."

"Sorry, nope."

"Look, why don't you take the day off tomorrow, spend some time with Karen and my sweet niece."

"At this moment, Shanty isn't being sweet. She's being two, as in terrible."

"Bet she'd give Ivan a run for his money."

"I don't need a day off."

"There's no reason for you to be sitting at the office twiddling your thumbs when I can do the same thing."

"Sadie—"

I cut him off. "I can't pay you, Blaine. And I feel guilty enough as it is. If something comes up, I'll call you."

I was saved from the depressing silence with a beep on my phone that told me I had another call coming in.

"Someone else is calling so I'll let you go. Don't worry about coming into work tomorrow. Just take the day off, okay. Please."

He sighed. "All right, but call if you need anything."

"Will do." I disconnected from Blaine and pressed my call-waiting button. "Hello?"

"Hi Sadie, its Clayton."

"Hi. What's up?"

"Cause of death came in on the body and I have some other news. If you haven't eaten, we could grab a bite or would you rather come into the office tomorrow?"

Although I'm sure they were all very professional, the idea of Clayton's coworkers eyeing me with suspicion, derision or just plain contempt and whispering about how he was representing his ex-wife, again, was about as appealing as having teeth pulled.

"How about Mick's, in an hour?"

"Okay. Did you want me to pick you up?"

"No, I'll meet you there." I headed to my bedroom to change.

"See you then."

I was beginning to question the frequency and location of our meetings. Was Clayton using the client/lawyer relationship to his advantage and wanting to spend time with me? Was he still interested? Was I? Or was I just delusional and seeing things that weren't there, making something out of nothing? Maybe I really did need to pick Tanya's brain.

Although Mick's was a bar, it wasn't the upscale lounge like Andro's. It leaned more toward the sports bar restaurant crowd, with one side being the restaurant where families could eat and the other where children weren't allowed. Decorated like a huge log cabin it had thick varnished beams of bleached wood, sturdy country style tables and chairs and dark wood flooring. Two televisions airing sports channels mounted high on either end on the bar side competed against country music coming from the speakers in the rest of the establishment. The chatter of patrons and cacophony of noise made it warm and welcoming. My kind of place.

Clayton had beaten me there, presumably coming directly from his work. I slid into the bench across the table, gave him a warm smile.

He leaned forward. "How are you?"

"Good, considering."

"Want a drink?"

"I'll have a dirty martini."

He arched an eyebrow at my selection. "Since when?"

"A friend introduced me to them." I wasn't about to say who and how. The lawyer in him would be inquisitive and resourceful enough to wheedle the details out of me and that would blow Will's operation. Look at me, using spy lingo.

I reached for the menu on the table. If I was going to drive home I'd better have some food in my stomach considering I hadn't eaten since breakfast and I'd already had a few of the delicious concoction I wanted.

When the waiter came Clayton ordered my martini and a draft for himself plus a steak sandwich. I had initially thought about pulled pork but visions of Hester popped into my brain and I opted for the same as Clayton with an extra side order of deep fried pickles.

I glanced at him, raised a brow.

"What?"

"So what is your news?"

He leaned back as the waiter returned with our drinks and left. "Thought you may want to eat first."

"Unless you're going to provide gory details, which you can spare me, fill me in."

My ex rested his arm on the table. "Coroner cited cause of death as blunt force trauma. He figures the body had been dead twenty-four to thirty-six hours give or take. The heat in the van may have accelerated the decomposition a bit. Also no confirmation on the identity yet. No hits on prints in the system, which I figured, and no dental records could be found. Whoever was in the crate had perfect teeth. Go figure."

"If we're going by the assumption the guy was Stanton that meant whoever killed him could have done so sometime after he contacted me."

"Possibly."

"Works in my favor since I was three hours away from Houston when he called."

"Still doesn't mean you didn't do it, or hired someone to kill him."

I glared at him. "Whose side are you on?"

"Just telling you how the prosecution will look at it."

"How tall was the body?"

"Not very, five ten maybe."

"There you go. I'm too short to be able to hit someone that tall over the head."

Clayton reached into the breast pocket of his jacket, withdrew a manila envelope. "Because no one has come to claim the body, police want me to get you to look at photos to see if you recognize it."

"Since I'd never met Stanton, what difference would it make?"

"I know but the body may be someone else, someone you might have seen in the building."

"Or it's some stranger and I just happen to be the lucky patsy the killer has pinned this on."

My lawyer said nothing.

"What about Rogers? Have you asked him to look? He would be a better candidate to know."

"He went out of town briefly."

I gaped at him. "How convenient." Maybe he's on his way to Pampa to get rid of the antiques?

"Personal issues and he's not a major suspect. Yet. Anyway, I'll get him to look at the photos as well when he comes back. Please, just take a quick look."

"Do I have to?"

Clayton shrugged, leaving it up to me.

I took a quick glance, making sure to focus only on the face and not dwell on the manner of this man's death. He was a total stranger to me.

I shook my head. "No. Don't know who he is."

Our food came and Clayton took the pictures back, put them away. I popped a couple of deep fried pickles in my mouth. Holy Hannah, they were hot. I grabbed my drink, gulped it down, and raised my empty glass to our server as a signal for another.

"You may want to take it a little easy on the drinks, Sadie."

I waved a hand in front of my mouth, and took a small sip from his beer. "Hot, hot."

He shook his head with a smile. "To continue our line of conversation, you may have been unable to bludgeon someone taller than you if they were standing, not if they were sitting."

His words of the body being clubbed to death on the head and the image on the film turned my stomach when I cut into my steak to reveal the pinky flesh inside. I pushed my plate away. Should have ordered the salad.

When my martini came, I told the young man he could take away my steak and pickles. The soft texture of the fried veggies wasn't going down well now either, think squishy brains, and asked for potato chips. Crunchy was fine. No blood either. I took another hefty swallow of my drink. Dang these were good. "And how, Mr. Brainy, did I get the body into the crate. I'm not Wonder Woman, you know."

"Your cohorts. Two guys could do that no problem."

"Cohorts? Who are you channeling, Perry Mason?" I didn't care if my tone was accusatory.

Clayton laid down his knife. "I'm trying to get you prepared. If this goes to trial, the prosecution will state these types of questions and scenarios."

I clung onto his word. "If. You're not going to let that happen, right?"

"Doing my best." He resumed eating.

The chips came. Munch, munch followed by more nummy drink. Oh, look, my glass is empty. I signaled the server again with a smile.

An idea sprang to mind, no small feat considering I was feeling a bit fuzzy at the moment. "What about manifestos? If Stanton was killed after he landed in Pampa that would help me, right?"

Another drink magically appeared before me. Man, they were fast here.

Clayton finished eating, quirked his lips and moved his plate to the side. "You mean flight manifests not manifestos."

"Pecan, pecaan." I elongated the word with a snotty English accent. I stared at Clayton's green eyes, strong jaw, nice clothes. It was a bit unnerving because he was wavering in and out of focus, but he was still good looking. No wonder I fell for him.

"We checked flights out of Houston that night, which brings me to the other news I mentioned when I called."

I leaned forward on the table, empty glass in one hand, chin in the other. "Doooo tell."

He drained the last bit of his beer. "Stanton isn't Stanton. There is no driver's license, no Social Security, no record of him whatsoever. By all intents and purposes, Lionel Stanton doesn't exist."

"Then whoosh body was shooow stinky in my van?" I mumbled as my head slid to the table.

CHAPTER FOURTEEN

Rule number one when out for a night of drinking – or eating but drinking instead – make sure you turn off your phone before you go to bed so no one could wake you up with the ridiculously incessant ringtone of your cell.

The caller, who had the nerve of repeatedly dialing so they could listen to *Take Me Out to the Ball Game*, never got the memo.

Rule number two – never mix dirty martinis and deep fried pickles on an empty stomach and expect anyone to answer said ringing phone in a reasonable time.

The idiot caller never got the amendment.

After the third installment of the classic baseball song, I rolled out of bed, literally, staggered upright from the floor and bumped my way to the dresser where the insufferable ringing came from. Light pierced through the window, landing on the phone so that it appeared like some celestial energy bolt made it jerk and dance across the wood top in conjunction with the ringtone. The gods had a sick sense of humor.

I quelled the desire to slam my fist into the unit, fumbled with the phone, pushed a multitude of buttons to end my torture and finally hit answer.

"Mello." That was all I could get out.

"Sadie?"

I grunted because although I knew who I was, I wished I were someone else. Preferably someone that didn't crave a lobotomy.

"It's Clayton. I've been calling every five minutes for the past half hour. You okay?"

"No."

"What's wrong?"

I opened my mouth to speak, swallowed a few times because there was zero moisture, ran my tongue over my gummy teeth, gross, and tried again.

"I've been decapitated. My head is sitting in some fella's vice and he's having a gay old time playing with it."

I heard muffled laughter – at least he had the decency to cover the phone when he roared – and his voice, softened somewhat, came back on. "Well at least you're in one piece."

"Not by a long shot. What happened?"

"You, my inebriated client, passed out at dinner last night."

Well, dang. And I thought it was a reenactment of me getting conked over the head, only I woke up in my bed instead of on pavement and without a nice looking officer bending over me.

"How'd I end up at home?"

"I drove you, of course. Your truck is still at Mick's. You'll have to either cab it over or ask Blaine to drive you. Or I could swing by after work and give you a lift to get it."

As much as I appreciated Clayton's act of kindness I needed to get to the office at some point today and my sibling would have a field day if he learned why I needed a ride. And his brotherly love would demand he know.

"Thanks but I'll just ask Blaine to take me," I lied.

His words about taking me home sunk in and I glanced down at my attire, still dressed in the clothes from last night. Count on my ex to be the consummate gentleman. Now if I could only decide if I was glad or not. Sigh. I needed to get my head screwed on straight.

"Okay. I have to get to court but wanted to check in on you. Try and have a good day."

"Sure. And thanks Clayton for, well…just thanks."

He paused before replying. "You're welcome," and hung up.

I slowly made my way to the kitchen using a hand along the wall to help guide me, did a silent plea to the cola gods that I'd stocked up on some, and opened the fridge to be greeted with half a dozen high octane cans of refreshment. Taking three, I poured them into a huge measuring cup, stirred with the utmost care to make sure the spoon didn't click against the glass until most of the bubbles were gone, heated the liquid in the microwave and added enough of the Live Wire ingredients to wake the dead. I forced myself to drink it all before going to the shower and standing under volcanic hot spray for a good ten minutes. When I emerged from the bathroom I felt and appeared somewhat human, except for the bloodshot eyes which looked alarmingly like I was possessed by some sort of demon.

A demon called a dirty martini.

There was no way in hell I was going to phone Blaine. I couldn't very well ask him to drive me to work after practically begging him to take the day off, plus I'd have to endure the inevitable teasing about how I felt this morning. I ended up taking three buses to get to my truck and by the time I did, my head had cleared enough that I wasn't going to be a danger behind the wheel.

The office was quiet when I got there and for once I was grateful. I spent the next two hours compiling a list of bills and tasks that needed to be done in priority order. When that was finished, and the precarious future of my business became apparent, I decided it was time to hand out those flyers to the campuses but first called up some of the competition and fleshed out their costs. My pricing would barely cover my costs with hardly any profit but it would get the word out and possibly garner future business. I was at my wits end about what else to do. I didn't have money for more marketing and the thought of packing in my business, having to go find work, felt like I was turning my back on my Uncle Stan.

I must have had at least one synaptic pathway working before I left my place because I had taken the computer file of my flyer with me. At the copy place while my job was being printed, I wondered how Will was making out in his search. Remembering he said he tried to phone me yesterday after I fled Whitestone's, I pulled out my cell and scrolled through missed calls. Tanya's was there and I figured I should phone her back but not right now, and there was also a display of a call coming in but no number assigned to it. The photocopier signaled my job was complete and I pushed the phone back into my pocket deciding I would figure out later how else to contact Will. I desperately wanted to tell him about Lionel Stanton being an alias but other than talking with Tanya, I had no way of getting a message to him. If Tanya ever found out he was helping me, despite it being his decision and he was over the age of majority, it would hamper our friendship. I'd just have to wait until he got a hold of me.

I ventured to the campuses armed with a staple gun and my flyers.

When I finally got home it was past dinner and I was hungry enough to gnaw the leg off a coon dog. I decided against getting a burger and fries from a place down the road and opted for scrambled eggs and toast. When I knew the contents of my stomach wouldn't visit me again, I went to see mom, taking extra time to tell her a few stories and playing a game of Snakes and Ladders. She won.

I went home to a silent apartment, my nerves edgy and tense, waiting to hear back from Will. When my phone rang sometime later I practically pounced on it, hoping my operative - more spy lingo - had news.

But the caller was Tanya.

"Hey. How've you been? Haven't heard from you?"

"Okay. I've been busy, trying to come up with new ideas to drum up business. How about you?"

The conversation was weird, stilted. Tanya and I never spoke in this manner, like we were testing each other's emotions over the line. There had always been a connection, some unseen thread that bound us together. But now it felt like that thread had weakened, had a kink in it, and I was dismayed at the thought. I knew it had to do with my request for her to do some behind the scenes checking into Back in Time. And if I could have erased those words, gone back to when I entered her office with bagels and coffee and never made the suggestion, I would have given my soul to do that now. I hated this walking-on-eggshells feeling.

"The usual," she replied. A slight pause. "Did you come up with anything while you were out pounding the pavement for customers?"

I filled her in, bounced some ideas off her which she thought were solid. "Listen, about what I asked you to do in your office, asking questions and snooping around at the antiques dealer, I'm sorry."

"It's okay, Sadie."

"I should never have put you on the spot like that, I really am sorry, but I was scared, still am in fact."

"I understand. It's okay," she repeated.

We talked for a bit more and although the conversation wasn't as awkward as when we started, there wasn't the usual warmth.

My phone beeped that I had another call.

"Tanya, I have to go. I'm waiting on another call from a potential client" – little white lie – "and I don't want to miss it. Call you soon, okay?"

"Sure. Take care."

She disconnected and I felt almost as bad as if she hadn't called. I hoped the separation feeling would dissipate over time.

I answered the call from a college kid who wanted to get his stuff moved the coming weekend so technically I hadn't lied to Tanya. I got his info, gave him a quick quote and he said he'd try and find another student to split the cost and get back to me. I sighed and hung up, wondering if plastering my flyers all over campuses had been such a good idea. Students had practically no money, something I had forgotten since being in school, and I had to contend with them trying to get the best deal.

My phone rang again.

"Hi Sadie. It's Will."

"Will! I'm so glad you called. I have some info for you."

"So do I but not over the phone. I know it's late but did you want to grab a drink or something and we can compare notes?"

"Coffee. No drinks." I didn't want to see another dirty martini for a long time. "There's a coffee shop on the corner of Almeda and Arbor. Can you meet me there?"

"Sure. See you in half an hour."

I grabbed my purse and phone and headed out the door.

When I walked into the Beanery most of the tables were empty except for a few twenty-somethings and an old guy who looked out of place in a coffee house like this. Will raised his hand from the back and I made my way to him. Smiling at the cloak and dagger stuff, I visualized dressing in a trench coat and sunglasses and meeting my informant. In reality, if I did find a trench coat that would fit me without cutting off a yard of material, I'd look more like a character in a *SpyKids* movie.

I ordered a cola on my way past the counter, paid the barista for it and sat down across from Will.

I wanted to say hi and ask how he was but excitement got the better of me. "What did you find out?"

He took some papers out of his pocket. "Some stuff. Nothing that sends any red flags. Business financials are okay, no massive deposits or withdrawals, that sort of thing."

"Wait, you looked into their finances...never mind. I don't want to know. Anything else?"

He took a sip of his coffee. "Pretty much matches what you told me. Staff consists of two part time delivery people, no cleaning staff, Mrs. Yates, the full time secretary, Ms. Ing who works only part time and two partners."

"Wait. What? Two partners?"

"Yes. Jeffrey Rogers and Charles Weckland."

"Mrs. Yates never mentioned another partner. Neither did Rogers. In fact when Rogers introduced himself he said *he* was the owner."

Will checked his notes, consulted a computer print out. "The registration for the business does list two people but most of the transactions are done with Rogers. Maybe Weckland is a silent partner?"

"But why not say so?"

"If Weckland fronted some or most of the money strictly as an investment there'd be no reason to mention him because he has nothing to do with the clients."

"True."

"Is there any way of finding out more about this Weckland guy?"

"I've researched as far as I can online. Because Back in Time is a small antiques dealership, they probably store all their files directly on their computers or an onsite server and the only way would be to get direct access to Back in Time's systems."

"Meaning getting inside the offices."

"Yes."

"No way. Uh-uh, no how. You are not going to do that."

Will sighed. "Sadie—"

"End of discussion, Will. I mean it. This has gone far enough. You've given me more than I had an hour ago but this ends here. Now."

My heart palpated in my chest in fear that Will wouldn't listen and try to get access on his own. I'd been stupid and selfish to involve him and I pulled the only ace up my sleeve that I had.

"If I find out you hacked into their system while on site I'll tell Tanya."

He reared back like he'd been slapped. "You'd do that? You'd rat me out?"

"To save you from something worse, you betcha."

He stared at me with hurt and confusion.

I leaned forward, tried to convey my fear for him. "I don't want you to think I'm ungrateful but you have your whole life ahead of you and yet you're willing to throw that away on something that potentially may not even be there."

"But we won't know until we try."

"Besides, how do you expect to get in? It's not like you can waltz through the door during the day and say, oh hey, I'm your computer repair man." It hadn't worked for Jim Belushi in *Jumpin' Jack Flash* either.

He merely shrugged and didn't look at me. "You said you had info too. What's your news?"

"Oh, I almost forgot. My lawyer said that Lionel Stanton isn't Lionel Stanton. The guy doesn't exist."

"So who's the stiff in the mummy case?"

"They don't know."

"Interesting."

I didn't like how he said that. He got a gleam in his eye, the same one he had when we first talked intrigue at Andro's.

"Will, what are you thinking?"

"Nothing."

"Horse pucky. I can see it in your eyes."

He laughed. "Horse pucky? Wait, I have an idea."

"I don't care. The answer is no."

"What if I told you I could get access to Back in Time's system without going in?"

"But you said you needed to be hands on."

"No. I said getting direct access. That can be accomplished without me physically touching their computers."

I sat back and sipped the last of my cola. "And how in Sam hell you gonna do that?" I was peeved because I could tell Will wasn't going to listen to me. His sense of obligation was clouding his judgment and in the end I'd have to squeal on him, which in turn would ruin my friendship with Tanya.

He reached into his shirt pocket, retrieved a small device no bigger than half my index finger and slid it across the table to me.

"As long as someone can insert this into one of Back in Time's computers, I can get into their system from anywhere I have access to my computer."

"This looks like a thumb drive."

"Sort of, but it's been modified by me to do more than just store info."

I picked up the sleek black object. "You're saying as long as someone gets into the office and can plug this baby in, you're in as well?"

"Yes."

I pocketed the object. "Then that would be me."

His eyebrows shot to his hairline. "How do you plan on doing that?"

"Let me worry about that. I'm not going to have you risk getting caught. I'm already up to my eyeballs in turd, might as well be in over my head."

"And if you can't get in?"

"I'll figure something out." Despite the false bravado in my voice, I frantically tried to plan a scenario but nothing solid was coming to mind.

"Give me three days. If I don't contact you, then we'll pack it in."

He ripped off a piece of paper from the computer print out, wrote down a number. "This is my private number. Very few people have it. Give me a fifteen minute heads-up before you go in. I'll know if you're successful or not. Any questions?"

"Yeah. Where can I get a kid's size trench coat?"

CHAPTER FIFTEEN

I tossed and turned the whole night, trying to find some feasible excuse to get into Back in Time without them either showing me the door or calling the police. I had a funny feeling if I asked Clayton if it would be all right to go there, he'd say an emphatic no. And as much as I could probably pull off some type of disguise, minus the trench coat, my size and stature was sure to be recognized.

If that wasn't enough to keep me awake for most of the night, I mulled over the info about the two partners of Back in Time, one who Mrs. Yates may have been seeing. In her conversation with the friend I overheard at The Maple Diner, she claimed her lover was going away without her. On the assumption it *was* someone from the antiques dealership she was having an affair with, it was feasible it could have been Weckland who was taking off. If Yates was that angry about being left behind, and Weckland was her lover, would that be grounds for murder?

I considered calling Clayton with the news about Back in Time having two partners but held off. He would want to know how I came about that information and I wouldn't divulge my sources. If the police started nosing around the antiquities dealer it could hamper my attempts to get into the establishment and place Will's modified thumb drive into one of the company's computers. So I decided to hold back for a few days until the right time came to reveal what I'd learned.

In the morning, I called Blaine and told him not to come in, to which he almost begged me if he could. My niece was in the midst of throwing a temper tantrum, but I held fast and said no. And added a witty comment about being a parent and for him to suck it up, then disconnected before he could fire a comeback. I listened to the peace and quiet of my place and took a moment to revel in the freedom of independency and lack of commitment, other than my business. That lasted about a minute before the reality of the charges against me and my lack of income smacked me in the head.

I was frustrated and at my wits end and when I was like this the only thing that calmed me down was hitting some balls. I changed into ball gear, grabbed a couple of bats and headed to a facility with batting cages on the corner of Jackrabbit and West Road that catered to diehard baseball fans.

When I got there, someone was already smacking a few at the end of the set of cages, so I chose the farthest one away and began to warm up. The stretching helped clear my mind, helped stow away the chaos of my life and sharpened my focus on only one thing, having the bat meet the ball. I did a few practice swings, the muscle memory coming automatically. I inserted my money, set the device for easy pitches to start, made sure my right shoulder was in line with the machine, breathed deep and let go.

The sound of a ball connecting with the bat has a beautiful echo. It smacks of childhood, of dreams and heritage, of freedom and most of all, of joy.

I could sense the rhythm returning, felt the blood pumping through my veins, filling me with life. Air went in and out my lungs at a steady pace, infused my blood with oxygen, set my endorphins free.

After a few minutes I changed the pitches to come at random and increased the speed. I was swinging with precision, my concentration so sharp I had tuned out everything. There was only me, the bat and the ball.

I don't know how long I was at it. I had dumped over thirty bucks worth of change and when my money finally ran out, I was drenched in sweat, my breath rasping in and out and my muscles burned from exertion. I felt happy, calm and centered for the first time in months.

I pulled the batting helmet off, wiped my brow with a hand towel I brought along and slapped on my cowboy hat, a leather dark chocolate brown, wide brim Stetson with a braided leather circle headband when my cell rang. The caller ID said it was a redirect from the office line. There were still a few people smacking balls in other cages, so I stepped into the hall that connected to another part of the building.

"Hawkins Freight."

"Is this Sadie Hawkins?" a male asked.

"Yes."

"Hi. This is Wayne Timmins."

I paused. The Good Samaritan cop. Did he have some information on my case? But if so, wouldn't he have contacted Clayton instead?

"My rescuer from Pampa."

"I wouldn't go so far as to say that," he chuckled.

"What can I do for you, Officer Timmins?"

"I…ahh…your hauling business. Do you do strictly commercial or can you move people as well?"

That wasn't the answer I expected. "Yes, I move people too."

"Great. I was wondering if you would be available to give me a quote on relocating to Houston."

"Umm, sure."

"I'm actually in the city. Finished a job interview and need to head back to Pampa. Can we meet now to get the ball rolling?"

I could imagine what I looked like, flushed, sweaty face that had no make-up, not even mascara. Scary. I sniffed delicately at my underarms. No smell but I certainly wasn't at my best.

I gauged how long it would take me to get home and take a shower. "I'm available in about an hour or so."

"Oh." Silence. "I have other appointments."

I thought for a second. What the hell, the guy had seen me unconscious, probably with my mouth open, not a shining moment.

"I just finished batting practice so if you don't mind a bit of sweat you can meet me here and we can talk particulars over a coke or something." I gave him the name and address of the facility and told him I would be inside.

"Perfect. I'll see you there in about twenty minutes."

I took that time to wash up a bit in the ladies bathroom and plunked the cowboy hat over my sticky hair. True to his word, Officer Timmins walked into the lobby a short time later.

"Hi. Thanks for meeting me. Cool place. I may have to try this sometime."

Now that my vision wasn't hampered with the thundering of jackhammers pulsing through my skull like when I'd first met him, I saw he was taller than me, most people were, but not overtly. I didn't have to crane my neck back to see his face, which was handsome, slightly rounded, in a boy-next-door kind of way. He had brown eyes, a shade lighter than his hair, which was straight, had golden highlights and cut short. A blue short sleeved buttoned shirt fit snuggly on his well muscled shoulders but he didn't have the physique of a body builder, more like someone who liked to keep in shape. Dark blue pants encased slim hips and traveled down to end just above polished black shoes. Nice, very nice.

"Do you play ball?"

He nodded. "You come here often?" He rolled his eyes. "Now there's a line if I ever heard one."

I laughed, knowing how he meant the question. "Sometimes. To relieve stress."

Now why would I say that? Like he would care.

"The case?"

I was about to ask him how he knew about that then realized Clayton had been in touch with him when I'd been arrested so of course this man would assume as much. I shrugged, not wanting to talk about my screwed up situation. I had come here to forget about that.

I changed the subject. "If you're here for a while Officer Timmins, are you going to sign up for some of the leagues?"

He smiled. "I'm not meeting with you on official business, so it's Wayne. I might look into leagues. You still play?"

"Not lately. Too much going on." Damn, seemed like there was no getting around the topic of my case. "With my business."

"Speaking of, I hope you don't mind that I searched you out. My transfer was already in the works when I first met you but that wasn't the right time to talk shop."

Was that the reason he hesitated before he left that night?

"No, it's fine. Surprised me, though."

He glanced away shyly, down at his watch then returned his gaze to me. "I don't have a lot of time but I'm a bit hungry. Did you want to grab a quick bite and we can talk preliminaries?"

As if the mention of food signaled my stomach, it gave a loud gurgle and I sensed the heat of a blush rising to my face. "Sure. How about grabbing something at the refreshment stand/café here?"

"Suits me." He grinned. He had nice teeth.

"I'll meet you there. I might have some spare contracts in my truck or at least some paper and a pen."

"Okay."

I jogged to my truck and rummaged around in the glove compartment looking for some paper and a pen. Found a pen but no paper. Not wanting to keep Wayne waiting, I headed to the refreshment stand and met up with him at the counter.

I read the menu. "I didn't realize how hungry I am. I'm starved."

I decided on a super sized cola plus a loaded jumbo dog minus the sauerkraut. Wayne chose a burger and a cola as well. The Texas heat would do its best to fry my brain so we opted for eating inside. As I left the counter I grabbed a stack of napkins.

We slid into a booth. I took a bite out of my dog, closed my eyes and practically groaned with pleasure. When I opened them it was to Wayne watching me.

"What?"

"Nice to see a girl who doesn't mind eating something other than salad."

Kudos for me. I raised my drink in toast and we touched cups. I spread out the napkins and grabbed my pen, poised to take notes.

He quirked a brow.

"No paper," I explained.

"Resourceful."

"It works. Now, what did you want moved."

We spent the next half hour talking business. There was comfortableness between us, an ease in our conversation, more like friends then proprietor and client.

"When did you want this done?"

He tossed our garbage into the receptacle and sat down. "I've actually got a house rented but am staying in a motel for now. I prefer the sooner the better. This weekend work for you?"

I hadn't heard back from the person who was hoping to get their stuff moved but I had to grab opportunity when it came. I was about to extend my hand and shake on the deal when I remembered I didn't have the van. It was still in the police compound.

Well, hell.

Wayne must have noticed my crestfallen expression. "What's wrong? This weekend no good?"

"No, the timing is fine." I sighed. "Problem is the police still have my van and I don't know if I can get everything you need in the back of my pick-up."

"I've got a truck we can also use."

I arched a brow. "Kind of defeats the purpose of hiring a moving company if you're doing half the work."

He lifted a shoulder.

I leveled my gaze on him. "I don't do charity."

"Think of it as helping the local economy."

"Wayne."

"Sadie, if I can get my things here in one haul instead of two or three with my truck, it will be worth it. I'll get reimbursed for the expenses."

I sat back and crossed my arms, not convinced.

"I have to hire someone anyway. I'd rather give the money to someone I know. Besides, I think it might be more enjoyable to work with you than strangers."

Well, well, well. Again my face warmed and I concentrated on rechecking the figures I'd written on the napkins even though I knew they were correct. I gathered them up in a neat pile and stuck out my hand.

"You have a deal, Officer Timmins."

He touched two fingers to the side of his head in a salute. "Thank you, ma'am. It'll be a pleasure working with ya."

* * *

Later, I phoned Tanya to see if she wanted to go for coffee but my call went directly to voice mail. I left a message for her to phone me back.

When my ringtone went off moments later, I expected it was Tanya but saw the call was a redirect from the business. I was at home because it was preferable sitting here than at work, in my tiny office, staring at a silent phone.

"Hawkins Freight."

"Hey. I've got your flyer here, from U of H and was wondering if you could move me."

Cool. Two jobs in two days. I crossed my fingers.

"Sure. When and where?"

"I have to be out of the room tomorrow so from campus to the other side of the city."

"Okay. Do you have furniture or mainly boxes?"

"Just my bed and boxes. Think you can do this?"

Perfect. I could handle this myself, well, maybe except for the bed, and should be able to squeeze it all in my truck. If not, two loads should do it. I mean, how much stuff does a student have anyway?

"No problem." I did a quick calculation on mileage and gave her a rough estimate depending on how many boxes. "Will there be someone to help me?"

"I can ask one of my friends and there aren't too many boxes."

"What floor are you on?"

"The ground floor."

I did a fist pump in the air. "What time tomorrow?"

"Say about nine."

I got her name and dorm room number. "I'll see you tomorrow at nine, Rachelle, and thanks for calling Hawkins Freight."

I had a shower and when I got out saw that someone phoned. The juvenile fantasy-land part of my brain hoped it was Jackson Steel calling to say he got my message. But it wasn't. Guess that ship had sailed.

The call had been from my sister-in-law, Karen, who'd left a voice mail message to ring her back. She picked up on the second ring.

"Hey, Sadie, how are you? Did I catch you at a bad time?"

"Never."

"Do you have any plans for tonight?"

"You're kidding, right. Why, what's up?"

In a plaintive, pleading voice Karen said "I need to get out of the house for something other than my class. I won two tickets to see a play being performed for the next couple of weeks. It's called the Mikado and you know how keen Blaine is to go to those sorts of things. Would you want to come with me?"

I could just picture my brother trying to worm his way out of something with so much culture.

"Sure, I'm game."

"Yay," my sister-in-law squealed. "I'll pick you up around seven."

"Sounds good, see you then."

When Karen picked me up later, a soft yellow blouse didn't quite hide the tell-tale baby bulge above her white capris. Brown eyes glittered from a face glowing with health and her auburn hair was held back in a ponytail by an elegant clip. She may be the fashion opposite of my semi-designer jeans, shirt and boots but we got along like a house on fire and she was primo in my book for making my brother such a happy man.

"Thank you so much for going out at the last minute. I'm overdue for some girl time."

I laughed after giving her a quick hug. "Anytime."

Once in the downtown core it took us a while to find a parking spot and then we had to hustle to the *Theatre Under the Stars* on Bagby to make it in time before the curtain went up. The cashier took the tickets from Karen and requested we take our seats as soon as possible as they don't allow entry into the theatre once the production started. Karen zipped into the bathroom while I found our seats and the lights were just dimming when she sat down beside me.

Over the next two hours the audience was entertained by Nanki-Poo who loves Yum-Yum but she's betrothed to Ko-Ko, the new Lord High Executioner. Between the hyphenated character names, some of the outrageous costumes and ditties like *I've Got a Little List* and *Three Little Maids From School Are We*, Karen and I spent most of the production laughing.

After a standing ovation, the full-house crowd made their way slowly into the aisles and out the theatre. Among the throng of people in the lobby, I waited to one side while Karen went to use the washroom again. There were half a dozen usherettes mulling about and cleaning up when, as one of them began closing the doors into the seating area, a man stopped her. He was Asian, good looking in a tough sort of way and dressed in casual clothes. He reached for her face, gave the young woman a deep possessive kiss and retreated back into the theatre. She said something to him that I didn't catch and as she reached up to lock the door to the top she turned and I sucked in a breath.

It was Ms. Ing. The young, imposter Ms. Ing.

I was too stunned to react before she slipped into the theatre and Karen took that moment to step out of the washroom. My mind tangled with wanting to race after the woman who was probably part of the reason my life was in such a mess and having to explain to Karen why I wanted to tackle a young woman and make a citizen's arrest. Not to mention the whole sordid story of doing my own investigating using less than conventional methods. As much as I hated to walk away, Karen and I exited the building but the whole time I was thinking how I would be back here tomorrow evening, early, watching for my quarry.

Imposter Ms. Ing was part of the theatre staff. I planned on finding out who she really was.

All I had to figure out is how I was going to do that without her seeing me.

CHAPTER SIXTEEN

When I arrived at the U of H campus dorm in the morning where Rachelle lived, there was no one to let me in. Repeated buzzing to her room proved fruitless so I started pressing every button at the security door before someone answered, swore at me, and released the lock on the main door.

I turned left down the hall, stepped over pizza boxes, empty beer bottles, a white sheet, a pair of lacy pink underwear and finally came to her room. I knocked on the door. No answer. I knocked louder. Still no reply.

Seriously? I'd been stood up by a college co-ed.

I thumped on the door and yelled her name to which I was told off by someone in the next room. I was about to turn away and chalk the event as a learning experience when the door opened and a slim, blond girl stared at me through eyes so red even Visene wouldn't help.

"Oh, hi. You're here to help me move?" She hung onto the door but still swayed back and forth.

"Yes. It's nine. Are you ready to go?"

"I think so. Come on in."

I saw the state of her room and knew there was no way she was ready. Bodies, living thank god, were strewn all over the floor, some in different stages of undress. The stench of stale beer, sweat and what could possibly be vomit filled the room like a dense curtain. My temper started to rise because I figured the time I had allotted for this job had just been blown.

Rachelle toppled a bit to the side. "Excuse me, I'll just be a minute," and stumbled to the bathroom where she proceeded to puke. Repeatedly.

At least she'd been courteous about it.

But that didn't stop my blood from beginning to boil. When I heard the retching stop for more than a minute, I marched to the bathroom door, knocked once and strode in.

"Hi again." She stood at the vanity, holding on for support and tried to focus on me.

She was still drunk and I didn't have the time or the patience for this.

"We had an agreement and a verbal contract."

"Yeah. Sorry but the gang sort of threw me a going away party, which, kind of, you know, lasted longer than expected. Umm, can we make it tomorrow?"

"I thought you said you had to be out of this room today?"

Her brows scrunched together, like she was trying to figure out a quantum physics equation. "Oh, yeah. How about later this afternoon?"

I wasn't coming back. "No. I've scheduled you for this morning. I have a business to run."

She pouted. "My daddy will pay you double."

"Darn straight he'll be paying double and we're doing this now." I reached past her to the stand-up shower, opened the cold faucet to full, pushed her in and held her under the spray while she wailed like a banshee and batted at my hands feebly. She stared at me with forlorn eyes, like a doe watching its mother abandon her but I wasn't about to be swayed.

"Is everything in this place yours?" I demanded.

Streaks of blond hair were plastered against her head. Her pink sleep shirt, the same color as the panties I saw in the hallway, clung to her like a second skin.

"Yes."

"Is everything going?"

"Yes." Her teeth began to chatter.

"Fine. I'll leave some fresh clothes out for you and box the rest." I gave her what my mother would call, a stern glare. "You kids want to be treated like adults, it's time you started acting like one and stand by your commitments. Sober up. I'll get everyone out of here."

I slammed the door on my way out.

Chalk it up to what was happening in my life but I had my fire on and showed no mercy booting Rachelle's party goers out the door. She'd said her friends would help but by the looks of them it would be hours before they were coherent enough to stand upright, let alone haul boxes, so I ushered them all out. I found a huge trash bag under the kitchen sink and crammed it full with garbage and empty bottles. Spying one of those single cup coffee makers in the kitchenette, I stuck a pod in and dialed it to strongest brew. When it was done I strode with cup in hand to the bathroom, knocked once, thumped the cup on the vanity and walked out. In her bedroom, where in the heck was the dang floor there were so many clothes on it, I selected what looked to be somewhat clean, grabbed some underwear, a pair of socks and a set of runners and brought those to her as well.

Most of the bedroom got packed in boxes I found in the corner when Rachelle finally came out of the bathroom. She stood in the doorway, cradling the coffee cup in her hands, silently studying me.

"What?" The word came out a bit harsher than I intended.

She tilted her head. "Why are you helping me?"

I straightened from the box on the floor. "Because we had a contract and I need the money."

She seemed to ponder that and gave a small nod. "Momma said daddy always pampered me too much. He said he did because he loved me."

I saw a young woman standing before me, about to step into a world that I learned from experience wasn't all peaches and cream. "You can love someone without coddling them. How are you going to learn to be independent, stand on your own two feet, meet challenges that you couldn't even dream about because they can come at you with the speed of light, if you're not taught commitment and determination. How are you going to get people's respect if you can't portray those things? How can you respect yourself if you don't?"

She stared at me for a long time before turning away. "I'll finish up the kitchen."

"Fair enough." I smiled at her retreating back.

It took two trips back and forth to get all of Rachelle's belongings out of her place and into a new apartment. By the end of the second run she and I were chatting like sisters. I learned her father was head of a huge advertising company and her mother was an architect. The parents stopped by at her new apartment and watched their daughter with a slight frown. When Rachelle was at the truck, the parents pulled me aside and asked if something had happened because instead of their daughter sitting back and having others do the work, she lugged and carted as many boxes as I did. I merely stated they had done a fine job raising their child and they should be proud, to which the father raised an eyebrow as if I wasn't telling the whole story. He did indeed pay me double the price and took a number of my business cards before I said my final goodbye.

When I got home the muscles in my shoulders and back roared in agony, probably from the combination of hauling boxes and batting practice the day before.

I checked my phone. There was a message from Wayne confirming a time and location to meet in the morning as we would tandem up to Pampa for his move.

No message from Tanya. I was getting worried.

More importantly, I still hadn't figured out how to get the small device into one of Back in Time's computers and my three days was coming to an end.

Since I was stalled on that try-to-make-sure-I-don't-go-to-jail part of my life, I figured I'd attempt to get closer to my mystery imposter.

As long as it didn't require anything physical.

Ms. Ing-the-younger had seen me in a tee and jeans so I gussied myself up a bit with black dress slacks, pumps, a lacy black blouse and the Cleopatra wig I used for my previous disguise. I studied my reflection in the mirror. I wasn't going hog wild and do eye make-up or the scar thing, that would be pushing it too far. But unless I didn't come face to face with Ms. Ing-the-younger - I'd have to come up with something else to call her - I should be okay. Besides, this was only a scouting mission.

Scouting mission. I was beginning to sound like a pint sized *G.I. Jane*.

I had to park several blocks away from the theatre. When I approached the building I did so from the other side of the street, hoping to catch a glimpse of who was in the ticket booth and my worst fears were confirmed. Inglette – I came up with that one on the drive down – was front and center. No way to get in the front doors without her seeing me. Even though I had a wig on, the lights from the overhang were bright and she'd have to look right at me. And then there was the body physique thing. I couldn't disguise that.

I melded into the shadow of the building behind me and edged away. There must be some other way to get in. Maybe if I waited until well after curtain, Inglette might close up shop and head inside. I mean, why would someone pay full price when half the show was over? Even if a staff member came into the lobby while I was there, at least I was dressed up enough to pass for an audience member. But I couldn't go in just yet so went back to my truck and waited.

When you're bored, time drags slower than a slug crossing a country lane. Every fifteen minutes I'd jump out of my truck and sidle up the street far enough to see if the light in the ticket window was still on. Yup. Back into my vehicle I went.

After forty-five minutes had passed I was rewarded with a dark ticket window. Yes! I zipped across the street, edged open the door and poked my head inside. My heart started pounding thinking someone would slam the door shut on my neck but the outer lobby was clear. Once in the inner lobby, which was also empty, I breathed a little easier. Upon slipping inside, I immediately took to the shadows of one wall and crept along the thinning dark maroon carpet on my tiptoes like a member of the *Scooby Doo* gang. There was a counter to serve refreshments, as evident to the locked refrigerated display cooler against the wall, but the standard red licorice and popcorn machine of a movie theatre was absent. A partitioned cloak room was located beside the doors leading into the theatre. Washrooms were on the far wall and anyone seeing me would assume I had just come from there.

All right, now that I was in, how would I find out who Inglette was? Staff lockers? I searched the room but the only door I saw read office. I went to it, tried the knob. Locked. Of course. What about the ticket booth? Maybe she left her purse in there. I tried that door but it was also locked. Dang it, people didn't trust anyone these days. There was a window near the top third of the door and although I jumped up and down, I couldn't see in. Frustrated, I snagged a box-shaped, vinyl covered lobby chair and, huffing and puffing, lugged it over to the door. I stepped up and inspected the enclosure. I couldn't see a purse but I did spy a uniform jacket. Peering close I made out a nametag – Sharon, but that didn't mean it belonged to Inglette.

The roar of applause startled me so much I almost fell off the chair. Crap, intermission. I scrambled down and began to drag back the chair when a leg got caught on a hole in the carpet.

"Come on, you stupid piece of horse shit!"

With a mighty yank, the captured leg sprang free with a resounding loud rip.

Ooops.

I pulled for all I was worth, got the seat relatively back to its former position and slammed through the bathroom doors just as the auditorium lobby doors opened. I dove into the nearest stall, locked it and stood hands on knees heaving my breath.

Too fricken close.

Women streamed in and out the washroom and at one point someone knocked on my stall and asked if I was okay.

"Fine. Constipated," I grunted out. It was the only thing I could think of.

I didn't want to chance seeing Inglette in case she was manning the front doors so I stayed where I was. Shortly, the bathroom emptied and I was about to exit my stall when the door opened again and I heard women talking.

"You were late getting to the lobby," woman number one said.

"I was back stage, talking with Russell," retorted woman number two. Inglette! I recognized that snooty voice anywhere.

Water running, then the *snuk-snuk* of what probably was the soap dispenser, followed by splashing.

"Careful Sharon, if the owner catches you slacking off he might fire you."

"I don't care," Sharon replied. "I won't be at this place much longer, have better things coming my way soon."

A *riippppp* from a paper towel dispenser.

"Really?" woman number one gushed, all excited. "Can you tell me?"

"Sorry no," she said, not very apologetically. "Time's up. We'd better get back."

"Nice watch. Are those, like, real diamonds?"

"It's a Cartier," Sharon bragged. "Someone special gave it to me."

"Wow, wish my boyfriend…"

And the rest of the conversation was lost as the door to the bathroom closed.

Inglette was Sharon! The voiced matched and the diamond studded Cartier I remembered seeing on her wrist confirmed it.

I waited another moment just to make sure no one else came in then got out of the stall and left the washroom. The lobby was again empty but I didn't want to take the chance that Sharon might be hanging around so I took off out of the place.

I sat in my truck, elated with my find but the joy was short lived. Sure I had a name, but only a first name. There must be thousands of Sharons in Houston. Hmm, maybe the theatre had a computer and a file listing their employees? But as soon as that thought came to mind I nixed it. How was I going to get access to their computer, even if they did have one?

No, this called for a more direct approach. I'd have to find another way to get into the theatre tomorrow night.

CHAPTER SEVENTEEN

Saturday morning dawned bright and early and before I left for Wayne's move I called Blaine, getting him out of bed, and asked if he'd mind going into the office just in case the gods were smiling on me and more of my campus flyers brought in other prospects. He thanked me profusely since Shanty was having two other kids over for a play date and this would give him a legitimate excuse for not being there.

My charge for his free pass was a weekend in Reno for Tanya and myself plus a case of high octane cola.

He promised one can and it would be on my desk. Take it or leave it.

As I drove into the motel parking lot of where Wayne was staying, talk about a clandestine rendezvous, he was leaning against his truck clad in jeans, a snug fitting tee and what appeared to be heavy duty hiking boots on his feet. Maybe he thought I'd drop a table on his foot. Still, the guy looked mighty fine. He straightened, grabbed two take-out cups from their resting place on his hood and gave me a lopsided grin when I pulled up beside him and got out.

"It's still pretty early, so I figured you might like a coffee. Don't know how you take it, though?"

What I almost said was 'any way I can get it, especially these days.' Instead, I lifted the lid and let the caffeine scented air waft into my brain. "This is perfect, thank you." Although I didn't drink the brew every day, I did appreciate a good cup of coffee occasionally, not to mention the gesture was really sweet.

His eyes crinkled when he smiled. "Did you want to catch a bite to eat or get going right away?"

"Since I'm not sure if we can get everything hauled in one load, even with both our trucks, maybe we should get started right away. Or if you're hungry, we can grab something to go?"

"I'm good, got some granola bars just in case."

"Always prepared. Let me guess, Boy Scout, right?"

He lifted a shoulder sheepishly.

I knew it. "Want me to drive lead?"

"Do you speed?"

My eyes widened in mock surprise. "No."

"Uh-huh. I'll drive point, Danica," he said in reference to the female race car driver.

"Where do you want to meet in case we get separated?"

He thought for a moment. "There's a restaurant just off exit 292A. We can stop there and get something to eat before we tackle the job. Sound good?"

I opened my door and threw over my shoulder, "Lead the way, Mario."

* * *

We made good time getting to Pampa but I was hungrier than a bear when I pulled my vehicle next to Wayne's and exited.

"Ready to eat?" He opened the door to the restaurant.

"Absolutely."

When the hostess seated us at a table, I asked for a cola right away, I was down at least one, and perused the menu. "I'm starving."

"Me too.

Wayne took a sip of his iced tea after the waitress left with our order and leaned back against the chair. "So, Ms. Sadie Hawkins, tell me about yourself."

I took a long draw from my cola. "Not much to tell. I'm from Amarillo, moved to Houston when I went to college. Divorced. No kids. Run my own business. That's it."

"Not many women in the moving industry. Was it a life-long dream?"

I stifled a laugh. "No. I took over the company from my dad's brother Stan."

"Does he give you a hand when you need a crew?"

"No, he died."

"Oh, I'm sorry."

"It's okay."

But it wasn't, because the business was all I had as a connection to happier times and it killed me that I stood the chance of losing it because someone might be framing me for theft and possible murder.

"Your accent isn't true Texan."

"Originally from Alabama."

"Thought I noticed a bit of a nasal twang."

I aimed my fork at him, glad the awkward moment was gone. "Hey, don't dish the voice."

He winked at me. "Never."

Was there some flirting going on here? My stomach gave a little flutter and not because I was hungry.

"Siblings?"

"A brother."

"Your parents live in Houston?"

"Mom does. My dad died when I was younger. Your turn with twenty questions."

A slight flush crossed his cheeks. "Sorry, it's the cop in me."

Our food arrived, burgers and fries for both of us and I watched with interest as Wayne removed the lettuce, tomato and onions.

"I'm mainly a meat and potato kind of guy."

"Why didn't you order it plain?"

He put the top bun back on his burger, took a few bites. "Because then they forget the cheese, ketchup and mustard. Easier this way."

I stuffed a fry in my mouth, chewed, swallowed. "I'm not letting you off the hook with the twenty questions."

He nodded and wiped a napkin to the corner of his mouth. "I grew up on a farm in Iowa with three sisters."

"That must have been fun." I downed my burger with a vengeance. Because of Hester I still wasn't up to eating pulled pork.

"At least we had two bathrooms. Both parents still alive."

"What made you decide to become a cop?"

Something, pain or anger perhaps, flashed briefly across his eyes and then it was gone. "Someone I cared about got hurt, beat up pretty bad. The culprit never had to pay for their crime."

The anger may have left his expression but the tightened muscles in his forearms still spoke of resentment.

"Amazing how people and events shape our lives, isn't it."

He stared at me and I saw the briefest flash of something I couldn't quite define again enter his eyes before the tension in his body left. "Yes, it is."

There was a pause in our conversation, deep, uncomfortable maybe, I wasn't sure, but I covered it up with draining the last of my drink and pushing away my plate. "We should get going."

He signaled the waitress and she came with the check, which he scooped up before I could grab it to see how much my share cost.

"Rate plus expenses."

Who was I to argue?

I followed Wayne to his place, a modest two bedroom bungalow with brown siding. There were no flowers or landscaping in the small yard but then with the type of work he did he probably didn't have a lot of time for upkeep. The house was located in a nice neighborhood with a park down the street and other well maintained properties.

The front door opened directly into the living room, with a decent sized kitchen beyond and laundry off that. Two bedrooms and a bath were down the hall on the left. Neat, compact, clean. Although not utilitarian, the place didn't have a homey feel either, which surprised me since Wayne came across as more of a homey type of guy.

No frilly curtains, no wallpaper borders. Not a single feminine touch whatsoever.

"Not a collector, huh?" I gazed around.

"Of house stuff, no, but I also have a garage."

He led the way out the back door to the yard that could have used a bit more grass seed. It wasn't a gravel pit or weed patch, but with a bit of TLC and some water, it would be a great place to hold barbecue parties and maybe even a dog and a white picket fence.

What? Where the hell did that come from?

I shook myself out of the daydream and followed Wayne to a single car garage. He swung up the wide metal door to reveal an inside stock full of outdoor gear, sports equipment, even a motorcycle.

I stared openmouthed at the contents. "Ahhh, I think you miscalculated on the amount of stuff you have. Big time."

"Yeah…I'd forgotten about a lot of this." He scanned the area. "We're not going to get everything in one haul, are we?"

"Not a chance. Especially not with the bike."

He slumped against the garage. "Damn."

"Hang on a sec." I went back into the house, took note of the already packed boxes, thank goodness he'd been prepared, walked to the vehicles, did some mental figuring and returned to the garage.

"You've got a couple of options. First, we take what we can, drop everything in Houston and come back for the next round. Second, you could coordinate any friends who have trucks who might be able to give us a hand or third, get a small trailer from a one way rental place.

He checked his watch. "It's a little late to try and scramble up some help at the last minute, people probably already have plans or are out, and I have no desire to swing back again today. Guess I'll head to the local rental place and hitch up a trailer to my truck."

"Okay and while you're gone I'll start loading boxes into mine."

He shook his head, frustrated. "I'm sorry, Sadie. I really thought we could get this all in one shot."

My hand rested lightly on his arm. "Hey, no worries. If all it takes is getting a trailer, this will be the easiest job I've had in a long time. See you when you get back."

He trotted to his vehicle. "There's bottled water in the fridge."

Although I had an inkling Wayne might have a slight interest in me, he gave off that sort of vibe, I wasn't about to go digging through his boxes to find out more about the man. Well, yes in truth I wanted to, but I hadn't known him long enough to start invading his privacy, so before I could succumb to me inner nosiness, I got down to toting and arranging boxes.

The Texas heat is unforgiving, especially in summer and while I was almost a native of these parts, no one gets used to it, they just live with it. With a river of sweat dripping into my eyes, I slammed on a ball cap – a change from my cowboy hat because it tended to get in the way - drew my arm across my brow and mustered on, dreaming of ice caps in Alaska.

When Wayne returned I had two rooms cleared out. He caught me crawling backwards out of the bed of my truck and I heard a low whistle. I stilled for a minute. Was he vocally commenting on how much I had got done or the state of my butt?

"You sure don't mess around when you have your mind set on something, do you?"

Dang, and here I thought he was appreciating my behind.

I grabbed the bottle of water sitting on the bumper and chugged half of it down.

"Tick, tock. Time is money."

His face fell. "I got here as fast as I could."

"It wasn't a comment on your part by any means." I peeked past him to his vehicle. "See you got a trailer. Perfect. I'll move my truck and you can back the trailer up."

"Yes, boss."

"Sorry. That didn't come out right." Did I really sound bossy?

He quickly flipped off my ball cap and ruffled my hair. "Relax. I'm only joking."

Okay, any guy that doesn't cringe from running his fingers through my sweaty hair is all right in my book. I snatched my hat, plopped it back on my head and jumped into the cab of my truck.

"Tick tock, my friend," I yelled, turning over the engine.

We worked in an easy rhythm. Grunting with effort when we manhandled his bedroom unit into the trailer and laughing because he kept an old lawn chair - the kind with the nylon ribbing – so long the next person sitting in it was bound to fall through. We talked mainly about sports, specifically baseball, but I was also surprised to learn how much he liked to read, mainly the classics, and that his favorites were Hemingway and Poe.

As the sun bent low in the horizon, we slammed the tailgate of his truck with a little pushing and coaxing and sat on his bumper.

"You're okay shortcake." Wayne nudged me in the shoulder.

My head snapped up to spear him with a glare.

He raised his hands in submission. "Whoa, didn't mean to offend you."

"I have issues with people making fun of my height."

His light brown eyes bored into mine with an honest, serious intensity. "I wasn't making fun. I was giving you a compliment. Not many women would have been able to keep up with me. You held your own."

I shrugged, looked away. My redhead temper had flared and I'd made something out of nothing and now regretted it.

He turned my face to his. "I've never met anyone like you, Sadie." The seriousness was still there but it had softened.

Air caught in my lungs and I couldn't breathe. Other than Clayton, in the first years of our relationship, no one had looked at me like that and I felt flustered and out of practice on how to handle it.

I bumped his shoulder with mine, jumped off the bumper and tweaked the bill of the ball cap he'd put on during the day. "We're good."

The smile was back on his face when he stood and consulted his watch. "Better make tracks to get back to Houston in decent time. You willing to tag along behind me, make sure the trailer doesn't yaw, or would the speed be cramping your style?"

"Very funny. Since you bought lunch, how about I spring for dinner?"

He checked the time again. "Rain check on dinner? We still have a few hours of driving to go."

I didn't take that as a rejection, not really. "Of course. You go first. But if a little old lady in a Model T passes you, all bets are off."

The trip back was smooth sailing. The trailer behaved itself and we pulled into the driveway of Wayne's new home as dusk was settling. He helped me unload my truck, which was mainly boxes and then tried to entice me to stay with pizza.

"I'm bushed." I sagged against the door of my vehicle, the heat of the door penetrating my clothing. "Rain check?"

He leaned against the vehicle beside me. "Well now, since we both have rain checks, how does that work, exactly?"

I reached for the truck handle. "Whoever calls first."

He straightened, stopped me from climbing inside, tilted my head up with his hand. His eyes traveled over my face, rested on my lips and held. My heartbeat kicked up a notch and when he lowered his head I wasn't sure if I was ready for a kiss or not. A second passed. Then Wayne simply placed a light kiss on my cheek and backed away.

"You're okay, shortcake," he said softly and opened my door for me.

After I clambered inside, he shut the door and gave me a wink. "Talk to you soon."

"You bet." I was a little breathless.

I drove out of his driveway, my head muddy with thoughts and emotions of the day and then I remembered that I'd wanted to stake out the amateur theatre downtown. I was too exhausted to try and play *Jessica Fletcher* and come up with a feasible way to spy on Sharon – aka Inglette – and get her last name.

I dragged my achy body into my apartment, stood wearily under a hot shower and flopped into bed. The last thing I remember was trying to figure out whether I was disappointed or not because Wayne hadn't kissed me.

CHAPTER EIGHTEEN

Sunday was the one day in which I tried not to schedule any jobs. It had nothing to do with a religious connotation, but when I grew up, Sunday was a day for family, for kicking back and spending time doing what you like, for you. So far it worked but if I was lucky enough to get busier, I was going to have to rethink the luxury.

Unfortunately I was wracking my brain, pulling my hair out trying to see how I was going to get the stupid little black unit into a computer at Back in Time.

I came up empty. Zero. Nothing happening.

The three day window I gave Will was over and I didn't know what would happen now. Would he go rogue, try and plan something on his own or would I have to step away and let the police totally handle the situation?

Worst of all there was no one I could talk to about this.

Clayton would start quoting the law and possibly have me confined to quarters. Wait, that was military.

Blaine would go all big brother protector on me and get into trouble himself. Wayne was new to the picture and besides not knowing him well enough, he was a cop. And Tanya obviously wasn't speaking to me.

Which left either asking Will for help or watch the rest of my life burst into flames like a fourth of July firecracker.

Not a lot of options.

With no other recourse I took out Will's private number, held it in my shaking fingers. In the other, my phone was grasped so tight, my hand ached. A raspy breath entered my lungs. My gaze zeroed in on the digits written in black ink and a thick dark wave of disbelief passed through me as I considered asking someone to do something illegal for me. The tide of emotion rose and collected my shame because despite my upbringing and preaching to Rachelle about respect and determination, I was so desperate not to go to jail that I would risk the future of an honorable young man. I squeezed my eyes shut and felt my world spin out of control.

My clenched hands pressed against my eyes, pushing back against the sting of tears.

A soft keen rose escaped my lips and the bitter taste of disgust lodged in the back of my throat.

Self preservation won.

It always did.

The phone started playing my ringtone and vibrating and it startled me so much I shrieked, almost dropping the unit. I stared at it for a moment before clueing in that someone was calling me.

"Hello?" My voice was thin and squeaked with tension.

"Sadie?"

"Yes?" I sounded like Minnie Mouse so I cleared my throat. "Yes?" That was better.

"It's Will."

"W..W..Will. Hi."

A pause. "You okay? You sound different."

"Ummm yes."

"I hadn't heard from you so I gather you didn't come up with any way to get into the antiques dealer."

"No." I sighed, resigned. "I'll get the device to you tomorrow."

"I may have found a solution. Can you meet me?"

My senses went on high alert. "Is it illegal?"

"Technically no."

Hmmm. "What is it?"

"Not over the phone. Come to the Beanery café, say about an hour."

His voice sounded upbeat, excited and a part of me clung to that thread of hope. Mind you, he was a computer hacker, they got their thrills doing nasty things.

"Will.."

"Trust me, Sadie. See you in an hour."

And he hung up. He didn't even wait to see if I wanted to go for coffee.

* * *

I walked into the Beanery which was busier than the last time I was there. Tables were filled mostly with young people and the old guy from the other night was nowhere to be seen. Will sat in the back at the same place as before, coffee in front of him. I ordered a cola with a double shot espresso because I needed the caffeine to calm my nerves. When I went to pay the barista said it was already covered.

Will. Such a gentleman.

I sat across from him and surreptitiously glanced from side to side.

"If we're going to keep meeting like this, perhaps we should have code names?"

He pulled out a piece of paper with a smothered laugh. "I think I've created a monster."

"Thank you for the drink. What do you have there?" I took a hefty gulp of cola coffee.

"Info and the solution to your problem."

"Okay."

He began. "I did a bit more digging. The general building does have a security system and a guard patrols at night."

Good thing I hadn't jumped the gun, got a Cat Woman outfit and tried to break in. Do they even make a leather jumpsuit in my size? And how would that look with cowboy boots?

"Is that good news?"

"Neither here nor there. But the good news is there is a cleaning staff for the complex and all the tenants pay a fee in their monthly rent to cover the service."

I nodded for him to continue.

"And best of all, they are short handed."

"Isn't that bad news?" He was losing me here.

"Bad for them. Good for us."

"Because…"

"Because we are going to provide them with a perfect employee."

My eyes narrowed. "How do you know all this?"

"Do you really want me to tell you?"

If your hand is caught in the cookie jar, my momma always said, you might as well make it worth your while. "Yes."

"I found out who owned the building, checked their business records, which they do keep offsite, and retrieved the name of the company who provides the janitorial service. From there…"

"I get the picture. I gather I'm going to apply for a cleaning job."

Will did a small gesture with his hand. "An employee file has already been uploaded into the cleaning company's database, and no, it isn't for you."

"It's for me," a voice said behind me.

I spun around and stared up at Rico, another member of the StreetSmart crew that had helped me with the move. The baggy beige pants and muscle shirt he'd worn then were replaced by a black tee shirt and black jeans. Not as tall as Will, he had a wiry body and reminded me of a young the actor who starred in *The Stream*. I gaped at him as he grabbed a chair beside Will and sat down with a cocky grin. He must have been sitting with his back to the door because I never even noticed him.

"Oh no, no, no. We are not getting anyone else involved."

"It's already been done."

I thumped my fist on the table. "You didn't even ask me!"

Will leaned forward, his jaw clenched. "You are running out of options, Sadie. I gather your lawyer hasn't told you there are other suspects because there aren't any. And you certainly can't work in the building because someone is sure to recognize you. Besides, Rico will actually be doing legitimate work and getting paid for it."

I whirled on Rico. "Why are you agreeing to do this? If you're caught you could be sent back to jail."

"Relax, little lady."

Was that a remark about my size?

"What's to get caught?" Rico continued. "I go in, clean out the garbage, stick the drive in a computer, do some vacuuming, take the unit out and I'm done. Hey I'll even clean the rest of the businesses just so no one gets suspicious."

It sounded so easy and perhaps that was why I started to cave. Technically Rico wasn't accessing anything, wasn't hacking into anything. Will was. And like I had thought before, self preservation always won.

My head rested on my folded arms. "I can't believe I'm letting you talk me into this."

When I looked up they were both smiling in satisfaction.

"What if they have security cameras in the office? They do have art and antiques there."

Will gave me an indignant look. "First thing I checked. Yes they have cameras but the security monitoring company is watching for things out of the ordinary. Cleaning staff is supposed to be there. Besides, Rico is so smooth you wouldn't be able to tell when he inserts the drive and takes it out."

Rico nodded. "I'll have the drive hidden in a rag and as I dust one of the computers I slip it in, do some vacuuming and when I come around the desk again I accidentally bump it and knock over a pen jar or photograph, whatever, and as I straighten it I palm the drive." He glanced from Will to me and back again. "So, are we doing this?"

I considered telling Will about Sharon, aka Inglette, but a part of me didn't want him to get even further involved and I also didn't have a last name. Yet.

I sighed, staring at their expectant faces. "You do realize they don't make prison garb that's going to fit me."

* * *

I left the boys a while later with a promise from them they were to keep me apprised the whole way. Actually I thought Will's plan was pretty sound. Talk about convenient that an opening was available with the cleaning service. At a red light my heart skipped a beat; Will or Rico didn't purposefully make sure there would be a position available? I mean, what did I really know about either of them?

A horn blasted behind me when I didn't move after the light turned green and I gave a quick shake of my head. Good grief, this wasn't a black ops mission, it was just fate finally giving me a glimmer of hope, like a peek at a rainbow. Hopefully it wouldn't be followed by a tornado.

I decided to spend the afternoon with mom. I went to the facility and with a nurse's aide, brought mom in a wheelchair out onto the covered patio. The sun was on the other side of the building but it was still warm out. She didn't seem to mind, her eyes capturing the scenery, landscaping and grass.

A quirky sort of smug grin started to spread across her face.

"What are you smiling about momma?"

She sat up straighter and gave me an almost haughty look. "We must be rich."

I tried not to let the confusion show. "Why's that?"

She indicated the wide expanse of lawn and the nurse's aide sitting a bit off to the side to give us some privacy. "We have staff and this huge yard and such a big house." She nodded as if convincing herself. "Yes, your daddy did quite well."

My chest tightened and I fought for a breath. I took her hand, squeezed it lovingly. "You're right momma. Daddy did just fine."

She turned inquisitive eyes to me, a hint of panic slipping in. "Where is Jerrald?"

I had to swallow past the lump in my throat. My voice broke slightly as I spoke. "Daddy's away working, but when he comes back I'll tell him to see you right away."

"Oh, that's right." She settled again. "I forgot he was off on business. He works too hard. Yes, please tell him to come see me, Sadie. I want something else done with the garden, maybe some Magnolia bushes. I sure do miss the Magnolia from back home."

"I will."

"I'm tired. Think I'll go lay down for a nap."

"Sure momma, let's take you back inside."

I held her hand as the aide pushed the wheelchair back into her room and we helped my mother into bed. I smoothed the covers near her chin.

"I'll visit again soon, okay."

She had a dreamy smile on her face as her eyes closed. "Okay Sadie, my little lady," and she drifted off to sleep humming.

I nodded thanks to the staff as I quickly strode to the truck, desperate to get out, away from people before it was too late. Inside I rested my head against the wheel and the tears I held so fiercely at bay began to slowly trickle down my cheeks. If Will and Rico failed, if the police couldn't find the real murderer of Lionel Stanton or whoever the hell the man really was, I would go to jail.

And who would look after my mother?

I had to do something. Mom was depending on me whether she knew it or not. Blaine couldn't afford to keep our mother in the facility and she required constant care. He had his own family to think of.

I had to get into the theatre.

Tonight.

CHAPTER NINETEEN

For the evening's reconnaissance mission at the theatre, I fell back on my outfit of the other night complete with the black wig, grabbed pen and paper and barreled to the destination. My plan was to get into the back stage as a reporter doing a news piece on local culture and since Sharon worked at the front as a cashier, I hoped she didn't do double duty and lend a hand backstage.

At the location, I disembarked and strode purposefully to the side door before I could talk myself out of it. I must have thumped for a good ten minutes before the door opened.

The guy I saw kissing Sharon the other night stared at me. "Yeah?"

I momentarily stammered, then cleared my throat and spoke with an assurance that I didn't even come close to feeling.

"Press. I'm here to do a local piece on the production."

"Russell, get your ass back here. We're about to do a scene change." A voice bellowed from down the hall, confirming the name Sharon had said while I was hiding in the ladies washroom.

Russell gave a frustrated glare between the stage crewman behind him and me. "All right, all right, get in here."

"Thank you."

I was in.

"Which paper." He led me down the hall, past a prop room and dressing rooms.

And…I was out.

Crap, what paper, what paper?

"The Chronicle."

It was the biggest in the city. Odds were he wouldn't even check for credentials.

He turned to me, confused. "Thought you guys were here on opening night?"

See, this is what happens when you ride without a saddle and you're not used to it. I was about to blow my cover and fall flat on my face. Sweat beaded under the wig, making my scalp itch.

"Sorry, I meant The Tribune. I do freelance for both. I missed opening night covering something else." I actually didn't know if Houston had a Tribune but seems most major cities used that moniker in some form or another regarding newspapers.

I hoped.

Russell continued to scrutinize me but his attention was required farther backstage.

Not giving him a chance to question me further I dove right in. "Opening night, I gather you packed the house? I see the set design is top rate." I peeked over his shoulder past the side curtains to the backdrop, quickly making notes.

"Russell, for god sakes!"

He grunted but turned, stepped away and I released a pent up breath in a low whoosh. I continued with my façade, taking copious notes, and while he was occupied, dug out my phone and took a few discreet pictures of him from a distance. I made a point of sketching a few things, asking for a program so I'd have the actor's names correct, all to make myself look legitimate. I scanned the names on the program, no listing of theatre staff.

Russell kept an eagle eye on me the whole time.

I pointed to the program. "I see you're listed here too."

His gaze shot to mine.

"Well, you are working back stage and I did hear your fellow stage crew member call your name. It is Russell right? I'll make sure to mention how helpful you've been in my article."

"Whatever. I don't care. It's mainly volunteer."

"Okay. No problem. What about others, like front theatre staff? I could do a side piece and possibly add some publicity for future productions." Hopefully he wouldn't catch on and just give me the names, Sharon's included.

"Maybe." Suspicion thickened his voice. "What paper did you say you were with again?"

Oh-oh. I repeated the name.

"Got any credentials?"

And just when I thought I would be riding off into the sunset I was about to slide off that horse and get trampled under its hooves.

"Yes, yes, sorry I should have presented them right off." I made an elaborate show of digging into my purse. "I have them right here."

The panic spiraling down my spine was enough to make me pass out. I clenched my teeth together to keep him from hearing me gasp for air. Why hadn't I thought of making fake ID beforehand?

"Russell! Intermission. On stage, now!"

"I'll be back. You stay right here," he demanded, jogging off.

"Absolutely!" I cheerily assured until he was out of sight then I sped out the door as fast as my legs could take me.

I didn't stop until I was in my truck and roaring down the street, tires squealing as I rounded the nearest corner.

Little rivulets of sweat trickled from beneath my arms. I yanked the wig from my head, tossed it onto the passenger seat, heaving great gulps of air. I didn't slow down until I was on my street and made sure no one was following me.

When I turned off the truck in the parking lot and forced my pulse to slow down, a smile of triumph broke across my face. Tonight's escape wasn't a total wash-out. My eyes scanned the theatre program I took. I may not have gotten Sharon's last name but I got something just as good.

Her boyfriend's name.

Russell. Russell Chen.

* * *

I woke up in the morning and made a decision. I needed to talk with Tanya, find out why she'd been AWOL in communicating with me. I couldn't handle this distance that had formed between us and I was going to confront her.

I didn't let her know I was coming, didn't stop to get the usual coffee and bagels. As much as I was concerned why she wouldn't talk to me, a part of me was ticked off. I thought our friendship went deeper than the teenage even-though-you-apologized-I'm-still-going-to-ignore-you stage.

Clouds had rolled in overnight and the humidity was so bad driving around in a bathing suit would have been preferable to the sticky, clingy feel of clothes plastered to my body.

I parked in the lot at Tanya's office, shoved a limp piece of hair off my forehead and headed into the building. Some of the StreetSmart crew milled about in the front office but I ignored them and went directly to Tanya's office and knocked.

At her greeting to enter, I stepped in and closed the door.

From behind her desk, Tanya's eyes widened but she recovered quickly and her lips formed a pleasant smile.

No warmth, no, hey girlfriend. Something was definitely up.

"Sadie. What a nice surprise."

"Is it?"

"What do you mean?"

I marched to her desk. "Why have you been avoiding me?"

She glanced quickly down at her desk, moved some papers into a neat stack. "I'm not."

"You haven't returned any of my calls."

Her lips tightened into a pinched expression. "I've been busy."

I slapped my hands on my hips. "Busy is a one-legged man in a butt-kicken contest. You've been avoiding me and I want to know why. What's wrong?"

Her gaze moved to her computer where she started typing. "Nothing is wrong."

This was ridiculous and my temper flared. "Don't you dare lie to me."

Her eyes snapped to mine; in them was suppressed anger and hurt. "What is going on with you and Will?"

I gaped like someone told me I'd won the Miss Universe Contest. "What!?"

"Will."

I pushed an exasperated breath out of my mouth. "Yes, I know who Will is. But have no idea what you're talking about."

"I've seen you two together."

Holy crap. Did Tanya find out that Will was helping me? That he'd hacked into several databases and files? Did Will know she suspected him?

My mind scrambled to come up with some plausible explanation.

"We had coffee." Which was true. "And how did you know?"

"I was outside the Beanery one night last week, walking to my car from a friend's," she said defensively.

One night. Only once.

"Like I said, we had coffee."

"Are you seeing him?"

"What!! Jeez Tanya, no!" Think, think. Think of something to tell her.

"Then why were you having coffee with him?"

Okay, now my temper not only flared, it spiked like a high striker game. "He's a grown young man. I can have coffee with whomever I like and besides what business is it of yours?"

She edged closer to me. "He's one of my charges. I'm very protective that he doesn't get hurt. Or worse."

I put my hands on her desk, leaned in. "Well, if you must know, I've asked him to come and work the few odd jobs with me when I need a crew. There are times when I can't do it by myself. Satisfied."

Phew, talk about thinking on your feet.

"Oh." Her cheeks reddened. "Oh, he never said anything."

"Should he have?"

"Well, no," she stammered, embarrassed.

"All right then."

We stood two feet apart but it felt like a hundred miles. Our eyes drifted to other places in the room but not to where they should have gone, to each other's face to try and reconcile.

My phone took that opportune time to ring. I glanced down; a redirect from the business. Saved by the bell.

"Hawkins Freight."

The caller was another student looking for a quote.

"Just a minute please." I put my hand over the mouthpiece, looked at Tanya. "I have to take this."

In a fluster she grabbed her briefcase, starting shoving papers inside. "Yes. I…ahh…I need to see a client about another possible charge. I…umm…should get going."

I walked to the door, phone to my ear.

Tanya called out when I was at the door, stopping me. "Sadie. Thanks. For coming by and…clearing that up."

I didn't say anything, just nodded once and walked out. Although I had accepted her apology, it seemed as if the gap between us had widened.

I continued speaking to the person on the phone, got a few details, gave a rough quote which was agreed upon and we set up the move in a couple of days.

In my truck I disconnected the call but pretended to still be speaking as Tanya strode out of the building to her car and I watched her get in. She knew I was still there because I caught her glancing toward my vehicle. We didn't wave to each other and I wondered who felt worse, her for mistrusting me or me for lying to my best friend.

CHAPTER TWENTY

I sat on pins and needles waiting to hear from my young partners in crime. I did text Will telling him if Tanya should bring it up that he was part of my moving crew when needed. I also gave him Russell Chen's and Sharon's name, explaining that Sharon was the young Ms. Ing, but he didn't reply.

Before long I was so antsy I couldn't sit still. I drove around looking for a league game to watch and once I found one, killed a couple of hours complimenting or picking apart various players on a team until the person beside me griped if I wanted to watch the majors to head over to Minute Maid Park.

I considered going back to the batting cages but couldn't afford depositing another thirty bucks just to calm my nerves. Instead I went to my office, scrubbed it from top to bottom, rearranged the filing cabinet, twice, then proceeded to clean the shop floor where Blaine worked.

I had just finished putting away all the cleaning materials when my phone dinged with a text.

From Will.

Success. Meet me at Beanery.

Heart galloping like a parade drum I texted back. *Different location.* I didn't want to even contemplate that Tanya might see us again.

Andro's?

Big surprise. *Sure.*

Drinks?

MAYBE!

He sent an emoji smiley face as a reply. Fresh young man. Why hadn't a girl snatched him up yet?

Traffic was light and I made good time. I didn't know where Will lived so wasn't sure who would get there first. As it turned out he did and was waiting by the door for me.

He wore chinos, Dockers and a nice shirt and I felt underdressed in my jeans and simple shirt but this wasn't a date so I didn't care.

We sat on the bar side, close to where we'd originally came up with the harebrained idea of infiltrating Back in Time's computer system.

"Drink?" The corner of Will's mouth tipped up.

"Cola. I might consider something stronger if I have anything to celebrate."

"So, Tanya thinks we're a hot item, does she?" Will commented when the waiter left to get our drinks.

My back stiffened. "Did she say that to you?"

He gave a short bark of laughter. "No. But I know her well enough that when she mentioned she was glad I would be helping on some of your jobs, the tone of her voice spoke of something entirely different. Thanks for the heads up by the way. At least I was prepared."

"I hated lying to her." It was still bothering me.

"Then don't make it a lie. If you need someone to help you, give me a ring."

I sent him a vexing stare. "I can't pay you, Will."

"No big deal, I can use some of the time toward community service served. We'll worry about that later."

Our drinks came and he raised his glass to touch mine. "To success."

"All ready?"

"Rico didn't let us down. Quick, in and out. In fact he's still working for them; specifically asked for night shift. They wanted to put him on during the day, to work with another guy but Rico told him he had another job. Too many people during the day for him to try and get access to a computer."

"You're sure there is no way anyone would find out you've been in?"

"Absolutely. Like I said, it's not like I was hacking into the FBI database. I went in through the back door and made sure no cookies or breadcrumbs remained and closed up tight when I left."

"You make it sound like you were literally in a physical room."

"In a manner of speaking."

"What did you learn?"

He spread out a piece of paper with notes on it in neat block lettering. After taking a sip of his drink he began.

"There is such a person as Charles Weckland. According to an email he sent to Rogers, the public owner of Back in Time, Weckland was scheduled to go away on extended holidays to Egypt. Funny thing though, I could find no record of him ever leaving the country. He wasn't listed on any flight manifest leaving Houston during the past month. Backtracking the email he sent to Rogers, I got into Weckland's email and found a hotel confirmation for Cairo but when I contacted the hotel, they said Weckland never showed. No record of any car rentals. Nothing. He just vanished."

I drummed my fingers on the table. "You thinking what I'm thinking?"

"That Weckland is your fresh mummy?"

I shuddered, remembering the foul stench. "Yes."

"I agree."

"Okay, we know who but we don't know how. And it's not like we can walk into the police station waving in the air saying, I know who the dead body is. And," I added with measure, "why didn't the cops come up with this?"

Will leaned forward, pointing to his notes. "Think about it. Weckland tells Rogers he'll be on extended holidays and from what I read in the email, Weckland said he didn't want to be contacted, maybe he wanted to be on a sabbatical of some kind. For all intents and purposes Rogers thinks Weckland *is* in Egypt. No one would be looking for him."

"We're still no closer as to finding out who killed Stanton, if he was indeed the body in the sarcophagus."

"True. But let's say for argument's sake he was. It might be easier to figure out why he was killed."

"Money?"

"That would be my first guess," he agreed.

"You checked Back in Time's financials. Did you see anything there that might be a motive for killing Weckland?"

He shook his head. "Nothing stands out."

I tapped a finger to my lips, thinking. "What about Weckland's financials? And Rogers?"

"I'll check them out. I didn't go that far yet, I wanted to talk with you first."

"Perhaps the murderer was someone on the outside of the company. Someone with something to gain."

"Or something to lose."

"Unless the murder wasn't done for money at all. Maybe it was done for love?"

Will raised an eyebrow. "Could be."

A previous conversation sprang into my brain, one whispered in secret. "Before we had drinks here the first time, I followed Rogers' secretary, Margaret Yates, to a lunch date with a friend of hers. I'd overheard a phone conversation she had the day I got back from Pampa while I was waiting for Rogers. She was very upset, said she'd done something awful and was scared she'd get caught. It had affected her so much she was considering going to the church to confess. I didn't learn anything about that but I did find out she is having an affair with someone she works with. That could be Rogers or Weckland then again she could also have another job and her lover might be someone else entirely. Are you able to find out if she has another job?"

Will frowned. "Other than hacking into the IRS to check her financials, which I really don't want to do, the only option I can think of is following her."

"When you first went into Back in Time's records you said someone worked part time. Was that only one person?"

"Yes. Ms. Ing."

"That means Yates works full time."

He waited a second. "I see what you're getting at but it is feasible Yates could work a second job, either on weekends or at night."

I sat back, deflated. "Damn."

"But odds are she doesn't and again for argument's sake for now let's assume she only has the one job and she is having an affair with either Rogers or Weckland. And since Weckland was using an alias with you, Yates didn't lie when she said there was no person by the name of Stanton working at Back in Time."

"Right. If it was Weckland she was seeing, she admitted to doing something that could land her in jail."

"Murder?"

"Maybe. At lunch with her friend she did say she wanted to go away with the lover and he supposedly laughed at her. Nothing like the temper of a jilted lover."

Will's mouth quirked. "Speaking from experience?"

"No comment." Like anyone wanted to admit they were jilted. "What do you think about the possibility that Yates murdered Weckland?"

"Anything is possible. But she could just as easily been talking about Rogers and the something awful she did was to him, which obviously wasn't murder." Will made a note. "You didn't mention this bit of info when we were there."

"Didn't think it relative at the time, it still might not be, but passion can be a strong motivator for murder. Especially when it doesn't go your way." Yet something didn't add up to me. "But then why steal the antiques?"

"Profit? Hide the original crime?"

"Possibly."

I sat back with a sigh. "More questions than we have answers."

"But more info than we knew before," Will assured.

"True."

"Ready for that drink now?"

I admired his optimism. "Not yet. When this is all cleared, maybe then. Oh, wait, what about the names I texted you, Russell Chen and Sharon?"

"Nothing so far. Unless I get Sharon's last name we're dead in the water there and so far Russell Chen is clean."

"Would a picture help?"

"If you have one, yes."

I pulled out my phone, brought up the few shots I took of Russell when he wasn't watching me and showed them to Will.

He studied them for a minute. "Send me these would you please. They are a little grainy and I may be able to clear some of the shots up with some software but I can't promise anything."

I took my phone back, forwarded the images and Will's phone pinged in response.

"Got them."

His phone chimed again that he had received a text message. "It's a text from Rico. He's got news."

"Is it about Back in Time?"

Another ding from his phone.

"He wants to meet. I have to go." Will stood and walked purposefully out the door.

By the expression on his face when he left, it didn't seem like good news.

I left as well because I felt uncomfortable sitting in an upscale place like Andro's by myself. As I neared my truck, my mind spinning a dozen different reasons why Will felt the need to take off like a coon dog catching a scent, my thoughts were interrupted by a phone call from Wayne.

"Hey, all unpacked?"

He scoffed. "Hardly. I think I'll be sorting through boxes for the next week."

"Awww," I chuckled in mock sympathy as I jumped into my vehicle. The guy really did have way too much sports and leisure equipment. But I did like the bike and I pictured him riding it. That brought a smile to my face. Then I pictured me sitting behind him, arms wrapped around his body as I hung on. That had me grinning wider.

"So much compassion in that one word," he joked. "I hear outside noises. You're not at home?"

"Not yet."

"Listen, I was wondering, remember those rain checks we have for dinner?"

I sat behind the wheel, a flutter of anticipation quivering in my stomach. Maybe I was going to go out on an actual date tonight. I mentally flipped through the clothes in my bedroom closet, thinking what I could wear.

"Yes."

"How about tomorrow night?"

That would work too. "Sure."

"Good. Great. Pick you up after I get off work, say around eight. That okay with you?"

"Perfect. Where are we going?" I heard the smile in his voice and matched it with my own.

"It's a surprise."

"Can you at least give me a hint? What am I supposed to wear?"

"Casual dressy and that's all I'm going to say."

"Okay. I'll see you at eight tomorrow."

"Since you're still driving, text me your address when you have a minute."

I told him I would and said I was looking forward to seeing him. With a 'me too' he ended the call.

I sat in the truck thinking that for the first time in months I finally had something positive to look forward to. The clock on the dash said it was almost quitting time and since Andro's was within a half block of Back in Time, and I didn't have plans for the evening, I thought I would wait and watch for the receptionist, maybe try to follow wherever she went after work. I had to agree with Will that Yates probably only had the one job but I couldn't discount anything.

It only took twenty minutes for staff to start filing out of the building and I slumped lower in my seat just in case someone saw me. I needn't have worried though, most everyone leaving wearing clothes of either business attire or casual dressy rushed to get home to their lives. I spotted Margaret Yates in a dark blue dress exit the building and head to a bus stop. That could make following her easier as even I couldn't lose a bus. Then I noticed Jeffrey Rogers depart and my eyes bugged out of my head.

On his arm, strolling merrily beside him with a big smile on her face was Sharon, the Ms. Ing imposter.

CHAPTER TWENTY-ONE

Slumped in the seat of the truck my jaw hit my chest as I watched the owner of Back in Time Antiques walk down the street with Inglette. Were these two in on the heist? Could they have orchestrated the whole theft and if so it was brilliant. Or was she having an affair with Rogers and he bought her the Cartier that she gushed to her coworker about in the washroom? She'd also been in a lip lock with Russell when Karen and I had gone to see *The Mikado*. Maybe she was two-timing. Considering she'd duped me I wouldn't put it past her. On the other hand, there might be a perfectly good explanation as to why she was coming out of the same building on his arm, something completely innocent, like going out for dinner or a drink or hell maybe she was dropping off some theatre tickets and since they obviously knew each other, decided to walk out the building together. Not everything was a conspiracy.

There was no toss-up between whether to follow Margaret Yates on the off chance she may be going to another job or tail Rogers and the young woman, even if whatever I learned turned out to be a dead end.

The couple crossed to my side of the street and once I was sure they wouldn't see me, I slipped out of the truck, ducked behind some people going the same way and followed at a distance. Unfortunately with me being so short I had to constantly peek around to make sure I didn't lose them but I had a hunch as to where they were going. And my hunch paid off when I saw the two of them enter the *Theatre Under the Stars* four blocks later.

I wasn't gutsy or stupid enough to pass through the doors as well because guaranteed they would spot me, instead took position in a doorway of an establishment across the street and waited. Was Rogers going to see the production? It was early considering the play didn't start for well over an hour. When he appeared a little while later and walked back the way they had come it seemed apparent he had merely dropped Sharon off, unless he planned on returning just before the musical started.

Now that I knew there was a direct connection between Sharon and Back in Time I was determined to get as much on this woman as I could. Unless she had to leave early, it was a fair bet she would be working until roughly the same time tonight as previously. And I was going to follow her home.

A glance at my watch told me it would be a good three hours before Inglette would leave so I could either take off and come back or grab a bite at the nearest cheap eating establishment I could afford.

The aroma of cooking drifted down the street and my stomach growled in protest to the lack of food at not having eaten for hours. I ventured back to my truck, scrounged through the glove compartment, between and under the seats, the catch-all in the center console and came up with a little under six dollars in change.

Hopefully enough for something.

Following my nose took me a few blocks up to a Chinese restaurant, where I bought a single order of white rice to go and went back to my vehicle to sit comfortably and eat while I waited for Sharon to finish her shift.

Darkness fell, time dragged, but I refused to leave the spot in case I didn't find another parking place or worse, got waylaid and returned late. Even the make believe game of this-is-your-lie Tanya and I did at the mall grew boring after a while.

To stop myself from going crazy, I checked periodically if I could get closer to the theatre and when a parking spot became vacant I tucked into that space. From here I could see the entrance and be able to immediately follow Sharon and whoever she was with to wherever they would go.

Nobody texted but then I didn't initiate contact either.

Eventually I saw a small group of people leave the theatre. Three older couples all talking amongst themselves, obviously knowing one another and had probably watched the production together. A few cars drove by. Another few minutes of inactivity. And then a sleek black Lexus drove up and parked directly in front of the doors. I straightened, ready, knowing sitting in the dark twenty yards down that I wouldn't be spotted.

Eventually my patience paid off.

Sharon came out the front of the theatre alone, slid into the passenger seat of the Lexus and the car eased into traffic. I hadn't seen the driver but put money on it was probably Jeffrey Rogers.

I pulled away from the curb and started to follow, then thought I might be too close, so hung back. My hours watching reruns of *Matlock* were good for something. With not many vehicles to hide behind, following someone is not that easy. To me the truck looked totally exposed with hardly any other vehicles in the street. The luxury car turned onto McKinney and then onto Main Street. Traffic was heavier and I closed up the gap, not wanting to lose them.

When the Lexus ventured into the residential district, I hung back, putting a half block again between their vehicle and mine. The auto slowed and pulled to the curb on the right. It did not go up the driveway which made me think the passenger would be disembarking. I made a quick right up a side street and parked. My truck was way too close to the corner but I couldn't take the time to find a parking spot farther up for fear that Sharon would reach her door before I could see which house she was getting into.

I jumped out of my truck and started to run when I noticed how quiet the area was. With my cowboy boots on, anyone could hear me coming. Dang it. Hopping on each foot, I tugged them off, tossed them through the open window into the truck and hoofed it round the corner, dodging from tree to tree, keeping to the shadows.

Sharon got out of the vehicle and walked quickly up a paved path to a narrow, brownstone house. I crept closer into the next yard. Dampness from the recently watered grass seeped into my stocking feet. All of a sudden she stopped, turned. I dipped back behind the tree I was peering out from. My heart blasted against my ribs. What would I do if she spied me and came looking? Take off to my truck? But she'd be sure to see me that way. Run to the back of the house whose yard I was in? Pretend that I actually lived in the neighborhood? Each option was bad. *Please don't let her see me, please don't come here.*

I pushed my back against the bark of the tree in an effort to meld with it. My left foot sunk into something soft. I didn't dare move to see what it was. I held my breath, waiting. After what felt like five minutes but was probably only five seconds, there were two short beeps of a car horn and a vehicle drove off. I still waited, not moving a muscle. After an eternity, I slowly pivoted. The stench of fresh dog poop wafted as my foot turned in the goo. Great.

My head inched ever so slowly from its hiding spot and I peered to the doorway I'd seen Sharon approach. No sign of her. Memorizing the exact house, I backed up and tiptoed-limped away. When I got a few houses down, I inspected the sole of my foot. Crap. Literally. The entire bottom of my sock was covered in dark brown dog poop. This much doggie-doo didn't come from any miniature poodle. What did those people own, a Great Dane on steroids?

When I reached my truck I peeled off the offending piece of clothing and flung it into the back. I'd throw it out when I saw a trash can. No way was I going to try and wash that out. At least I hadn't been wearing my Post's. The few pieces of napkin I had from the Chinese food place took care of wiping the bottom of my foot and they followed the sock into the back.

I backed up around the corner, kept my lights off, and drove by the house Sharon had gone into, making note of the address. Perhaps Will could get more info on Sharon with this bit of news. Once out of the area I texted him but got no reply. Maybe he was still dealing with the text from Rico while we were at Andro's.

I got home, having dumped my ruined sock and dirty napkin into the trash at a convenience store and paced the floor, waiting for Will's reply to my text. Nothing. I tried to make sense of what seeing the owner of Back in Time and the Ms. Ing impersonator together meant. Obviously Jeffrey Rogers and Sharon knew each other but in what regard? Had Rogers orchestrated the murder and antiques theft from the very beginning?

CHAPTER TWENTY-TWO

It has been my experience that fate has a very warped sense of humor, which is what I thought when, the next morning, with notions of my upcoming date, an occasion that I haven't had a chance to go on for a very long time, I got a text from Will.

About time. I hadn't heard from him since he left the lounge so quickly last night.

We have a problem.

Okay. What's up?

We need to talk.

I felt like saying, so phone me already, but knew he wouldn't.

When and where?

The usual place. ASAP.

I couldn't see an establishment like the Andro's being open before noon. *They serve breakfast too?*

Damn. No. Beanery, then.

My radar went on high alert by the use of his expletive. Something was obviously wrong. I checked my watch and made a time to meet when I figured

Tanya would be in the office. Just to be safe. He sent an emoji thumbs up sign in reply.

Less than two hours later at the café, I walked in to see Will with Rico. And they both didn't look happy.

A seed of unease formed in my stomach. I bypassed the coffee bar and headed straight for their table in the back.

"Hey, guys."

They both nodded as I sat down. Two cups of coffee stood untouched in front of them.

"What's wrong?"

Will glanced at Rico who shrugged and motioned for him to proceed.

"With tweaking the photos you sent we got an ID on Russell Chen." His face was dead serious.

My brow puckered, confused. "Well, that's good, right?"

"Not in this case. We're pretty sure Russell Chen is actually Russell Chang, a big player with a sheet from here to the West Coast. Nothing came up when I did a search for him before because of the different last name."

"Okay. But we can go to the police now that we have a name."

"With what? All we have is his association with Sharon, aka your young Ms Ing. Just because he has a record doesn't mean he's tied to any of this."

I felt the need to defend my position. "It's obvious to me."

"But not to the courts," added Rico.

"What about the info I texted you with last night, that Jeffrey Rogers and Sharon know each other? And the address of where she lives?"

"The address is from a rental agency," Will said. "I couldn't find any connection with that agency to Back in Time. It took me most of the night but according to their records, the lease is in the name of Sharon Marsden. Whether that's her real name or not, I have no idea. She has no police record and I'll need more time to see about any other type of connection between her and Rogers."

"And Rogers' financials?"

Will shrugged. "His personal accounts have had a few hits. Checking them and his credit cards, I think he's got some gambling problems."

My ears perked. "Weckland could have found this out, accused Rogers of skimming from the company. That would be a motive for murder."

"True, but I didn't see any indication of that when I went through the company's records."

"Unless Rogers wasn't taking cash. Maybe he was stealing the antiques, fencing them to pay off his debts," suggested Rico.

"Or maybe Weckland wanted to double cross Rogers," I added. "It was Rogers' signature on the bill of sale of the antiques that were stolen although he claims he didn't sign for them. Weckland could have framed Rogers but taken the money for himself instead."

We all three agreed with a nod.

"Are either of them married?"

"No. You still thinking the lover scorned angle?" Will asked.

"Maybe, but how about this. Yates and Rogers are having an affair, Weckland finds out, there's a fight and Rogers kills him."

"Better. But that still doesn't account for the theft."

"It does if the guy has gambling issues," added Rico.

"Does this mean we're dead in the water? Again?"

"No," Will assured. "It means we just have to keep digging."

"Can I give the police Sharon's address? Maybe she stored the antiques there?" I was grasping at any type of life line.

Rico shrugged. "Maybe. But the cops would need just cause to search her place."

"But we know she impersonated Ms. Ing. She is tied to this thing because she knew about the antiques. She may even know about the murder," I reminded them.

Will glanced from Rico to me. "Well, we could phone in an anonymous tip, hope they get a search warrant. Could take a day or so."

Something dinged in the back of my brain. "When I was hiding in the bathroom at the theatre, I overhead Sharon talking to another woman saying she was leaving. It could be just her job but maybe she plans on skipping town. Since I know where she lives, I could always go and see if she has the antiques."

"And add break and entering to your list of charges?" Will said with an arch of his eyebrow. "Besides, if she really wanted the antiques, she could have taken them before you arrived for the pickup that morning. Why haul them across the state only to have them come back?"

I conceded the point.

"Unless the crates were empty," Rico pointed out.

I stared at him. I'd never thought of that.

"Did you see any of the items?" asked Will. "I know we certainly didn't when we got there."

I shook my head. "I only saw what you did. Everything was already packed. The crates were heavy."

"They could have been filled with anything. Books, paper, rocks, anything to add weight," Rico said. "Seems a bit extreme though."

"And if the load was empty or filled with junk, why have someone break in at the drop off in Pampa?" I added.

No one could come up with an answer to that question.

"Guess I'm not trying my hand at cat-burglaring."

Rico smirked. "It might be a better idea, conejito, to tell your lawyer that you know Sharon was the imposter."

I inwardly winced. That would mean I'd have to tell Clayton *how* I knew Sharon had impersonated Stanton's secretary. After he warned me to let the authorities handle it. But that was the problem, it seemed to me they weren't handling it.

"Maybe you should, Sadie," Will agreed.

I mulled it over, could see no other alternative and knew I had been sitting on some pertinent details the authorities should be aware of long enough.

"Okay, I'll tell him but he's not going to like how I got that information."

I watched the two young men glance at each other, saw the flicker of resignation in their eyes before it faded.

I cut our café rendezvous short, citing my need to get to work when in actual fact I had other ideas. Out of the Beanery, we went our separate ways and I waited until I was in my vehicle before texting Blaine that I felt like I was coming down with something and therefore not coming into work. He replied *wimp* but added a sad emoji with a face mask and said to text him if I needed anything.

I then placed a call to Clayton but since he was in court, left a message with his secretary for him to phone me.

The move I had set up a few days prior from the college student got cancelled through no fault of mine. He decided to stay where he was.

I spent the rest of the afternoon setting up a scheme and searching for items I would need for my next sleuthing escapade, finding most of the necessities at a couple of secondhand stores.

Clayton phoned as I let myself into my apartment.

"Hey. Got your message but didn't have time to call until now. "

"That's okay. I've been busy," I stalled.

He waited.

So did I.

"Sadie, you contacted me remember. What did you want to talk about?"

I dreaded telling him what I knew then decided I would start with the more irrelevant news item.

"Did you know that Mrs. Yates was having an affair with a co-worker? Perhaps even one of the owners of Back in Time?"

A short pause.

"What do you mean, *one* of the owners?"

So much for easing into my confession.

"There are actually two partners."

"According to what we have records, there is only one owner. Jeffrey Rogers," he said, sounding confused.

"Dig deeper."

"Sadie…"

"I can't tell you how I got that info but it is valid."

Silence.

Oh well, might as well go all the way.

"And the partner's name isn't Lionel Stanton, it is Charles Weckland."

"How in the hell.…"

"Please, Clayton. I can't tell you. I'm sorry. And while you're checking, Yates has done something serious enough she believes could land her in jail. Maybe she killed someone."

"That's a pretty serious accusation. Next you're going to reveal who the murderer is." No mistaking the anger in his voice.

"I wish."

"Have you been nosing around in this case after I specifically asked you not to?"

This time it was my turn to be quiet. I heard him sigh over the line.

"I don't know if this can help you or not."

"Why do I even try," he muttered then added. "Anything else?"

"No."

"Sadie…"

"I have to go, Clayton. I'll call you later. Thanks." I hung up.

I didn't want to give Clayton any more. If I told him about Russell Chang and Sharon Marsden he'd be down to my place faster than a hot knife through butter.

Besides, I had other plans. Despite what I'd told Will and Rico, I was going to break into Sharon's place tonight. I didn't tell them because I knew they would try and talk me out of it and I might have listened, but somehow she was mixed up in this whole scenario. I could feel it right down to my Dan Post cowboy boots.

I glanced over to the articles I had picked up, checking the items off my mental list.

Piece of cake, I'd seen it done on TV a million times. How hard could it be?

CHAPTER TWENTY-THREE

"Why does everything have to be so god dang hard!"

I was fuming and worst of all, stuck.

Literally.

It was dark. My legs were on the ground, sticking out of the rectangular hole, while my butt was wedged into the doggie door in Sharon's back door.

I heaved and pushed yet again to no avail. Should have brought Crisco.

After I had left the Beanery, I cased Sharon's house – who knew I would catch on to this investigation lingo so quickly – while posing as a dog walker in the neighborhood. With a couple of phone calls I found a small non-profit shelter that was in desperate need of volunteers. I filled out a form, paid a deposit, left them my driver's license and took two excited canines on an extended outing. Channeling my inner *Cagney and Lacey*, I needed the dogs for a ruse and because the shelter wasn't near where Sharon lived, I parked the truck a few blocks away so the staff wouldn't think I was stealing them. I was nervous driving without my license but that couldn't be helped. I made sure not to walk past Sharon's house more than twice in a joggers disguise complete with a hideous blond wig and other items from the second hand store. When Sharon had finally left, wearing her theatre uniform, I returned my four-legged accomplices after texting the animal shelter a little white lie that I was having car trouble because I had decided to take the dogs to a dog park. Despite the donation of a bag of dog food and telling them they could keep the deposit, the cool reception I received from the staff when I did hand over the dogs made it clear my days of animal service were numbered.

From there, I went home and changed into black jeans, black long-sleeved tee, black runners and used back yards and alleys to get to Sharon's place. An inspection of the doors and windows showed no easy access, except for the doggie door. This was one of those few times I was grateful for my petite stature. Unfortunately, my hips didn't quite fall into the petite classification.

After another heave proved fruitless in releasing me from the predicament, I figured I'd better come up with something before Sharon and possibly Russell came back from work and did the only thing I could think of to free myself. With cell phone clutched between my teeth, I lowered the zipper of my jeans and shimmied out of the denim encasing my legs. It wasn't easy. I flipped out of my sneakers and use my toes to hold down the hem of my pants while I wiggled and grunted. The procedure took so long that when finished, I was sweating and swearing and partially indecent lying on the floor. But I was free.

Light from a street lamp the next house over filtered in through the frosted window in the door, throwing shadows around the room. I was in a laundry/mud room.

Once I stopped gasping for breath, I got dressed and tiptoed in my stocking feet, sneakers in hand, to the door that connected to the house. I inched open the portal slowly. Although I hadn't noticed anyone else in my surveillance that afternoon – another investigation word; I should hang up my shingle – I didn't want to take any chances. Well, more than I already was. I was as nervous as a member of the bomb squad working on their first live device. Hearing nothing, I eased into the house proper, leaving the connecting door slightly ajar in case I needed to make a quick exit.

A shallow beam of yellow illuminated the linoleum flooring in the hallway. I paused. Waited. Nothing. And for some reason I felt like I was forgetting something.

I rounded the corner, heading to what looked like the kitchen where the light was coming from, when I stopped.

In the middle of the hall was a bear.

Or what looked like a bear in the gloom. The black silhouette was that huge. In some far off part of my brain that wasn't panic induced with thoughts of I-am-going-to-die, my mind couldn't correlate the size of the doggy door, which I'd gotten stuck in, with the behemoth sitting motionless before me.

I heard myself swallow in the silence. Holy crap.

We stood staring at each other, motionless, its eyes reflecting eerily in the lack of light. Did he have any relation to *Cujo*?

Then it moved.

I sucked in a breath through my nose and shut my eyes. My stomach plummeted then vaulted into my throat and I swallowed hard, the acrid taste of fear coating my mouth. Oh god, I was going to be eaten alive.

My feet were frozen to the floor and I shook from head to foot.

Until a slight whimper broke the stillness and a wet nose nudged my gloved palm. The whimper intensified and a soft, wet tongue licked the wrist of my hand that had a death grip on my phone.

I slowly opened my eyes and peered down to the massive bulk sat at my feet, its head just past waist level, sniffing and licking my hand. I moved my hand an inch, waited to hear the responding growl or snap, feel the agony of crunched bones but it didn't come. With infinite slowness, I touched the top of the dog's head. The whimpering grew louder, accompanied by panting.

I tried to speak but my throat was so dry nothing happened. Swallowing, I tried again with a dry croaky voice that came out as a whisper. "Hey, fella."

The dog emitted a soft whine, and I could hear the faint swish of its tail as it swept across the floor.

As I petted it more, the dog's tail increased in speed. It gave a low woof.

"Shhh. Are you a good boy?"

Woof.

Okay. Do not engage the four-legged security guard in conversation.

I inched around the dog and made my way to the kitchen as it was the room directly in front of me. The canine followed, trotted past and sat its big rump in front of the refrigerator door. The light from over the stove reflected in its brown eyes and I could see the massive dark brown head which melded into a deep tan then white of a Saint Bernard. The dog cocked its head, stared beseechingly from fridge to me and back again.

My heart started to melt.

"Are you hungry, baby?"

Another woof.

"Shhh. Not so loud. Did your mom forget to feed you? Has she been a bad mommy?"

What the hell was I doing? This wasn't my dog and why was I even talking to it like I cared?

He pawed at the fridge door.

I scanned the floor and spotted an empty food bowl and a water dish that didn't have enough water to cover the bottom.

Awww, jeez.

Figuring if the dog was occupied eating it might let me investigate the rest of the house, I shrugged and pulled open the fridge. I didn't spot any open cans of dog food but did notice the remains of a beef roast sitting on a plate covered with plastic wrap. A slow evil smile spread across my face.

I whispered to the dog while reaching in and taking the plate out. "Poor baby, Auntie Sadie will give you something to eat."

I peeled off the plastic wrap, stuffed it in my pocket, put the meat on the floor, turned the plate upside down in front of the fridge and added a bit of water to the water bowl while the dog happily chowed down. The scene made it appear the dog pulled the food out of the fridge himself, which could happen, and most people don't notice the water level in their pet's bowl. If I had left the plate near the dog's food bowl, the owners would surely suspect someone had been in the house.

I didn't want to think what the repercussions would be when Sharon came home and saw what happened, but if she did raise a hand to the sweet, loveable mini pony happily eating the morsels of meat, I hoped he'd bite her hand off.

As Moose was dining, that's what I decided to name the dog because he seemed to be as big as one, I hurried up the stairs searching for some place that could be an office. I had no clue exactly what I was looking for but if I could find any connection with Back in Time Antiques or its owner, Jeffrey Rogers, I would take what I could get.

The upper floor consisted of two bedrooms, a bath and an extra room that held boxes marked clothes, storage and miscellaneous. A quick scan of the miscellaneous box didn't come up with anything that could be used as evidence.

What the boxes did show me was that it appeared Sharon was getting ready to move. Looked like she was going to take off out of town.

I quickly ventured into the two bedrooms, cautiously moving items on dressers and bedside tables. Nothing. A quick search of the closet and drawers came up empty as well.

As I passed the bathroom doorway, the radio clock showed the late hour. I had better hurry.

Back on the main floor I halted, scanned the area. No land line. And I didn't see a phone upstairs either. That meant any communication would be through cell phones and text messaging. I ground my teeth in frustration. If they had to write something down on a piece of paper they would need a pen and since most kitchens had a junk drawer for extraneous stuff, maybe I'd get lucky and see a scrap of paper lying around with messages, notes, any hint of a connection to the antiques dealership.

Moose wagged his tail when I entered the kitchen.

"Good boy. Did you enjoy your treat?"

He burped.

The kitchen table held a deck of cards, some flyers, a folded newspaper and a takeout menu from the same Chinese restaurant where I'd gotten the rice. Considering how close it was to the theatre it seemed logical Sharon might go there, perhaps with some of the stage crew or cast. An article in the newspaper was circled. It was about Stanton's murder.

Coincidence? Not likely. But still nothing concrete.

However something written on the takeout menu did catch my eye; Pampa and the date of when I arrived there with the antiques delivery, plus the initials J.R.

J. R. Jeffrey Rogers?

I peered at the message. This was conclusive evidence linked to the theft, if not the murder. I stuffed the Chinese menu into my pocket, hoping Sharon wouldn't notice it missing and if she did, perhaps pass it off as misplacing the piece of paper.

But I didn't worry about that now because something more pressing required my attention.

The slamming of a car door outside the house.

CHAPTER TWENTY-FOUR

The echo of the slamming car door from outside reverberated through my gut, and the sound of voices sent my heart slamming into my ribs.

One higher voice, one lower. Sharon, and possibly Russell, was back.

And I was inside their house.

Uninvited.

The Saint Bernard gave a joyful woof and trotted to the front door. I raced to the laundry room to make my exit out the back, hopefully unseen. I closed the connecting door to the hallway and zipped to the outside door, praying they would use the front entrance. As my hand gripped the knob, thankful I didn't have to exit the same way I got in, I paused.

Wait a minute. The occupants of the house didn't know I was there and they might, just might, start talking about Stanton and the missing antiques. It was obvious they were planning on leaving so this could be the perfect opportunity to learn what their plans were.

On the other hand, I was in the lion's den and if caught, I was pretty sure they wouldn't let me go. No, they would probably kill me then dump my body in the Chihuahuan Desert. But if they left town, as evident from the boxes upstairs, and I didn't find out where they were going or get any solid evidence to link them to the crime, I was probably going to spend the rest of my life in jail.

Two options, bad and worse.

Great.

I figured I might as well go for it and stay to see what I could learn. I put my sneakers on, then infinitesimally turned the doorknob connecting the room to the hallway and inched it slowly open.

Sharon was in the middle of scolding Moose for his late night snack.

"Bad dog!" she hissed in a low tone. "Can't let Russell see this."

From my hiding spot I could hear the soft rip of what I guessed was paper towels and running water.

"How on earth did you get into the fridge?"

"What's that?" A man's voice called.

"Ahh, I said want a beer from the fridge?"

"Sure."

I heard the snap and hiss of a twist off cap.

"You not having one?"

"No. Got a headache."

"Who wouldn't after having to watch the same performance of a bunch of amateurs in ridiculous costumes singing night after night? And I'm not even getting paid. Should never have let you talk me into volunteering."

There was a pause as the couple moved farther away. I inched the door open a smidge wider. Moose sat looking at me, his head cocked to one side.

My whole body quaked. I could be outed by a dog. I squatted down, pet his head. "Shhhh."

Voices carried from the living room.

"I'm worried, Russell. I think we should leave."

"We will, babe. Soon."

"No, I mean, now. Like tomorrow."

"Why?"

"I don't know. I get..I just get the feeling someone's watching me, watching us."

My eyes widened. Had I been spotted the other night while standing behind the tree?

"No one is watching us, Sharon. You're just being paranoid."

Her voice rose, agitated. "I'm not. There's no reason for us to sit around here. I swear I can feel eyes on me."

My heart rate kicked to the next level. Could she hear me breathing? I pressed my lips together, tried to calm myself by taking very slow but deep breaths. Moose panted enough for the both of us.

"Come here, babe." Russell consoled, soothed. "If you're that freaked out, okay, we'll take off tomorrow. You got most of the stuff packed already. We can leave the rest. You going to tell him goodbye?"

"No."

Rogers? Somebody else? The dog?

I stared into Moose's warm brown eyes. Don't tell me this wicked witch was going to leave him?

I heard rustling. They were on the move! Although I didn't have any more information than before, it was time to go.

Saying a silent apology to the dog, I eased the inner door closed and crept toward my escape. With my hand reaching for the doorknob I came eye level to a glowing panel mounted on the wall.

An alarm. And the black lettering on the glowing green screen said activated.

I began to hyperventilate. I was freaking stuck in the house with two possible killers and they have an alarm?

Well, hell.

"Bernie needs to go before bed," Sharon called, her voice trailing away. "Just let him out the back for a pee."

Out the back, as in the back door. Panic seized my lungs, refusing to let in any air. When I got here earlier, I saw there were only two ways into the house;

the front door and the one with the doggie flap that I was currently standing in front of.

I spun, searching for a place to hide.

Any place.

A muffled grumble came from the other side of the door. "Yeah, yeah. Stupid dog. Come here, mutt."

A large, upright laundry hamper stood against the wall, between the dryer and the door. It was tall, made of canvas, and supported on a metal frame. I didn't have the luxury of hoping it would hold my weight. I reached in grabbed a large handful of towels and stepped in.

"Move out of the way, you stupid dog, you're blocking the door."

I crouched down and threw the towels on my head as the door opened.

Nails scrabbled on tile.

I squeezed my eyes shut, as if not seeing anything would make the panic spiraling through my body evaporate. My heart was pounding so fast it actually hurt. Heavy breathing rasped close to my head.

Moosie was sniffing the laundry hamper.

I stifled a whimper. Oh god, oh god!

"Get away from the hamper! Sharon must not have washed the towels from your barfing session this morning. Come on, idiot!"

More scuffing of nails.

Four high beeping tones. Russell had punched in the security code on the panel. When I had closed the connecting door I couldn't hear if they had worked the alarm upon entry. A click, then cooler air wafted, bringing in the evening's scent – and the slight stench of doggie barf from the towels on my head.

Freedom was within feet but I was trapped.

"Go on. Go pee. And hurry up, I want to get to bed." Russell mumbled under his breath, "Fat load of good renting a house with a dog door already in place when the hole is the size of a Pekinese."

Seconds ticked by with agonizing slowness. I took slow, light, shallow breaths.

"Keith? Yeah, it's me." Russell must be on his cell. I strained to listen.

"I could give a crap what I'm interrupting. Look, I'm calling cause we're taking off. Tomorrow. Yeah, that's right, tomorrow."

"I want you to meet me at José's. Should be there late afternoon." Pause. "To fence the stuff, stupid."

Proof! Yes! I very slowly wiggled my cell phone out of my pocket and went to activate the screen to find the recording audio app but then paused. Once I took my phone from sleep mode the screen would light up which would mean Russell might spot the muted glow. Apprehension made my legs twitch and I inwardly screamed at them to hold still.

"Well hurry the hell up and get a pen for christ's sake," Russell growled. "Fricken moron."

I'd have to take the chance. I cupped the phone to mute the glow and with shaking gloved fingers, switched on the screen, found the app and tapped the button. A small dot of red showed my cell was recording.

"You ready? Okay, one-five-one-seven-eight Desert Sands Road. Got that? Good. Meet me there with the stuff at four tomorrow afternoon. What? No, don't take it out of the crates. Jeez, think man. José needs to see that we haven't tampered with them. Get a brain."

Bernie the dog, aka Moose, came galloping through the door.

Beep, beep, beep, beep. The security panel was activated.

Terrific. I was hoping Russell would forget. Now I'd have to wait in this eight by ten room until they were asleep for a bit and I could make a run for it because there was no way I was going to spend the night here.

"Come on, stupid, go lay down on your bed." Obviously Russell had hung up on Keith and was planning on going upstairs to bed. All I had to do was wait.

I stopped the recording, hoping I had enough evidence to at least get the police involved in an ambush.

I could hear the door beginning to shut when it happened. When I finally remembered what it was that I should have done when I first got here earlier.

I had forgotten to put my cell phone on vibrate and my ringtone of *Take Me Out to the Ballgame* jangled loud and clear, breaking the silence.

CHAPTER TWENTY-FIVE

The door to the laundry room where I hid in the hamper slammed against the wall with a heavy bang but didn't drown out the expletive.

"What the fuck!"

I desperately jabbed at the ignore caller button on my phone but I knew it was too late. Bright overhead light seeped through the stitching of the canvas laundry bag I was crouched in and less than three seconds towels were ripped off my head, exposing me to Russell Chang.

The man who framed me for the theft of Back in Time's Antiques and, in all probability killed Lionel Stanton in the process, reached in and pulled me up by my hair.

"Who the hell are you?" he demanded.

"Uhhh…"

I'd always thought I would be able to come out with some witty comment in any situation, some sublime remark that would sound great in a movie script. You know, the comebacks you think about after the moment had passed. But this was no movie and my throat closed in such fear I couldn't utter a word.

Russell released my hair, clamped onto my upper arm and hauled me out of the hamper, tipping it over in the process. I sprawled onto the floor but was immediately forced upright.

His face moved within an inch of mine, eyes blazing with fury. "I'm not going to ask you again." His anger was so intense it was almost tangible.

Sharon came careening into the room, sliding to a stop in her stocking feet. "You!"

Russell whipped his head to face her. "You know her?"

"She's the stupid bitch from the moving company, the one we took the antiques from."

Wait a minute, did she just call me a bitch? And a stupid one to boot?

My cell phone, which I had tried vainly to hide by pressing it to the back of my leg, vibrated with a muted buzzing sound of a text. Russell reached around with his other hand and yanked my life line out of my hand. He glared at it, threw the phone on the floor and drove the heel of his shoe into the lit up screen.

"I've got a bone to pick with you, chickie," he growled out with a menacing grin. "You put one of my bros in the hospital. I don't like it when my friends get hurt."

I was in trouble. Deep, deep trouble.

"What do we do with her?" Sharon eyed me with a mixture of anger and dread.

My legs refused to work properly as Russell dragged me out of the small laundry room to the kitchen and shoved me onto a chair. It almost toppled to the side but I clung on and steadied the piece of furniture.

"I'm not sure yet but I know what will make me feel better." With a swiftness I didn't see coming, his hand connected with my cheek, sending an explosion of pain straight through to my skull.

"That's for smashing Vince's knee."

Another hit and the sensation went from pain to absolute agony. I tasted the coppery tang of blood on my lips.

"And that's for the inconvenience you've already caused me."

Sharon pulled Russell back. "Enough. We don't have time for this. She might have told people where she went. We have to leave. Now."

Russell's face hovered above mine. Tears of pain made his visage slightly blurry.

"Did you tell anyone you were coming here?"

Since the whole point was for me to stay alive, I nodded my head. Big mistake. It felt like a sword entered my skull with each movement.

"Yes."

If I hadn't been in such a serious predicament, I would have been dismayed at the ragged whisper in which my word came out instead of the firm determination I had wanted.

My attacker pierced me with a threatening glare. "Shit."

Although I never thought I was going to get caught, because you don't break into a place with the sole purpose of that happening, I wasn't stupid enough not to let Will know where I was. Before I snuck in I had phoned him and despite his repeated attempts at talking me out of it, he made me promise to contact him as soon as I was in the clear.

Russell reached behind him, withdrew a gun. "I say we kill her."

My focus pinpointed to the cylinder's round hollow end aimed at my face. The dim lighting in the kitchen didn't reflect off the barrel but seemed to be absorbed by it, not only into the metal but also the blackness of intent it represented. At that instant I heard nothing else except my breathing, as if I was underwater. Although my heart ricocheted against my ribs it seemed I only heard every tenth beat, like time had slowed and the sound was akin to my life draining away from a bullet wound.

My life didn't flash before my eyes, like they claim in books and movies but what did enter my brain was regret. In the two-point-three seconds it took between breaths, my thoughts went to my mother. Who would take care of her? And how would my brother explain that her only daughter was no longer alive because of cocky recklessness? Would my mother even comprehend she'd never see me again? The burden of care would have to fall on Blaine now because he couldn't afford to keep our mother in the facility where she currently was. The pressure of caring for her plus two kids would put a strain on his marriage and it would all be because of me. And then there was Clayton and the unresolved issue of how I still felt for him.

My focus went again to the end of the weapon pointed at me and bile slid up my throat, launching my fear factor off the charts.

Sharon pushed his arm down. "We can't kill her here. They'd pin the murder on us for sure. Don't forget my name is on the lease, people have seen us come and go."

"Then we take her somewhere else and do it."

The female of this Bonnie-and-Clyde team spun her partner around. "You think she's going to go along quietly. We're in a crowded residential neighborhood and people could see us. We might as well wrap ourselves up with a bow and turn ourselves over to the cops. We don't have time for this crap. Tie her up, knock her out, I don't care, but I'm leaving before anyone suspects she's missing."

Russell wasn't about to be swayed. "She said people know where she is. How do you know the cops aren't out there right now?"

A look of incredulity crossed her face. "Do you honestly think they would allow a suspect in a murder investigation to break and enter into a house?"

He stared at Sharon, nostrils flaring with each heated breath. I tried not to make any noise while getting oxygen into my lungs. The tenseness of Russell's arms and the vice-like grip he had on the gun spoke of how difficult it was keeping his temper under control.

"We'll get nailed with forcible confinement," he argued.

"By the time she comes to and someone finds her, we'll be long gone. If we leave now, we can get the antiques and be in another state before noon tomorrow. I'm sure you can find another fence to dump them."

He considered her suggestion for a minute then nodded. "Get me some rope and duct tape."

I almost sagged with relief but when Sharon turned away she met my eyes and the cold emptiness that resonated in her gaze froze the blood in my veins.

While Sharon searched for duct tape and something to tie me up with, Russell placed a call, all the while keeping his gun trained on me.

"Things have changed. We're leaving now. I'll call you on the way for a time to meet." He paused and I could hear a man's voice on the line but before the guy was finished, Russell ordered through clenched teeth before disconnecting "You don't want to piss me off right now. Just be ready."

I gathered the conversation was with Keith, the guy they were scheduled to meet tomorrow, who had to be notified of the change in timeline.

Sharon returned with items clutched in her hand, passed them to Russell while she trained the gun on me. Once he was finished, she walked behind, bent down for a minute, tested the ropes, then rose and checked the duct tape across my mouth. Russell stood in front of me, a smirk across his face.

Sharon moved to the right. "Perfect. Thank you, honey." Then she leveled the gun and shot him point plank in the chest.

The reverberation of the shot was muted but it didn't stop me from jumping so hard in the chair that it moved a good six inches. Drops of warm liquid hit my face. Russell fell backward, arms wide, shock registering on his face as he tumbled to the floor. Air rushed in and out of my nose, short, fast, making my head swim. Sweat broke out along my hairline and upper lip and I had to swallow quickly not to gag. Every nerve ending in my upper body felt like they were electrified and I forced myself not to pass out.

Sharon moved around, a wicked icy cold smile spreading across her face.

"Oh, don't worry. I'm not going to kill you."

She unscrewed the silencer which she must have hidden in her palm when Russell passed her the gun so he could tie me up then attached it when she was squatting behind my back.

"That would raise too many questions. Instead, the police will get an anonymous tip in a short while about a possible intruder at this address." She removed Russell's cell phone from his pocket and left the room.

My head was spinning. This woman was either certifiable or so smart that I had totally underestimated her role in this whole thing. I wrenched at the rope binding my hands but there was no way to get free.

Sharon returned with a small statuette of the ancient Egyptian God of Bes. Gold filigree glinted in the kitchen's light, bouncing off the little man's head and rotund body. She pointed to the body on the floor. "This turned out perfectly. I've been trying to figure out how to get rid of him for days in a way that won't implicate me. How does this sound? You caught Russell with some of the antiques you'd help to steal. He wanted to keep some for himself." She wiped off the antique with a towel, took Russell's limp hands and pressed his fingers around the item, then let it drop beside him. "You didn't like that. A fight broke out. You shot him." Using the same piece of linen, she wiped the gun clean, holding it in the fabric. "You're my scapegoat."

My eyes narrowed as she reached over and yanked the duct tape off my face. I clenched my teeth a moment against the flare of pain. "The police aren't going to believe that. This is your place."

She made a tsking sound as she shook her head like I had no clue what was going on. "Do you honestly believe I would use my real name?"

My mind raced, trying to figure out how to deflect the blame from me. "People have seen you together."

"Yes." Her voice changed with false astonishment. "And as soon as I found out about Russell's role in the theft, I left him. I can't be associated with a thief and murderer."

I stared up into the woman's cold conniving face, motioned to my tied up hands. "Kind of hard to be your scapegoat tied up."

"Not for long," she said and pistol-whipped me on the back of my head.

And then my world turned black.

CHAPTER TWENTY-SIX

"Sadie. Sadie wake up."

Someone was harshly whispering in my ear but it felt like they were using a megaphone. My head hurt so bad I hoped whoever was yelling at me had an axe to lop it off. All I could do was groan in reply.

"Come on, Sadie. Wake up."

A hand shook my shoulder, jostling my head. I hissed in pain. "Nooo."

"At least she's not dead."

A different voice, familiar. Welcoming.

Arms slipped beneath my shoulders, hefted me upright. I swayed on my feet, clutched my head. God damn it hurt.

"Please stop the merry-go-round, I'm getting off." My voice was thick. I licked dry lips, winced as my tongue made contact to my split lip.

A pair of hands cupped my face, turned it upward.

"Open your eyes. Look at me, Sadie."

I slowly opened my eyes, shut them again as the glare of a flashlight stabbed into them.

"Will?"

"Yes," he said. "We need to leave. Now."

Rico pointed the flashlight away from my face. "You've got one hard head."

"Sharon. Took antiques.." My thoughts were garbled and I had a hard time focusing on putting one foot in front of the other.

"Explain later." Will maneuvered me into the laundry room. "Time is of the essence."

I stopped his hand as he reached for the doorknob. "Alarm."

"It's not activated."

Sharon must have left it unarmed giving more evidence to the scenario she was going to paint for the police of fleeing from an intruder in the house.

They ushered me outside, mostly with Will's support, strode quickly through the back and into connecting yards. Each footstep reverberated through my skull. I slowed, felt like heaving.

"Just a bit farther," Will coaxed.

When we came close to a car, he turned to Rico. "Take Sadie's truck and follow us."

"Keys." Rico held out his gloved hand.

"Under the seat," I groaned out. "It's parked—"

Will cut me off. "We saw it already. Get inside. I'm sure the cops are on their way."

Rico raced off. I practically fell into the front seat of Will's car. He jumped into the driver's side, whipped off his gloves, turned over the motor and sped away, checking his rear view mirror every few seconds. The world pitched and turned, sending my stomach with it. I clenched my teeth, breathed through my nose, determined not to hurl.

"You have blood on you."

Will's voice was steely hard and I turned to see his jaw set in stone. He didn't look at me, kept his eyes on the road, but from the expression on his face he was angry. Very angry.

My fingers connected with wetness on my face. I pulled them back. They were sticky but not warm. In the darkened interior of the car the blood appeared almost black against my white skin.

White skin.

"Where are my gloves?"

"What gloves?"

"I wore gloves tonight so I wouldn't leave any prints."

Will's jaw clenched again. "Thank god for small mercies. There were no gloves at the scene, Sadie. Someone must have taken them."

He turned sharply right, stepped on the accelerator. Sirens wailed in the distance. The vehicle veered left and I hung onto the door handle to keep from falling into him.

"Will, I—"

"Not right now. Wait till I get you somewhere safe, then we can talk about tonight and how you could have died."

Yup. Definitely angry.

I kept my mouth shut which was fine with me. It took all my concentration to keep the contents of my stomach where it belonged and my head from spinning every time the car swerved. The silence gave me time to think, as difficult as that was, and put things into some semblance of order.

The clock on the dash read after midnight. I couldn't remember exactly what time I'd broken into Sharon's house but from her comment about a headache and Russell's reply about amateur actors, it was plausible they went home directly from working at the theatre. I figured Sharon had about a two hour jump on getting to the antiques.

And any evidence that would exonerate me.

"We need to contact the police. I know where Sharon is heading."

"Soon. We're almost there."

A few minutes later we pulled up at the back of a nondescript small building. A single light bulb over the door threw a weak halo to the ground. My truck arrived less than a minute later and Rico jumped out. After unlocking a door, we hustled into the building, down a darkened hallway and Will opened another door on the right. He flipped a switch.

The room was small with a desk that held a computer and a cot that hugged the back wall. Along another wall, a rack of steel shelving housed an elaborate array of computers, monitors and surveillance equipment.

Very *Lone Gunman*.

Will marched me to the cot. "Sit."

If I hadn't been feeling like dog shit I would have barked at his command. The thought did make me realize I smelled something foul emanating around me. I sniffed, sniffed again. Wrinkled my nose. Yuck.

"You have stuff in your hair, conejito." Rico pointed to the top of my head.

How did I get stuff...

Laundry hamper.

Moose barf.

Great.

Rico grabbed a stool. Will sat in the office chair from the desk, arms folded, glaring at me.

My eyes went from one to the other and finally rested on Will. "Don't be mad."

He said nothing.

"We need to call the police, to set up some type of trap for Sharon. She's heading to Pampa, the address is..." I went for my phone in my pocket only it wasn't there. "My phone?"

Will reached into the pocket of his jacket, pulled out several pieces of shattered plastic. "You mean this? I had a feeling you didn't want it left behind as evidence."

My eyes slid shut. Damn it.

"My phone had the recording of Russell's call and the address of where he was to meet someone. That's where Sharon is going to get the stolen antiques. Now I have nothing."

"Do you remember the address?" Rico asked.

"Desert Sands Road, in Pampa. One something, something." I sighed. "Sorry I don't remember." I stared at what was left of my cellular device, then at Will. "Can you fix it, get anything from it?"

"Not enough time by what you're saying," he said. "Did you happen to hear a name?"

"One was Keith and the other…" My head was pounding a relentless staccato, making it hard to concentrate. Russell had said a name. What the heck was it again?

"Something tequila."

Rico smirked.

Will cocked an eyebrow.

"A name. Like a tequila brand."

"Don Julio?" suggested Rico.

"No."

"José Cuervo?" Will tried.

"Yes, that's the name. José. If I remember right, the guy that Russell was talking to, Keith, was supposed to meet him and Sharon tomorrow at José's place to get rid of the stolen antiques."

Will turned to Rico. "A fence?"

He nodded. "That would be my guess."

"Anyone you know?"

Rico pursed his lips. "Possibly. When I ran with a gang we didn't fence a lot of stuff. But I did remember hearing the name José Ramirez once. Could be him."

José Ramirez. J. R. The J.R. on the Chinese food takeout menu?

"Can you find out?"

Rico rose. "I need to make a few calls. Be back in a minute." He left the room.

"Reception is better outside, unless you use my cell, which I'm not willing to give him and knowing what I can do, he's not comfortable giving me access to his phone," Will said.

A heartbeat of silence. Two.

Will stared at me with a mixture of exasperation and worry. "I should never have let you go in alone."

"I wasn't going to drag anyone else down with me if I got caught and there was no other way I could figure out to get information. But I was right in assuming Russell and Sharon were planning on leaving. They had boxes packed and ready to go. It was just stupid bad luck I got caught. Besides, we had no other leads."

When he just shook his head in resignation I added "At least I told you where I was."

Rico returned and Will went to meet him near the door. They talked in low tones for a minute then Will went over to his computer station, pulled out his cell phone, plugged it into a cord that was connected to the computer and started dialing.

Rico came to sit with me. "You okay, conejito?"

"All right I guess. Okay, you've called me that a few times. What does that word mean, conejito?"

He smiled, his whole face lighting up, making him appear even younger. "You sure you want to know? You may not like it?"

My spine bristled. "Why? You making fun of me?"

He laughed. "No way, Sadie. You're all right. Conejito means little bunny."

My insides warmed. Rico thought enough of me to call me by what seemed like an endearment. It was sweet. Only I wouldn't tell him that. And I couldn't let him totally off the hook. "Little. Is that a comment about of my size?"

Although I tried to make it sound like I was offended, the smile I tried unsuccessfully to suppress gave me away.

He winked but didn't reply.

Will came over and sat back down. "I put a call in. Whether the police act on it in enough time, I'm not sure. I had to reroute the call through a few servers so they couldn't trace it back to this location, and I used a voice changer so they might not take it seriously. But I think they will."

I stared at the both of them "Now what?"

"We take you home, I guess. And wait," Will said.

"By the way," Rico asked. "Were Sharon and Russell in the house and that was how you got caught?"

"No. My phone rang."

Will's mouth opened in surprise. "You didn't think to turn off your phone?"

I stared at the floor, embarrassed. "I'll remember next time. You didn't call me did you?"

He shook his head. "Had no reason to. You said you'd contact me when you got what you needed."

"I did have what I needed. I had evidence both on paper." I remembered the Chinese menu with writing on it and whipped it out of my pocket, waving it in front of Will. "And a voice recording. I was free and clear. All I had to do was wait until Russell and Sharon went to bed and was fast asleep and I would have left."

"And the alarm?" Rico asked.

"To heck with the alarm. By the time they got down the stairs I'd have been long gone. I was one of the fastest runners on my ball team. But when someone phoned me, Russell was just about to head upstairs and he heard my ringtone."

We rose and headed for the door when my brain started to work again and I stopped before I made it to the entrance.

The scene before I was knocked out played again in my mind.

"The statue."

"The one we saw by Russell's body?" asked Will.

"Yes. Why would she go upstairs to get the statue?" I mused out loud, trying to tie the pieces together.

"To take it with her?" suggested Rico.

"But she left it."

"She could have forgot."

I turned to them, shaking my index finger back and forth slowly, trying to work it out.

"No. She didn't. She specifically went and got it, wiped it down with a towel, then put Russell's fingers around the antique before placing it beside him."

Rico and Will spoke at the same time.

"Sounds like a frame-up."

"The murder weapon."

"Exactly. Her explanation of the scenario was that once the cops came they would conclude Russell and I had an argument about the antique and that I shot him. But why keep *that* antique? The only reason would be if it was Stanton's, aka Weckland's, murder weapon and putting Russell's prints on it would implicate him as the murderer."

"Which means Sharon killed Weckland," finished Will.

"There's still the gun, the one Russell was shot with."

"What about it? Did you shoot him?" Rico's eyes widened.

"No! Sharon did. She wiped her prints off the gun after she shot him. I was still tied up. After she smacked me in the head and before I passed out, I thought I felt my hands being untied from the chair. And my gloves were removed, which are now missing. If she follows what she did with Russell, she probably put my prints on the gun."

My eyes darted to both of them. "Did either of you remember to pick it up?"

Will and Rico exchanged nervous glances.

"There was no gun at the scene Sadie," Will said softly.

CHAPTER TWENTY-SEVEN

It felt as if the concrete floor I was standing on, in an unknown location where Will did his technological magic, started to shift beneath my feet.

"What do you mean, there was no gun? Sharon shot Russell right in front of me. She wiped her prints off the weapon before knocking me out with it. Why would she take it with her?"

"Plant as evidence at your place?" Rico wondered.

"She doesn't know where I live. Besides, it would take too much time. She's on the run, remember."

"My guess is she'll loose it close to the house, make it look like you dropped it, or put it in a garbage close by, perhaps a storm drain. She might dump your gloves with it too," Will added.

I stared at my two cohorts in dismay. I was being set up. Again. My world began to crumble and I wanted to crawl into a hole and never come back out.

"Come on." Will took my elbow. "I'll take you home."

As we headed to the door of the room I turned to Will. "How did you know to come get me? I hadn't texted you."

As if it was the most basic answer in the world he said "You'd already given me Sharon's address before but to double check I tracked your phone. I was parked three blocks away the whole time. Thought it best to wait in case you needed a hand."

My ego took a hit. "Are you always going to cyber stalk me?"

"For as long as I need to."

Rico chuckled and I stared at them. These young men had become my friends and they were both risking so much to help me. I pulled out of Will's grasp. "I can't go home."

"You have to, Sadie. The police will come looking. If you're not there it will only make things worse."

I glanced over at Rico who nodded in agreement.

"But..but they'll arrest me and this time there's no way Clayton can get me out."

Will handed me his phone. "Then you'd better call and get him to meet you at your place."

"You haven't got much time. It may already be too late," Rico agreed. "Make the call."

The whole situation made me feel like I was being pulled down a long tunnel. With more trepidation than I cared for, I phone Clayton. He answered on the third ring, sounding groggy. Of course. It was the middle of the night and I had woken him.

"Hello?"

"Clayton. It's me."

"Sadie? What's...what time is it?"

"I'm sorry to wake you. Can you come over please?"

"What? Now?"

"It's important. Please, Clayton. I'm in trouble."

I disconnected before he could ask any more questions and handed the phone back to Will.

"Let's go."

The guys followed me in Will's car while I drove quickly to my place. I needed to beat my ex-husband to my apartment or there'd be way too many questions asked and not enough time for answers. I kept off the major streets and made good time because of the lack of traffic. When I arrived at the parking lot of my complex, Will kept going and I was glad. I didn't want him or Rico anywhere near me when the police came.

I hustled up to my apartment via the back entrance and made it into my place with enough time to wash my face, rinse out the muck in my hair, change and throw my blood-spotted tee in the washer. I tossed in my jeans and socks for good measure and started the unit.

Five minutes later the buzzer rang.

Was it Clayton, my knight in shining armor who would save me yet again, or the police?

"H..hello?"

"It's me."

I let him into the building, went to the kitchen, grabbed two glasses and a fifth of Wild Turkey and walked into the living room as he knocked on the door. When I opened it, his green eyes, filled with worry and confusion, scanned me from head to toe.

"What the hell is going on, Sadie?"

He must have donned on clothes in a hurry, because his usual wardrobe of suit and tie was replaced with jogging pants and a sweatshirt. I pulled him into the apartment. "Come in. Sit down and I'll explain as much as I can."

In the living room, I splashed generous amounts of alcohol into both glasses, passed him one.

He stared at me strangely.

"Trust me, you're going to need it." I tossed mine back, poured another.

Clayton sat, took a hefty swallow. "All right. I'm here, now tell me what happened?"

And I did. I explained everything but made sure not to reveal how I got my information. I had to protect Will and Rico. Starting from Sharon killing Russell and working backwards, I told him about my break and enter into Sharon's house, looking for anything that would tie her to the antiques theft and

Stanton's murder. Clayton took the Chinese menu that I had shoved back into my pocket after I showed Will but he said nothing, motioning for me to continue. My eyes kept darting to the window, expecting to hear a voice on a megaphone telling me to come out with my hands up.

I got as far back in my story as seeing Jeffrey Rogers and Sharon together when the knock on the door came. I guess the police didn't need a buzzer to get in. They probably contacted the super of the building first.

I rose to get the door but Clayton stayed me with his hand. "I'll handle this. Say nothing, understand."

He introduced himself immediately and let the police through the door. They came in, walked straight to me.

"Sadie Hawkins, you are under arrest for the murder of Russell Chang."

One officer read me the Miranda while the other placed my arms behind my back, and although this wasn't the first time in my life I had been in this type of situation, it still didn't make it any easier.

* * *

Over two hours later I was sitting across from Clayton in an interview room identical to the one I ended up in for Stanton's murder.

I felt like crap, probably looked like it too, but at least I had the time to wash up first and toss my blood stained clothes into the washer. Having that much evidence against me including the murder weapon, which now had my prints all over it, would have been a slam dunk as far as the police were concerned.

I looked at Clayton who sat across the table, all showered and changed into semi-business attire, and wondered if my life would ever be normal.

I said as much.

"Normal isn't in your DNA," he replied with a half hearted grimace.

My mouth didn't even quirk at his attempt of levity. I was exhausted, both mentally and physically.

"First off, the body in the sarcophagus was Charles Weckland. Rogers did a positive ID on the photos we showed him after he returned from out of town. Also, I followed up on the anonymous phone tip the police got earlier regarding Sharon and the antiques in Pampa. Local law enforcement has the location under surveillance and will call me if and when they learn anything. You want to tell me how that piece of information got relayed?"

I met his penetrating gaze. "No clue." No way was I bringing Will or Rico into this.

"Sadie."

"Must have been a neighbor."

He stared a moment longer, sighed, and flipped through some papers. "Police located the gun and a set of gloves in a trash can a few houses down the block. The fingerprints on the weapon were a match to yours, since they had them on file."

"Of course. I told you Sharon put them on the gun."

"According to what you told me, you weren't awake when that happened."

I gaped at him. "I didn't kill Russell Chang."

"I know that." He tried to reassure me. "But the police will see your statement as being flimsy at best."

"What now?"

"We wait and hope Sharon and the others involved go directly to where the antiques are hidden."

I nodded.

"Do you know anyone that can corroborate your story?"

"No. I was there alone." Unless you counted Moosie. "Did the police find a dog?"

Clayton's brows lifted, slightly confused. He scanned the report, nodded. "As a matter of fact, yes. A Saint Bernard."

So the witch did leave the dog. Typical. "What happened to it?"

"I don't know. They'll probably take it to a local shelter."

My heart sank. Poor Moose. Looked like he'd be spending time in confinement like me. Hopefully his fate would turn out better than mine.

"Did you want me to call Blaine?"

"No."

"You sure?"

"No, Clayton. Blaine doesn't need to know right now. If nothing comes of the tip, then I guess you'll have to contact him. But not until then."

"Don't you think he'll be a bit concerned when you don't show up for work?"

"I texted him yesterday that I wasn't feeling well."

Clayton's cell phone pinged. He checked his message, his face unreadable, then gathered his papers. "I have to go."

"A development?" I prayed for good news.

"Possibly. You'll have to go back into holding. Sorry."

I nodded. He rose and made his way to the door.

"Clayton."

He paused, turned. "Yes."

"I…I'm sorry."

He tilted his head slightly. "For what?"

"For…everything. For us." And I was. I was sorry that our relationship hadn't made it. I was sorry I still depended on him. And most of all, that I couldn't categorize or understand my feelings for him.

His eyes softened briefly. "Me too."

His knock on the door brought the guard who came in, handcuffed me again, and led me back to my cell.

I lay on the cot and stared at the concrete ceiling and walls. The mumblings and snoring of a few other inmates hammered home just how screwed up my life really was. Even though I was innocent, there was still a very real possibility I would never get out of here. If the police didn't get Sharon, it was over. There was enough circumstantial evidence to charge me and no matter how good Clayton was, with my past record regarding Ricky Best, it would take a miracle to get me out.

Depression washed into me, moving through my body until it settled in my heart, drowning it in anguish. I envisioned my business closing, Blaine needing to find a job, wondering who would look after my mother, and if I didn't land on death row, I would be past middle age before I was free. Unless I got out early on good behavior.

Where would I work? I'd have to start my life over, and I could pretty much guarantee I'd spend what was left of it alone because who'd want to date an ex-con that was convicted of theft and murder.

Date.

I swallowed a low groan.

I was supposed to have gone on a date with Wayne tonight, or more precisely last night, but I'd been so caught up in trying to find evidence against Sharon and Russell that I'd totally forgot. And since Russell obliterated my cell phone, Wayne wouldn't have been able to reach me. Maybe he was the person who called while I was hiding in the hamper. He probably thought I'd stood him up.

Might as well take him off my dance card from now on especially once he learned I ended up here instead.

Well, hell.

CHAPTER TWENTY-EIGHT

I didn't get released from jail until three days later. Although Clayton had stopped by once to tell me the police in Pampa did have Sharon Marsden in custody, Houston officials still wanted to keep me until they had enough evidence to exonerate me and charge her.

I hoped the witch was stewing. Or even better, freaking out.

It was Blaine who sat outside the police station in my pickup truck when I exited the building into the warm Texas evening air. I let the sinking rays of sunshine seep into my skin, penetrate through to my soul, while I stood on the sidewalk, eyes closed in thankfulness. I heard a door slam, lowered my face and let my gaze settle on my brother as he leaned against the hood of my vehicle. My heart swelled in gratitude and tears filled my eyes when he straightened, held arms out and I walked into his comforting embrace. We stood there for a moment, saying nothing, until he placed his hands on my shoulders and pulled me away.

"One of these days, Taz."

I nodded, palmed away the few tears that had slipped out and squeezed him quickly before stepping to the passenger door.

"Take me home, please, Blaine."

"You may want to rethink that." He got into the truck. "Reporters have been phoning work looking for you. They may be at your place. Why don't you come home with me, stay with us for a day or two, get your bearings."

"Reporters?" What the hell could they want?

"Yeah. According to the news, you were pivotal in cracking the case of finding the missing antiques and of Lionel Stanton's murder."

"Charles Weckland's murder," I corrected him.

"Yes. Anyway, I figured you probably needed a few days to decompress."

As much as I wanted to lock the doors, pull the shades and sleep for a week, I wanted to be surrounded by the people I cared about, and almost lost.

"I'd love to."

* * *

After steak, potatoes, salad and half a dozen beers between the two of us, Blaine and I sat alone on his deck. My sister-in-law, Karen was giving Shantelle a bath. We hadn't talked about the case during dinner; the topic not something Blaine, Karen or I deemed appropriate to an impressionable two-year-old. But now it was just the two of us and I let myself relax for the first time in almost two weeks.

"I'm sorry, Blaine." I sighed, took another sip of beer.

"You should be."

My expression must have said how much I didn't appreciate his tone because he elaborated. "I meant about not calling me."

"I knew I was innocent. I didn't want to worry you."

"With you, worry is part of the territory."

My mouth twitched.

"Clayton didn't say a lot about the case, so maybe you can fill in the blanks."

I tilted my chin toward the house. "Don't you want to wait until Karen gets back?"

He shrugged. "I'll give her the condensed version."

I corralled my thoughts. As much as I wanted to give credit to Will and Rico for their help, I would not be able to without implicating them. I knew Blaine wouldn't purposefully let their names slip, even if I asked him to keep them a secret, but I didn't want to put my brother in that position.

I leaned back, trying to spot some stars in the Houston sky but failing. "Apparently Sharon Marsden is actually Sharon Martin, Jeffrey Roger's niece by marriage. She was adopted and since they live in the same city, she knew Rogers traded in antiquities."

"Okay. And the shipment?"

"Russell Chang, who worked as a janitorial staff member cleaning the building where Back in Time Antiques was located, overheard Stanton, aka Charles Weckland, setting up a deal with a fence in Pampa for the stolen antiques. Weckland was planning on an insurance scam."

My brother reached to a cooler between our two chairs, pulled out another beer and cracked it open. "With you so far."

"Wanting to get in on the deal, Russell and Sharon met Weckland in the loading bay before I got there. Of course, Weckland denied the allegations until Russell produced a cell phone recording of the conversation Weckland had with his fence. The police confirmed this from Russell's phone which they confiscated from Sharon when they arrested her. Anyway, there was a struggle and Weckland fell and hit his head on a crate only he didn't die. Knowing Russell was still on probation and any slight infraction would get him arrested again, and losing a chance to score some considerable cash, Sharon took one of the statues that hadn't been sealed into a crate yet and killed Weckland."

I drained the last of my beer. Blaine retrieved another from the cooler, opened it and handed it to me. "Continue."

I took a long pull. "Russell panicked, knew he'd be sent to prison for a long time now, so he and Sharon took the mummy out of the sarcophagus and put in Weckland's body instead. They unloaded the antiques from the crate that had Weckland's blood on it, dismantled it, repacked the articles into another, then hauled the mummy and the broken down bloodied crate into their vehicle. By this time, I was on my way there."

"You'd think Weckland would have had the antiques boxed up beforehand," Blaine suggested.

"Rogers' would have seen the items missing. That's why Weckland went in to work early. But Russell and Sharon caught him."

My brother wrinkled his brow. "Obviously they knew you were coming if Russell had overheard Weckland's conversation to his fence the day before, so how did they explain his absence when you got there?"

"Once they killed Weckland they didn't have a lot of time. I'm assuming that Sharon came up with the idea of posing as Ms. Ing. Don't forget, Jeffrey Rogers was her uncle and I did see them together that one night coming out of the building and going into the theatre. It's conceivable that she visited him at his office, maybe on multiple occasions and got introduced to the staff. With Weckland dead, who else would be able to speak for him but another dealer, or in this case, his secretary Ms. Ing. Russell had keys to the offices because he was part of the janitorial staff, so it would have been easy for him or her to get a blank check."

Blaine pursed his lips for a second. "Remember when you called me from Pampa, said there was no one there to pick up the load?"

"Yes."

"Did Russell and Sharon know Weckland's fence?"

"I don't know. But Clayton told me the address where I went, which was a house, is owned by Sharon's parents, Rogers' sister and brother-in-law. Sharon knew they would be away on holidays."

"Sounds premeditated."

I shook my head. "I don't think so. I think it was a crime of opportunity. Remember, Russell and Sharon didn't plan on killing Weckland. It just happened. They were lucky there was a place they could drop off the shipment in Pampa where no one would question it. Including me. Sharon merely wrote her parent's address on the envelope with the documents before she handed it to me."

"That's taking a huge risk. If the guys who stole the antiques just took off with them, Russell and Sharon wouldn't know where they went."

"Clayton said police eventually found traces of Russell's DNA inside the crate. That would mean he stayed in the crate when I drove to Pampa and the reason his two henchmen came and got him out."

"Henchmen?"

I stared at him in fake haughtiness. "I'm tapping into my inner *Snoop Sister*."

"If he was in the crate and the antiques were there it would have been the perfect opportunity to take the stuff and run."

"True but since he had a long history of crime, and was on probation, if he magically disappeared all of a sudden, it would look pretty suspicious considering he worked in the building. He'd have to sit on the antiques for a while. You just can't peddle those types of things anywhere."

"Sharon probably drove to Pampa, got him and brought him back," Blaine commented.

We were quiet, taking comfort in the simple pleasure of sipping a beer in the warm Texas night.

Blaine grunted but said nothing.

"What?"

"Was wondering why they didn't get rid of Weckland's body in Pampa when they had the chance."

"Logistics. And also timing. To move the whole crate with the sarcophagus they'd need a forklift and well, most homeowners don't have one in their garage. And considering the drop off was in a residential neighborhood, I'm sure the rest of the street would notice a forklift driving down the block in the middle of the night. Then there was the problem of disposal."

I shuddered but carried on. "Sharon, Russell and their gang would have to bury the body, or transport it somewhere, maybe out in the desert and that would mean the possibility of leaving trace evidence in their car. It was easier for them to leave Weckland's body in my van to point the suspicion on me. In their eyes I had motive, means and opportunity."

Blaine was silent, digesting it all. He lifted the index finger of the hand wrapped around the neck of his beer. "Hang on. Clayton told me they found enough evidence to drop the suspicion of Weckland's murder against you. Did they find the mummy and crate?"

"Yes, in a dumpster near the theatre where Sharon worked as a ticket agent. Police actually had to stop the garbage truck a block away. The dumpster had just been emptied so the contents were sitting on top. Good thing they didn't have to go to the dump and sift through all that garbage. Although tossing the stuff into that dumpster wasn't the brightest move they made, I also don't think they had a lot of time. I mean who wants to drive around with a mummy in their vehicle. Anywhere they parked the car, people could see inside. In the end it was the statue Sharon kept that eventually implicated her."

My brother turned his head from where he was staring out into the yard and looked at me. "I thought it got put in the crate?"

"No. My theory is that in the craziness of getting rid of Weckland's body, the mummy and the bloody crate, they forgot about the statue until it was too late and I was almost there. So she kept it."

"But why would she do something so stupid as to keep a murder weapon?"

"I doubt she gave a reason, but Clayton thinks Sharon was already figuring on framing Russell at this point. Apparently she wasn't planning on going down for his murder." I snorted sardonically. "She almost got away with it too."

"Almost?"

"Besides finding traces of Weckland's blood on the inside lip of the base of the statue, forensics also found a minute amount of foundation nestled in the eye crease of the statue, probably came from underneath her fingernail when she was applying her make-up that morning. They matched it to the makeup with her stuff she had packed in her car."

"Okay." Blaine nodded. "That cleared you for Weckland's murder but what about Russell's?"

I went silent, reliving the short, high pitched retort of the silencer, the hot, wet spray of Russell's blood as it hit me, the shocked wide-eyed expression frozen on his face. Although I claimed I was okay to everyone, I hadn't slept much in jail and knew I would have nightmares for a long time because of what I had seen and experienced.

"They found two small drops of Russell's blood on her shirt. It was dark, she probably didn't notice."

Blaine sat up straighter, shocked. "She admitted to being there?"

"Kind of had to at that point. However, she claimed I had the gun aimed at her and was going to kill her too. She said after I shot Russell she attacked me, wrestled away the gun, knocked me out and fled in a panic. When she realized she still carried the weapon, she tossed it into the garbage instead of coming back and taking the chance that I had woken up."

I didn't mention my gloves the police found with the gun. Sharon's story about knocking me out with the gun and fleeing with it in panic was plausible, but Clayton believed scooping up my gloves and disposing them with the gun appeared like circumspect behavior. Another slip up on her part.

"That still doesn't prove she killed him."

"True. But in her statement she said I had the gun in my right hand. Specifically my right hand." I grinned in satisfaction.

"And you're left-handed." Blaine matched my smile.

"The prints on the gun matched my right hand, not my left. And since only about ten percent of the population is left-handed, Sharon automatically pressed the weapon into my right hand while I was unconscious. That plus what I said in my statement that I was sitting and she was standing, which matched the bullet's angle of trajectory, Russell's blood on her shirt, her being caught with the antiques in Pampa along with two other guys, who rolled over on her to save their own butts, and the makeup on Weckland's murder weapon, they let me go. I'm sure Clayton used his persuasive talents and convinced the District Attorney they didn't have much of a case based on prints alone."

"What about the antiques?"

"The police are keeping them as evidence for when Sharon goes to trial."

Blaine reached over, touched my hand. "So, you're cleared? Of everything?"

I clasped his fingers, held on. "Yes. Of everything."

We sat, silent, holding hands, gazing into the night. I don't know who was more thankful.

I didn't care.

CHAPTER TWENTY-NINE

I slept for twelve hours straight, only waking when Shanty barreled into the room and jumped on the bed, bewailing that her Auntie Sadie was a sleepyhead. Her continuous leaping made it impossible to ignore and sink back into dreamland. I dragged myself to the bathroom, took the hottest shower imaginable, and emerged in the kitchen to Karen plating scrambled eggs and toast. She placed the food beside a can of cola. Bless the woman.

We chatted about everything except the case. My guess was that Blaine, who had left for the shop, had already given his wife the sordid details and she didn't want me to rehash them. Another reason why I loved her, besides putting up with my brother.

She told me Clayton had left a message since I didn't have a cell phone and that became the first order of the day. I took my truck, bought a new phone, which depleted my bank account to less than a dollar, and called Clayton.

"Hey. You okay?" he asked when he picked up. I was lucky he didn't have court.

"Thanks to you, I am."

"Just doing what I get paid for."

"But I'm not paying you."

"I'll get payment sometime."

His comment was to make light of the situation because I could hear the ease in his tone but for some reason we both paused. I wondered exactly what that meant and he wondered why he said it.

He cleared his throat. "We still have a few things to go over. Can I buy you lunch?"

Considering I had just eaten, I opted for coffee and we agreed to meet at a café near his office.

When I arrived, Clayton was already there, looking handsome and professional in his suit, a dark grey with moss green tie which accented his eyes. The young woman took my order of a cola with double shot espresso chaser and we sat in companionable silence until my beverage arrived.

He broke the quiet. "Jeffrey Rogers from Back in Time asked if he could meet with you."

My eyes widened in alarm. Not again. What now?

Clayton must have seen my panic because he quickly assured me. "It's not what you think. He wants to say thank you."

"Tell him to send me a card."

"Play nice, Sadie. He wants to apologize in person."

"He should. Manhandling me that way."

"And to give you a reward. The antiques were recovered, which saved the insurance company a considerable amount of money and exonerated him regarding the theft."

That perked me up. "Considering I'm out the cash from the original job, it's the least he could do."

"Send him a bill," Clayton drawled, knowing I probably wouldn't. Well, not unless the reward didn't cover my expenses. "And he wants the media there, make a big show about it."

I stiffened. "No way. No press. Tell him to give the check to you and you can pass it along to me." I did not want my picture in any papers, especially something that could be picked up on the wires and a case about locating stolen antiques was sure to pique the human interest angle. My face didn't even make the papers when I was charged with the theft and possible murder of Charles Weckland.

"I figured as much." He reached into his breast pocket, withdrew a white envelope and slid it across the table to me. "But I wanted to give you the option."

"You know me well."

"We were married."

I smiled tentatively and took the envelope. "Do you know how much?"

"None of my business."

I lifted the flap, pulled the check out slowly and gasped. The amount was more than I could have hoped for. Tears pricked my eyes and I closed them quickly so Clayton wouldn't see. This amount of money would wipe out my current bills, pay Blaine for his hard work, and tie me over for the next few months. I took in a deep breath, then another and let the hope that had been suppressed since I reopened the business, shine again.

"Police have also released your van from impound. I guess that means you're back in business." Clayton grinned.

"I guess that does." I beamed at him. "Thank you, Clayton."

He studied me, still smiling. "You're welcome."

"What happened with Margaret Yates, the receptionist?"

"She was having an affair with Weckland but, as you know, did not murder him. Using the tip you gave me, she confessed to slashing the tires of his car at the airport. That's what she was worried about getting arrested for."

Wow, if she was that upset thinking she'd get arrested for something so trivial, albeit not very nice, she was a highly strung woman.

I mentally backtracked. "The airport? Since Weckland was killed in the loading bay of Back in

Time, and presumably he drove his car to get there that morning, how did the vehicle get to the airport?"

"Sharon's prints were found in the car so she must have driven it there after you loaded the crates into your van. Keeping it at the office would cause suspicion because he was supposed to be on a sabbatical and since Russell Chang had overheard Weckland's plans for leaving, the two of them decided to put it in long term parking, less security than in the underground lot."

"And Yates, thinking Weckland had left the country, drove all the way out to the airport to slash his tires in retribution?"

Clayton nodded. "She also surmised the car would be in long term parking because he had told her he was leaving for a while."

"Seems the no-nonsense Mrs. Yates has a temper. How much trouble is she in?" Considering the kind of guy Weckland turned out to be, maybe it was best he didn't take her along.

"Since Weckland is dead and can't file charges, she'll get a slap on the wrist."

Clayton's cell phone rang and he took the call. It was brief and when it ended, he rose. "Sorry, Sadie, but I have to run."

"Saving the next damsel in distress." I couldn't resist the quip and stood.

A lopsided grin creased his mouth. "Something like that." He kissed my forehead. "Take care of yourself."

"You too." I smiled and watched the man who had first been my lawyer, then my husband, then my ex-husband, my lawyer again and now my friend, leave. I still hadn't figured out exactly how I felt about Clayton but he held a very special place in my heart and maybe one day, when things had settled down for me, I would revisit that place and come to some conclusion.

I finished the last of my cola-coffee and left the café.

Although I didn't want a media fanfare, I couldn't, in all conscience, not thank Jeffrey Rogers for his generous reward, so I drove to Back in Time. Upon entering the building, I had the weirdest sense of déjà-vu. I hadn't stepped foot in the place since I was charged but despite me having been there before, I saw it with different eyes, like from another lifetime. In a sense it was another life, one prior to seeing a man die before my eyes and being incarcerated. Both of those things had changed me but I survived and had to believe they would make me stronger.

Mrs. Yates was at the reception desk and her eyes widened slightly upon my entrance. I wondered how she was coping knowing she had been in love with

Weckland yet not realizing what he had planned. Maybe we don't know people as well as we think.

"Ms. Hawkins." She nodded when I approached the desk.

"Mrs. Yates. Is Mr. Rogers in? I would like to speak with him."

She didn't keep eye contact, merely called his office, told him I was in the waiting area, then returned to her typing. Part of me felt sorry for her. I wondered if her husband ever found out about her affair.

Within a minute, Jeffrey Rogers appeared, smartly dressed as before, a welcoming smile upon his face. Certainly better than the last time we spoke.

"Ms. Hawkins. How nice to see you again." He clasped my hand.

I returned the gesture. "Mr. Rogers."

"Please, call me Jeffrey."

I was taken aback by his geniality. Did the guy forget he charged me with theft?

He must have noticed the subtle change in my expression because his voice lowered, became serious, apologetic. "I feel awful for the stress I may have caused you. I am so sorry but I had no clue what Charles was up to." He led me aside, motioned to sit in one of the two chairs against a wall.

"Your gift of the reward was more than generous."

"The least I could do considering. How are you doing?"

"Getting better. I want to put the whole situation behind me."

"Yes, I understand that well."

It felt a bit odd, having an almost stranger ask about my well being, but I had to remind myself that he had been duped as much as I. Even more so considering Sharon was his niece.

"This whole situation must have been quite difficult for you too."

He looked away momentarily and a flash of pain crossed his features. "As you can imagine, my sister Lillian, Sharon's mother, is devastated. I had gone to Pampa to visit her last week because I had become deeply concerned about Sharon and her association with Russell. Their relationship had been going on for a while and I didn't feel he was the right person for her. Unfortunately, it was a little too late for any type of intervention."

"I'm sorry. Although the stolen antiques were returned, you also lost a partner."

"A dishonest one," he pointed out sternly. "Embezzlement, false insurance claims, fraudulent documentation, and forging my own name on top of it."

I gave him a moment.

"Are you going to look for another partner?"

"Perhaps in the future but for now, Ms. Ing is being promoted from secretary to a part time broker. She will be able to find and acquire some items."

I thought back to the middle aged woman who I'd seen in Whitestone waiting on a client with a Ming vase that never showed, the real Ms. Ing. "Good for her."

"Yes. Funny how it worked out. I had noticed her dedication and with Weckland planning a sabbatical, which we now know was bogus, I didn't want to be caught short handed if some pieces came available out of town. I approached her before this whole situation blew up."

"She must have been thrilled."

Rogers blushed slightly. "Surprised was more like it. That probably had to do with the dinner meeting. Perhaps she thought I was hitting on her but I figured she deserved the good news in a nice setting."

My eyes flicked over to Mrs. Yates. Her frosty attitude toward Rogers when she reminded him of that meeting the day I came in made perfect sense now. She was probably jealous of the promotion.

He paused, took a deep breath and smiled. "I'm glad you stopped by. I was thinking, if there was a time that we may be in need of your services, if I could call on you?"

"For moving?"

"Of course. What did you think I meant?"

"Well, definitely not stealing." I forced laugh and started to fidget. This was getting uncomfortable.

He took my hand again, placed it between his. "Sadie. I truly am sorry for what you went through. Please let me help you in whatever way I can."

I hesitated, startled by the sincerity in his eyes that matched his voice. Maybe things were starting to go my way. Maybe Hawkins Freight did stand a chance of making it out of first gear.

I smiled, stood. "That would be great, Jeffrey. I'd appreciate it."

"Terrific. Do you have any business cards?"

Dang it. Never thought but then I didn't expect this type of boon either. "Not on me, no."

"Next time you're close, drop off a stack and we'll hand them out to clients as well."

"Thank you. I appreciate that." I extended my hand which he shook.

"Think nothing of it. We'll talk again." He turned and strode away down the hall to his office.

I left the establishment in a bit of a daze. In the span of a few days I went to being jailed and almost broke, to having enough money to pay my bills with a possible client on retainer. I felt like I'd just stolen the captain of the football team away from Mary Sue Watkins, a cheerleader when I was in high school.

The bank was my next stop, then on to try and make amends to a friend.

* * *

I stood at Wayne's door but didn't knock, my stomach twitching in nervous apprehension. What if he wasn't home, since I hadn't called I didn't know if he was or not. Or worse, what if he didn't want to answer the door? I did stand him up on our date, although not on purpose, and it was an outing I, and hopefully he, had been looking forward to.

But standing there like an idiot wouldn't solve anything or give me any answers so I knocked and held my breath.

Footsteps approached and when Wayne opened his door his brows rose but that was the only change in his expression. His brown eyes were pinched, his lips level, neither smiling or unsmiling. Perhaps he didn't know what to make of me. That's okay, at times I didn't either. But I was really glad to see him.

"I can explain." I hoped he wouldn't slam the door in my face.

The corner of his mouth lifted sardonically. "I actually already heard."

Of course he did. How stupid of me to think he wouldn't know. He'd have seen or heard my name because even if he didn't work at the same station, Houston cops talk to one another. Although I was dressed in my usual attire I felt like I was appearing before a judge in striped prison garb.

I scuffed my boots, jabbed my hands in the back pockets of my jeans, my gaze flicking to his face then away in embarrassment. "Sorry about missing our date."

"I actually phoned you because you didn't come across as being someone who would stand a guy up."

So he was the call that got me in hot water. Oh well, couldn't fault him for something he didn't know.

"Yeah, I was...tied up."

A few seconds ticked by. He snorted, then broke out laughing. "Shortcake, you do keep me amused." He opened the door wider, inviting me in with a sweep of his hand.

I smiled from ear to ear, relieved this handsome boy-next-door-type hadn't washed his hands of me. "Actually I can't come in and am hoping you won't want me too either." Anticipation made my fingers tingle as they slid out from my jeans pocket, withdrawing a set of tickets. "They're just above Diamond Club. Best I could do on short notice."

Wayne's mouth dropped. "Wow. Those must have cost you a pretty penny."

"Yeah, well I had a few extra dollars. Strictly legit," I rushed on as he narrowed his eyes. "Am I forgiven?"

He reached behind him, flipped off a ball cap resting on a wall peg, and slapped it on. "Throw in a few Little Bigs and some brew and call it square." He closed the door behind him and we headed down his sidewalk.

CHAPTER THIRTY

The next few weeks after my make-up date with Wayne, which turned out to be more fun than I expected, were busy fielding calls from the persistent press, paying off creditors and generally trying to get my life back on track. I did a few small moving jobs, nothing major, and truth be told I was glad. I was able to spend some quality time with Blaine, Karen and Shanty, fulfilling my role as Auntie for them so they could take in a movie or dinner.

I also completed an obligation I had made to myself while I spent those days in jail. On a sunny afternoon - in Texas most afternoons were sunny - I parked outside a brick building, jumped out of my truck and heard the yapping and barking of dogs begging to be taken home. I entered the building on a mission.

A young woman behind the desk glanced up at me expectantly. "Hi there. Are you looking to adopt a dog or a cat?"

"A dog. A specific dog, in fact. A Saint Bernard that came in a little over a week ago."

She checked her files, nodded and said for me to follow her.

The noise level rose by a few decibels as we passed through a metal door with a window from the outer office to the caged area. Dogs of all shapes and sizes, some sleeping, considering all the noise I had no idea how, some eating, but most running to the front of their cages hoping for a kind stranger who would take them to their forever home. The staff member led me down toward the end and stopped, pointing to the cage on the left.

There he was, lying with his head on his paws, looking miserable. He must have sensed we were there to see him because his ears twitched and he raised his head.

"Moosie!"

The dog's ears perked, he took one look at me and bounded forward, tail wagging, a loud and happy woof escaping his smiling mouth.

"Hi boy."

His whole body shook he was so excited.

The attendant reached for the latch. "You may want to take a step back."

"Why? Has he been aggressive?"

"No, but by his reaction, which is the first we've seen since we got him, he's thrilled to see you. Is this your dog?"

"No. He belonged to a person I knew but she left him behind and won't be back."

She nodded, opened the gate and I prepared to be steamrolled. Moose zipped out but instead of bowling me over like I expected he sat at my feet, staring with those adorable brown eyes. I lifted my hand for him to sniff but he didn't need to. He bumped my fingers with his head and then licked them with his big, soft tongue. I squatted down, rubbed his ears and I swear I could almost hear him purr, even if he was a dog. My heart melted all over again.

"Is he available for adoption now?" Most surrenders had to go through a quarantine period which was another reason why I waited to check on him.

"Yes."

"Great. I'll take him."

She closed the cage door. "Awesome. Follow me."

We went to the front, Moose trotting beside me, his head continually bumping my hand in search of a pet. My heart was practically flying.

At the reception area an older woman was behind the desk, her back to us. She turned and her eyes narrowed, took one look at me, then the dog and said "That dog is not available for adoption."

"Yes he is," the other corrected.

"No it isn't." The sergeant behind the desk stated, her eyes still pinned on me. "Especially to you."

The young woman and I exchanged a glance of surprise and I blurted "Why not?"

"Because I was at the shelter when you brought those two dogs back after having them way too long. This SPCA works in tandem with other smaller organizations across the city, which was why I happened to be there. Regardless that they were returned happy and unhurt and your donation of the dog food, it seems apparent you do not have the best interest of an animal in mind."

The tension in the room rose and I knew if I had any chance of rescuing Moose it would have to be when Cruella de Vil wasn't there.

I checked my watch. "I see. Perhaps if I could prove to you that I am totally sincere. I do have an appointment but maybe I can return tomorrow and we can discuss this."

Cruella didn't respond either way. The young woman gave me a confused shrug and took Moose away. His feet scrabbled for purchase as he whined and tried to resist. I headed for the door, not wanting the woman to see how angry and hurt I was.

I got in my truck, muttered to the fates about having the worst luck in the world, drove out of the parking lot and stopped at a convenience store a block away. When I had those two dogs for a walk, I made sure to take extra water for them, kept to the shade as much as possible, gave them a few treats and played ball after the surveillance of Sharon's house. When I returned them there were a few people milling about and I don't remember seeing the drill sergeant because I had been in a hurry but obviously she had been there. I understood where she was coming from but I wasn't about to try and prove how much I cared for Moosie only to be rejected in the end because the woman didn't know all the details. And if I told her I had been on a scouting mission to break into a house, she'd show me the door faster than I could blink. I pulled out my cell phone and dialed. The call was picked up on the second ring.

"I need your help."

* * *

It took some convincing, actually a lot of convincing, on both our parts but at the end of the day, Moose had a new forever home. A place he would be fed well, cared for, allowed to run around imitating a pony in the back yard and where he could practice his guard dog skills, which needed some work. But most of all he would be loved.

At Blaine's house.

Between working, doing my part in the canine version of *Free Willy* and teaching Shanty to play catch with Moose – Blaine and Karen kept his name in deference to me, the angels – I spent extra time with my mother in an effort to appease my guilt over the lack of visits. Most days she was good, cognizant, even cheerful, but those instances were getting shorter in length and farther apart.

After a few misfires, Tanya and I reconnected again. We were still best friends, hopefully always would be, but an underlying veil of caution was present when we were together. I almost got the sense she was holding something back but I figured one day that veil would eventually disappear, it would just take time.

The phone in the office rang and I hustled over from where I was cleaning out the inside of the van.

"Hawkins Freight."

"Sadie?"

"Yes, this is Sadie Hawkins."

"Hello, hello." The woman's voice lowered on the second greeting. "It's Sylvia Brady. Remember me?"

Sylvia Brady? The name was familiar and I wracked my brain until it came to me. The four-legged Brady bunch.

"Yes, of course I remember you, Ms. Brady. How are you and the dogs doing?" I couldn't hear any barking so I hoped she still had them.

"Fine. Well, sort of." She paused before continuing. "Mercury is in retrograde and things haven't panned out here in Amarillo. The city has too much of a bad vibe and it's messing with my aura. I'm calling to see if you would be able to move me and the dogs back to Houston."

I held the phone, speechless for a second. Her aura?

"Ahhh...I don't know if I can get the same person to help me on the trip." I doubted Tanya would fall for the same thing a second time and the way our friendship was on tender hooks I didn't want to ask her.

"Oh, don't worry about that. I can drive back with you to keep an eye on the dogs. That is if it's okay with you?"

"Ummm..."

"I'll pay extra. Actually my uptight sister will be footing the bill. She laid down the law of either getting rid the kiddies or me finding another place to live. Can you imagine?" The last was spoken with such incredulousness I almost broke out laughing.

"That is hard to imagine." Though, personally, considering the calamity of the trip there, I figured the sister was a saint to take in all the dogs.

"I'll have to see if I can get the same vehicle." I was sure Blaine would loan me his van, for a fee, which would be probably taking Moose for a walk, or in his case, a gallop through the park. "How soon did you want to move?"

"As soon as I can. I don't trust my sister not to bring my dogs to an internment camp."

"Internment camp?" What kind of person was her sister?

"A kennel!" gasped Sylvia, mortified. "Please, can you get here in the morning?"

"Give me your number and I'll get back to you."

Sylvia disconnected and I called my brother. He did agree to loan me his van and his fee was what I had figured plus a bag of dog food.

I called Sylvia back and told her I could be in Amarillo in the morning. She was so relieved and excited about the way back, stating she'd bring veggie snacks for the trip. I didn't ask if they were for the dogs or us. Although a drive from Houston to Amarillo and back was doable in a day, it could be tiring and including the dogs it was more than my patience could stand at the moment. She asked if I'd like to stay at the house, since I would be arriving later that night, but I lied and said I would be staying with a friend. I had no desire to get caught in the middle of a feud between sisters. The seats in the van reclined and it wasn't the first time I'd have to sleep in a vehicle or probably the last.

I called Tanya to see if she wanted to go out for coffee before I had to leave but she didn't pick up. I left a voice mail message saying I was sorry I missed her and maybe we could get together for a drink or a movie soon.

I finished cleaning the inside of the van, returned a few phone calls, booked another job. It was a referral through Rachelle the drunken co-ed's dad. I drove the cube van to Blaine's, grabbed his vehicle and headed to Amarillo armed with a cola double shot espresso and two Live Wires, just in case.

This was the third time I had driven the Interstate north recently and I was beginning to remember where the troopers liked to hide for speeders so I minded my lead foot and cruised along. As I neared Amarillo I tuned the radio station to KRDL for no other reason than in hopes of hearing Mr. Sexy Voice, Jackson Steel. If I couldn't connect with him on the phone, at least I could over the radio.

On the outskirts of the city, I pulled off into a rest area to stay overnight. At first I was a bit leery, me being a single woman alone in a van despite having my pal Louis with me but after a while a family hauling a tent trailer pulled in as well as an elderly couple in a camper and I nestled the van between them. I figured if I didn't get the best night sleep because of the noise, at least it was somewhat safe.

The ten o'clock news came and went, then a few songs and I listened, hoping Jackson didn't have the night off. Hearing his voice would make the perfect end to an otherwise boring, normal day.

And with the single utterance of the letter *g* in his greeting of good evening, I sighed. His deep voice soothed me, infused my blood like liquid honey and I closed my eyes in bliss. I thought about what he looked like, how he would present himself, in other words, fantasized like a teenage groupie.

"Good evening, Amarillo and all you classic rock fans. Welcome to the show. This is Jackson Steel and I'm hoping you'll stay with me so we can share some good tunes and good times."

I would stay with that man for as long as he'd have me and it definitely would be good times.

He laughed at something and for a crazy minute I thought Jackson had either heard me speak out loud or read my mind. I smiled at the sound of his deep, resonating laughter.

"We'll start this evening off as I have been for the past couple of weeks with an invitation to a certain mover and shaker to give me a call and let me know she's all right."

My eyes snapped open and I bolted to a straight sitting position. What did he say? A certain mover and shaker? My brain cart wheeled back to the conversation I'd had with him just before my two midnight visitors stole the antiques from the back of my van. At that time Jackson had called me a mover and a shaker. Was he referring to me now? He did say she.

I had to wait a good twenty minutes before Jackson rattled off the number to the station if anyone wanted to request a song. The phone rang a number of times and I was beginning to think he was too busy to answer when he finally did.

"Thanks for calling KRDL. This is Jackson."

I swallowed past the dryness in my throat. What if I was making a fool out of myself, reading something into nothing? What if the person he was referring to wasn't even me?

"Hello?"

"Ah, Jackson? Hi. This...this is Sadie."

"Sadie."

He didn't say my name as a question, as in who are you, just merely repeated it.

Oh man, I made a mistake. It was stupid of me to call.

"Sadie? As in moving company, Sadie?" he asked.

Okay, still couldn't tell if that was who he wanted to call. "Yes."

"Hey! You finally got my message. I'm so glad you called."

A flushed roared to my cheeks and I was grateful Jackson wasn't there to see it.

"Well, umm, I wasn't exactly sure it was me you were referring to."

"Hang on, I have to set up a few more songs. Don't go away."

He put me on hold and my heart began to flutter in my chest. This was ridiculous. Why was I even excited? He probably just wanted to know that his good deed turned out okay for me.

He came back on the line. "Wow, I can't believe you're finally calling. I've been trying to get a hold of you since that night we talked. You okay?"

"Ah, yes, I'm fine. Thanks."

"When I didn't hear anything back, I'd feared the worst."

"Oh. Didn't you get my message?" I brow knitted together.

"What message?"

"I stopped by the radio station the next morning to say thank you for calling 9-1-1 but you had already gone so I left you a written message and gave it to the clerk at the reception desk."

"I never got it."

"Oh. Well..it said thanks for sending in the cavalry and…ah…I jotted down my phone number."

"Hmmm. Looks like I'll have to have a talk to Tiffany about making sure I get my messages." He did not sound amused.

"I'm sure she just misplaced it." Not.

He didn't reply for a second. "So, you gave me your phone number."

I heard the suppressed chuckle in his voice, making it sound all sexy and low. Oh lordy.

"Well…I…I.."

He let the chuckle out. "No worries. I'm just sorry the message never got to me."

"So…um…because of your gallantry can I at least buy you a drink, or maybe coffee as a way of saying thanks?"

Silence.

"Ah…I don't know."

Dang it, I blew it. He's probably used to women trying to throw themselves at him so of course he won't meet with a total stranger.

"That's okay." I assured him. "I get it. I…well I just wanted to phone and let you know that I'm fine."

"It's not that. I have…reasons why I don't meet up with people who I don't know."

"Did someone go all *Play Misty for Me* on you?" Oh my god, I can't believe I just said that! My hand clamped over my lips in horror. This was going from bad to worse. Hopefully he didn't make the connection to the movie.

"No, no nothing like that." There was a beat of silence before he spoke again. "Will…will you promise me one thing?"

All of a sudden my phone beeped in my ear. I had another call. I frowned, checked the time, it was past eleven thirty. I didn't recognize the number so let it go to voice mail but did wonder why anyone would be calling at this hour.

"I'll try. What's the promise?"

"I have to go but will you promise to call me again. Here at the station."

"But I'm not from here. I live in Houston and I can't get KRDL on my radio there."

"Oh." He sounded disappointed. "Well, I work eleven till six, Monday to Friday, if you want to call."

Now it was my turn to be hesitant. I chewed on my lower lip. "I don't know."

"Please, Sadie. I want to talk to you some more and I'd like to hear about how you got away from the bad guys."

I hesitated a moment longer then relented. "Sure. Okay."

"Great." He rattled off the station number again, making sure I programmed it into my phone. With a last quick promise from me that I would call again, he said goodbye and hung up.

On the radio, his smooth voice sounded more open and happy. "Hey classic rock fans, this is Jackson Steel and I'm going way back into the vault for this one. Not my usual fare but I'm sending this out to a friend of mine because I'm glad we connected. Hope she still has her ears on."

Shake it Up came blasting out through the speakers and I couldn't hold back the giggle. Mover and shaker indeed.

After the song ended I switched off the radio because tomorrow would be a hectic day and I needed to get some sleep. I noticed someone had indeed left a voice mail message. I pressed the buttons on my phone and listened.

"Sadie. It's Tanya." Her voice sounded odd, strained.

There was a short pause but I could tell she was still on the line.

"I...I need...I need to see you. Call me tomorrow, please. You won't be able to reach me tonight." Another short pause. "It's important."

I stared at the phone, confused. I'd never heard the slight tremor in Tanya's voice before and I immediately wondered if something happened to Blaine or Karen and she was in charge of contacting me. But then one or the other would have called.

Unless they both couldn't.

If my family wasn't safe I couldn't wait until the next day to find out so I phoned Blaine who picked up after the fourth ring.

"Hello?"

"Blaine. Is everything all right?"

"Sadie? Yes, everything is fine. What's going on? Are you okay?"

I had probably woken him and now he was worried at the late hour of my call.

"Yes, sorry. I got a call from Tanya and she sounded different, off. She said it was important and I immediately thought it had to do with you. You're sure everything is okay with you, Karen and Shantelle?"

"Yes, we're all fine."

Then what was the urgency of Tanya's call?

"Did Tanya say what she called about? Why aren't you phoning her back?"

"No, that's the thing, she said she couldn't be reached tonight, told me to phone her tomorrow."

"Did she say it was an emergency?"

"No."

"Well, I'm sure it's nothing. If it was an emergency she would have said so, right?"

Yes, she would have, even though our friendship had hit a rough patch, she would have put that aside if it was critical.

"You're right. Guess I'm just tired and paranoid."

"Get some sleep and drive safe tomorrow with the dogs. You can phone Tanya when you get back. You may not want to call her before you hit town because whatever it is, there's nothing you can do about it from Amarillo."

"True. Okay, thanks, Blaine. I'll see you tomorrow."

He clicked off after saying goodnight and I shut off my phone to preserve the battery. I stared out the windshield of the van into the night. Perhaps Tanya finally wanted to clear the air, really talk about the gulf that had formed between us. Unfortunately, I wouldn't be able to be totally honest with her regarding Will and Rico. She could never find out about their involvement in the Weckland murder case against me. Maybe one day when they weren't under the StreetSmart umbrella, but not until then.

I reclined my seat. It had been a good day. I was on a job, had another booked in a few days and I noticed the phones had begun to ring more frequently. I talked to Jackson who seemed to want to continue some type of friendship, on his terms, but a friendship nonetheless. Even Wayne and I had made a bit of progress.

And Tanya wanted to talk, although it did sound a bit serious.

Oh well, nothing I couldn't handle.

I closed my eyes and hummed *Shake it Up* until I drifted off to sleep.

About the author

Pat is a playwright and award winning author who has had a love affair with the written word since childhood, many times immersing herself in the stories of Enid Blyton and Carolyn Keene. An active imagination gave inspiration to short stories and her first play as a teen.

Her full-length play *The Truth About Lies* was staged at a regional theatrical competition in 2006. She was selected in the "One of 50 Authors You Should Be Reading" contest in 2012. One of her novels achieved a finalist slot in the 2013 International Book Award Contest - fantasy category. *The Daughters of the Crescent Moon Trilogy* garnered 2nd place for best series in the 2016 Paranormal Romance Guild's Reviewer's Choice Award. She was also one of the winners of the 15th Annual Writer's Digest Short Story Competition for *A Holy Night*.

Although still in pursuit of a place truly called home, Pat shares her life with her husband and three cats, all of which claim rule over the house at one point or another. Besides dreaming up her next novel, Pat enjoys traveling, baking, camping, wine and or course reading - not necessarily in that order.

You can find her on Facebook, her website patriciaclee.com or send her an email at authorpatriciaclee@yahoo.com

CPSIA information can be obtained
at www.ICGtesting.com
Printed in the USA
BVHW071544080920
588050BV00003B/187

9 781777 156305

Being Witty, Petite and Feisty has its Benefits

Recently divorced, petite and feisty Texan, Sadie Hawkins, struggles to get her newly established logistics business off the ground and when the opportunity to haul antiquities, including a mummy, drops into her lap, she jumps at the chance. But when her cargo gets stolen and a fresh corpse mysteriously replaces the mummy, Sadie is arrested for theft and suspicion of murder.

Out on recognizance thanks to her lawyer ex-husband and not willing to watch her business sink farther in debt while the police search for clues, Sadie yanks up her cowboy boots and does some investigative work on her own. Stymied by her lack of success, she reluctantly enlists a few members with specific skills from Streetsmart, an organization made up of rehabilitated young adult offenders.

While taking whatever moving job she can to keep her business from going under, Sadie endeavors to uncover the truth, the whole time wondering if this crime is some form of retribution for an incident in her pa̶s̶t̶. As things spiral out of control and Sadie̶ ̶e̶n̶t̶e̶r̶s̶ the killer's crosshairs, it appears ̶h̶e̶r̶ accomplices in Streetsmart will be ̶s̶a̶v̶i̶n̶g̶ her now.